IN TIMES

And oth(

Marie O'Regan

To lovely Alexandra,

Lots of love,

Marie O'Reg

xxx

Hersham Horror Books

HERSHAM HORROR BOOKS
Logo by Daniel S Boucher

Cover by Edward Miller 2016
Copyright 2016 © Hersham Horror Books

ISBN: 978-1530485079

Collection.
First Edition.
First published in 2016

Also from
Hersham Horror Books:

Alt-Series

Alt-Dead
Alt-Zombie

PentAnth-Series

Fogbound From 5
Siblings
Anatomy of Death
Demons & Devilry
Dead Water

The Cursed Series

The Curse of the Mummy
The Curse of the Wolf
The Curse of the Ghost
The Curse f the Zombie
The Curse of the Monster
The Curse of the Vampire

Contents

Foreword

The irony about being asked to write an introduction for Marie O'Regan is that she really should need no introduction; not in terms of the British horror writing scene at any rate, and I imagine across the Atlantic too. Marie has been a firm and active member of the BFS and the Horror Writers' Association for many years, and is passionate about both the genre itself and those who work in it. Her soft spoken voice conceals both a wicked sense of humour and also a core of steel. To Marie, the genre and its reputation are her family – like a mother lion, she'll do anything to protect it. She'll also do anything to protect *you*. A rare trait in the world these days and even rarer in a genre that so often threatens to destroy itself from the inside.

Marie and her then boyfriend/now husband Paul Kane were two of the first people I got to know when I started going to conventions in the UK, and they were already established stalwarts of the scene, known not only for their writing and their organising of conventions and open nights, but also for being two of the nicest, kindest people you could meet. Niceness probably isn't what the book-buying public immediately think of when they think of horror, and certainly won't be foremost in your head when reading the tales within these pages –

which are far nastier than nice – but if any darkness lives in Marie's soul she keeps it very well hidden.

As well as writing her own fiction and screenplays, Marie is also an accomplished editor, having put together several high profile anthologies, including the *Mammoth book of Ghost Stories by Women* and *Hellbound Hearts*. In the latter all the stories had to be influenced by the original Clive Barker work, 'The Hellbound Heart', which spawned the iconic *Hellraiser* movies, and it is in both of these works that Marie's influences and story preferences, to me at least after reading this very collection, become clear.

'In Times of Want' is what I would call, in my very professional way, an 'old school' collection. Before you throw your hands up in alarm, this does not mean old-fashioned or out-dated, but instead is a collection that harks back to those short stories where I, and many of us, first learned to love horror. They are stories of creeping dread. There are echoes of Barker's *Books of Blood* and King's *Nightmares and Dreamscapes* to be heard as you turn the pages. A hint of M R James. A flavour of John Connolly. A nod to a Pan book of Horror.

What can you expect from 'In Times of Want'? Well, you won't be left wanting. There are ordinary people drawn into horrifying situations; for example the psychiatrist with the OCD patient who gets far more than he bargains for when treating her. There are tropes you will recognise before they lead you down their own, new, dark paths. The mystery deaths on train tracks with a family secret at their core. The broken down car that leads to a monastery in the middle of the night. Dreams of losing one's teeth that have far, far reaching consequences. These are stories you can sink into and relish, perhaps one a night by the fireside or in bed, just before turning the lights out. Ghostly tales that send a shiver through you, and finishing with a story of a haunted cradle that couldn't help but make me think of a blend of *Rosemary's Baby* and *The Woman in Black*.

There are other stories with more modern concerns however, and the collection opens with one such, 'The Real Me' about the dangers of plastic surgery and this obsession with perfection that has gripped the world. There is also a tale of domestic violence - and the horror in that is perhaps more of the real than the unreal - and how it can ultimately trap both partners, just not perhaps in the ways you might think! There are dark crime stories, and battles of good and evil, and in some a wickedness that will make you smile.

So, when I say 'In Times of Want' is old school, that is a compliment. There are stories here to sink into with relish; familiar tropes in unfamiliar territory. The kind of stories you want the lights turned down low to read and to be curled up in an armchair reading, just the right length for reading each to be like selecting a chocolate from a box and savouring it.

This, of course, isn't Marie's first collection. A prolific short story writer, her first collection is called *Mirror Mere*, and I suggest that if you enjoy the stories you find here, then you go to the PS Publishing website and grab a copy of the ebook of that. Because Marie O'Regan, for all her kindness and charm, has a dark side that clearly needs to be vented on you, dear readers, and as you will see in the tale of Robert Leary towards the end of this collection, repressed darkness can be bad for the soul.

So, go ahead and turn the page and let the nicest

woman in Horror freak you out for a while.
Happy Reading!

Sarah Pinborough
2016

.

For Paul, for everything.

THE REAL ME

Grace stared into the mirror, looking for some sign that the changes she'd so recently and enthusiastically wrought had changed her. Had changed *her*, the sense of self that one intrinsically has, from the very first inkling that there *is* a self: something separate and alone.

Her eyes were the same. Pale blue-green, staring coldly back at a face that seemed – on the surface, anyway – only subtly altered. At twenty-five, the lids had not yet started to droop. Her lips were slightly fuller, it was true; the result of minor collagen injections she felt sure were almost imperceptible; her skin alabaster smooth now, thanks to a chemical peel. This second procedure, in particular, had been painful – and there were times, as she peeled off the strips of blackened, charred skin, that she had wondered what on earth all this was for – but there was no denying the end result. Smooth, shiny skin now covered her face, and Botox had taken care of the slight frown line that had been developing. All in all, she was pleased with the results of her latest efforts.

The bathroom door opened, and another of the hospital's patients entered. Mia was small, only five foot three to Grace's five eleven, and her hair was short, dark and spiky – the opposite of Grace's flowing, honey curls. Yet Mia was the striking one. She bounced into a room and filled it with energy, while Grace's entrances were quieter affairs, more subdued and almost reticent. It irked

11

her that, although she had always prided herself on her manners and her appearance (ladylike at all times, in all things, as per her mother's instructions), it was Mia who people remembered. Mia who people warmed to.

Grace who people ignored, or failed to notice.

Mia ran her stubby fingers through her own spiky coiffure and her cheerful reflection grinned at Grace. "What's the matter? Something else need fixing?"

"No! Why, what have you seen?" Grace pored over her reflection anew, convinced she'd missed some overlooked imperfection, and Mia roared with laughter.

"For God's sake, aren't you *ever* going to be happy?"

"You can't talk, Mia Ryan. You've just had a tummy tuck."

Mia's face darkened. "True. I have. But only to fix the mess left after losing five stone. I'm happy now." She stared at herself in the mirror, grinned, and her reflection winked at Grace, taunting her. "What's your excuse?"

Grace couldn't say.

Mia moved closer, stood on tiptoe, and brought her mouth close to Grace's perfect, shell-like ear. "When are you going to be happy with who you are? When are you going to be *happy*?"

Grace had no answer.

A tear rolled down her cheek, and she marvelled again at the dewy complexion magnified underneath, Mia's annoying presence temporarily forgotten.

She left the bathroom and went back to her room, eager to see the doctor and be discharged, a disgruntled Mia staring after her. But try as she might, Grace couldn't get Mia's question out of her head. *"When are you going to be happy?"*

Five days later, back in the sterile environs of her loft apartment, she still had no answer. She lay on her black leather recliner and gazed at the white walls and floor, devoid of decoration – save for mirrors artfully dotted here and there. Who was she? What made her so quintessentially her, Grace Byrne? A thought flitted across her mind's eye and she tried unsuccessfully to frown, wincing at the slight pulling sensation. Was she even real? She lay there, perfect in every way thanks to the efforts of numerous plastic surgeons, and couldn't remember what was actually her now; as she'd originally been. What was pure, unadulterated Grace, and what was plastic? And did it make any difference anyway?

She felt the skin on her forehead strain once more as it tried to crinkle, and smoothed her brow with her fingertips, taking care to be gentle with the papery membrane. Feeling slightly disgusted with the sensation, she moved to the bathroom, poring over her reflection as closely as she could. She looked beautiful. Flawless. Yet the nose wasn't hers, not really – not the way God had intended. Neither were her lips, or her forehead... she even had cheek implants!

"What are you obsessing about now?"

Grace jumped, the gruffness of her husband's tone jarring her out of her reverie. "Nothing, I just thought..."

"What? You saw some miniscule wrinkle and you'll just die if you don't have it fixed?" Mike pulled his tie loose and undid the top button of his shirt, groaning as the reddened flesh of his neck was released. "Newsflash. You're perfect." He disappeared from view, into the adjoining bedroom.

Grace hesitated, then followed, unsure of his mood.

Mike glanced briefly at her as he hung his jacket over

the back of a chair and eased his shoes off, sighing with relief. He undid his trouser belt, then went to the bed, looking for his pyjama bottoms. Mike liked to be comfortable. Grunting as he struggled into his pyjamas he said, "You were perfect when I met you, I spent fortunes on you, and you're even more perfect now. Apparently." He turned to her, his face stern. "There. Is that enough support? Enough comfort for you?"

She cringed as she answered, "I don't know why you're angry, I was just looking. That's all."

"At what?"

She hesitated. This was going to sound crazy, she knew, but the seed had been planted. And so... "I know I've fixed everything."

Mike added, "Nothing needed fixing," in an undertone, but she chose to ignore that. Steeling herself, she carried on.

"I know I look... better, now. But..."

"But what, Gracie?" His tone had softened, somewhat; he could see she was nervous. Just not why.

"But what if I'm not me anymore?" She gazed at him, trying to gauge his reaction – to see if he understood. He just stood there, perplexed – and a little scared, too, she thought.

Finally, he took a step closer, smiled; his posture designed to soothe, to calm. "Honey, I don't know what you mean. You're beautiful." He stroked her hair, tried to ignore the slight flinch as she automatically protected the new skin of her face. "You always were... to me." He pulled her close, nuzzled her neck, and she tried to relax into the comfort of his embrace. "What's this all about?"

She moaned. "I don't know, really. It's just... Mia at the hospital asked what would make me happy, and I can't stop thinking about her."

"Aren't you happy?" Although he was still holding her, Mike had stiffened at her words and his tone had hardened a little. Thin ice.

She snuggled into his chest, eager for his warmth, and smiled as his arms wrapped tightly around her; holding her safe once more. "Of course I am. I love you, you know that. But... I look in the mirror and I'm not sure if it's still me staring back. Does that make sense?"

Mike released her then, and sat down heavily on the edge of the bed, just staring into the distance. When he looked at her again, he'd aged ten years at least. He looked old and worn. And frightened. "Honey, you're the woman I married. The woman I promised to spend the rest of my life with, 'from this day forward', the whole nine yards... So, you've fixed a few things. Who hasn't these days?

Grace considered this. Was she any different to the myriad others who sought to improve their lot through surgery? A nip here, a tuck there? Did it affect who they were? She wasn't certain. She smiled down at her husband, ruffled his hair affectionately. "*You* haven't, thank God."

He placed his arms around her waist, pulled her close, leaning his head against her taut, flat belly – the liposuction had obliterated all trace of softness here, and his face ground against her muscled abdomen. Still, she smelled wonderful. "I don't have to, do I? I'm happy as I am. Long as you love me."

She kissed his head, noting the beginning of a thin patch at the crown. "Of course I love you. I always have." She made a mental note to make an appointment for him with a trichologist. Plugs had improved so much; they were barely noticeable these days.

Over the next few days, Grace observed those around her. Working as she did in the offices of one of London's more successful modelling agencies, she was surrounded by the surgically enhanced, day after day. Tuning out the inane chatter of who was doing what, and to whom – what was 'in' this week, and who hadn't noticed so was '*so* over' – she took stock of the faces and bodies of these, her workmates, her supposed friends. And one thing hit her immediately.

There was a homogenous quality to all of them that she found disturbing. Male or female, many had the same mouth, or chin. No one could frown or do more than twitch an eyebrow. Nobody looked *real*. After a while, she became aware that they were watching her, too, and she was convinced that they knew she was seeing them properly, maybe for the first time. Coffee cascaded across her keyboard as she scrambled to her feet, and files clattered to the floor.

"Are you okay?" Her supervisor, Ms Gleeson, was staring at her over her half-rimmed glasses, her expression slightly wary.

Grace nodded. "I'm sorry, I just… I'm not feeling very well."

"Then you should go home, dear." The voice came from behind Grace, silky smooth. Turning, she saw the office manager, Ms Kenyon, staring at her. She smiled, and Grace felt her insides turn to ice. "We can't have you here if you're sick, can we?" She took a step back, her tone harsher as she went on, "You might be infectious."

The room emptied as if by magic – infection was worse than imperfection, but only just. Grace nodded.

"Thanks, I will." She cleared her desk, put on her coat, and headed for the elevator – unmolested by anyone in the now barren office. As the elevator doors closed she glimpsed the first of her workmates venturing out of their cubicle, a handkerchief clamped to her oh-so-perfect nose as she sprayed disinfectant into the air.

Back in the safety of her home, Grace flicked channels on the TV, seeing for the first time how similar everyone was there as well. All the size zeros, with their uniform smiles and teeth, hair teased into whatever style was currently fashionable. Where were the individuals? Where were the real people?

Mike called to say he was delayed at the office, not to wait up. Bored, she gave up watching TV and went to bed.

She woke when Mike slid into bed beside her, some hours later. His breathing grew softer, shallower – Grace was surprised he hadn't kissed her on the neck, his usual habit when coming to bed late. "Mike?"

No answer.

"Mike? Honey?" She switched on the bedside lamp and sat up, tapped his shoulder. Sighing, he rolled towards her, and she recoiled. "What did you do?"

Mike sat up in bed, embarrassed. "I fixed stuff. Like you." His face was clean, unlined. His laughter lines – that she'd loved to stroke – were gone. His frown, the same. Mike's face was plastic, shiny. "I thought you'd like it."

"You thought wrong!" She got out of bed and backed toward the door, horrified. "What did you do?"

"It's just a little Botox, some filler, nothing you

haven't been doing for ages. What's the big deal?"

Grace stared at the bland face watching her, realising how little she could actually see of his intention. Was he angry? Sad? It seemed these days as if the only signifiers of emotion – in virtually everyone she knew – were the eyes and the voice. Other than those, she might be talking to a mannequin, for all the reaction she could see. She took a deep, surprisingly shuddery, breath and tried to smile. "You're right, I'm sorry." Her voice steadied, and she relaxed slightly. "It was just a surprise, that's all."

She stared back blandly as Mike appraised her response – and prayed he couldn't tell she was still horrified. Aware of the hypocrisy in her reaction she smiled at him again, and resolved to accept this change in Mike: her rock. How could she criticise him for, as he'd pointed out, something she did regularly herself? Aided by the substance in question, she was able to keep her features relaxed; and although she was grateful for that fact, the irony of their situation was inescapable.

"I guess it was." He smiled warmly at her and patted the bed. "Come back to bed, babe… please."

She smiled shakily and climbed back under the covers, lying rigid beside him. Neither dared move, and the similarity to a pair of dolls didn't go unnoticed. Minutes passed, and the silence grew unbearable. Finally, Grace turned over, her back to Mike – and relaxed as she felt his body mould itself to her contours, familiar as ever. She smiled as he kissed her neck, and whispered, "Night, babe."

"Night," she answered, but her voice was crystal clear – she was far from sleep. She felt her husband's body relax against her, his arm grew heavy over hers; and finally she allowed herself to react. A perfect tear formed in the corner of each eye, and rolled down onto the pillow. She made no sound. Mike was the one solid thing in her life, faithful and unchanging.

What was real now?

Over the next few days, Grace tried hard to reconnect. She gave up attempting to have proper conversations with anyone at work; it was all the usual gossip from expressionless clones, as far as she could see. No, she tried to talk to *people*. The man at the station's ticket office, tired and grumpy yet desperately trying to stay polite to the mass of people herded past his barrier each day; the woman at the newsagents', whose smile Grace had been pathetically grateful for when she'd paid for her weekly dose of tabloid gossip; the man she'd bumped into when entering the lift to her floor at work, who'd glared at first then smiled when he realised the person who'd annoyed him was an attractive woman. At least, she thought he'd found her attractive. He'd smiled, eased his shoulders back, made some inconsequential flirty comment when she'd apologised – but all she could think of with these people was: *How does it feel, when your face creases up like that? When you laugh, shout, smile, cry? How does it really* feel*?*

She was devastated when she realised she couldn't actually remember those feelings first-hand. How anything that felt real on the inside translated into external sensation. Sitting at her desk, staring blindly at her monitor, she ran her fingers over her face; nothing. Trying to keep tears at bay, she bit the inside of her cheek… and winced at the sweet, sharp pain as blood flooded the inside of her mouth. At last – this was what reality felt like, this was the real thing! She dabbed at the wound with her tongue, and was rewarded with a fresh lance of pain. Over the course of the day she occasionally probed at her cheek, savouring the sensations she felt at each fresh disturbance of the wound. Several of her workmates looked up as she gasped in delight, but quickly bent their heads to their work again when Grace smiled at them; her eyes glassy and way too bright, her laugh brittle.

While cooking dinner that night Grace 'accidentally' dipped her hand under the hot tap. She hissed at the way her nerve endings leapt in response to the heat, pain racing up her arm, leaving her breathless.

"What's the matter?"

Mike's voice in the doorway made her jump, and she hid her hand quickly in the folds of a tea towel, the seared skin rasping against the cloth. She swayed a little, and leant against the worktop to disguise it. "Nothing... I just... the water was hotter than I expected, that's all."

Mike came forward and examined her hand, cooed over the marks and took her fingers into his mouth. She gasped as his tongue lapped against the skin in an effort to soothe.

He looked up, concerned. "Did I hurt you?"

Her breathing quickened, just a little. "No, no, I..."

His lips found hers, and she groaned as he kissed her, his tongue finding the sore spot there, too. She shivered as his hands roamed over her body, and she responded eagerly as he pulled her down to the floor.

Despite Mike's ardour, Grace quickly grew frustrated as she realised that all the enhancements had an undesired side effect. Although she was bigger (or smaller) in the appropriate places – firmer, more supple – she had lost a significant degree of sensitivity, and found herself exaggerating her responses to Mike's touch so that he didn't suspect. She was forced to spur him on to being more forceful, almost rough, in an effort to really feel *something*. As he lay atop her prone body, she found herself disconnecting. Life wasn't real anymore; nothing was.

Everything was so remote…

Two days later. A Bank Holiday loomed. Three days away from work, alone together. Mike relished the prospect. Grace had seemed almost like her old self the last couple of days, less introspective, almost eager to try new things, seek out new experiences. He hadn't wasted the opportunity – each night had brought them to new peaks of pleasure, or so he thought; she certainly seemed to be enjoying herself as much as he did. Only one comment had been unusual, and it returned now to haunt him as he waited for her to wake up from their evening's lovemaking. "Did you really feel that, babe?" He'd looked at her, bemused, wondering what she'd meant. She'd smiled a little at his expression, and tried again. "Was it good? Was it *really* good?"

"Of course. Wasn't it good for you?"

She'd smiled and reassured him, her lips curving gently. Although they'd barely twitched, Mike knew how much effort had been involved even to make such a small movement, and had appreciated the apparent warmth of her response. But there'd been something about her expression, hadn't there…

He put it out of his mind as she sighed and rolled over, her eyes blinking open and her gaze not quite focussed as she tried to orient herself. She saw him sitting there, beside the bed, and her eyes opened a little wider.

He tried to tell himself he was imagining the vacancy of her expression.

"Mike," she purred.

"Hey, honey; enjoy your sleep?"

She nodded. "I did. I feel so tired, though, still." Her gaze went to the window, and the rain streaking the glass. "Oh, not a nice night."

"No," he agreed, "it really isn't. Good job we don't have to go out, I suppose."

"I don't want to go out tonight. I don't want to go out *at all*."

He paused, watched her more closely for a moment – that emphasis had been strange, hadn't it? Mike wasn't just imagining things, he was sure. Grace was staring at the rain, mesmerised, her face perfectly still. And blank.

He shivered, and Grace turned her gaze briefly on him. "Cold, honey?"

"No, not cold." He cleared his throat. "A goose ran over my grave, I think."

She giggled. "Such a silly phrase…" Her face fell again, and all of a sudden Mike was very sure that Grace was no longer with him. He was all alone with a mannequin that, God help him, he adored.

Later that night, Mike stirred to find the bed empty. The curtains were open, and rain still bled down the windows, gleaming in the light that seeped into the room from the hall. He heard the sound of a drawer slam in the kitchen.

"Grace? Honey, is that you?" A choked laugh was his only reply, accompanied by more banging of drawers and clinking of implements as his wife rummaged through them, looking for… what, exactly?

Silence fell. Listening to his own rapid, shallow

breathing, Mike slowly came to realise the depth of his terror. He felt the skin on his face stretching in response to that fear, try as it might to remain calm. He wondered what he actually looked like; remembering the sight of an elderly actress he'd seen once, Botoxed to the hilt. Asked to emote fear she'd merely registered slight surprise – unless you looked into her eyes. In them, you could see terror; as if she were screaming on the inside *all the time*, only no one could hear. He heard the sound of his wife padding down the hall towards the bathroom, accompanied by a scraping sound as she hummed tunelessly. The bathroom door slammed, and he heard the light clicking on.

"Grace?" His voice was quivering now, his fear rising by the second. He heard his wife moving around in the bathroom, her voice high and shrill as she crooned something to herself. What was she saying? He got out of bed and inched towards the door, hardly noticing that he was holding his breath, goosebumps rising in the chill air. Light gushed under the door, rendering his feet white and bloodless as he stood there, trembling.

Standing outside the bathroom door, he could make her words out clearly. "Not real, not real," she muttered, as something metallic clinked against the counter top and liquid splattered into the sink. He shifted from foot to foot in the cold, his bladder shrinking by the second, both from the cold and the horror that his wife seemed to have become. Taking a deep breath that was almost a sob, he took a shaky grasp of the door handle, and tried the door.

Grace was staring blindly into the bathroom mirror, oblivious to the door opening just a crack behind her. Her nightdress lay in a bloody heap on the floor, her perfection laid bare in the glare of the bathroom light. In one delicate hand she held a paring knife, small and extremely sharp; and she was singing softly as she slowly flayed herself, strip by strip. "Not... real, not... unhh..." A bloody strip of skin slapped wetly into the basin in front of her, gore spattered onto the floor unnoticed. "...Real!" Her arms were so much raw meat, and she was gradually paring away the skin from her face.

Mike saw a strip of flesh hanging from the counter and recognised the freckle cluster there – he'd nuzzled it while kissing her shoulder just the night before. His stomach clenched, and he vomited onto the floor. Grace turned, gazing dispassionately at her husband as he knelt on the tiles and retched. "I told you."

Mike fought to keep his nausea under control, and avoided looking at the thing that was his wife as he answered, "Told me what?"

"That I didn't know if I was real, after all..." She gestured at the flesh adorning the counter. "...All that. I couldn't *feel* anything, not properly." She shuddered, and a cry of pain escaped her as her raw hip nudged the counter behind her. She smiled, and did it again.

"And can you feel now, babe?" he asked, wondering how bad this really was; and whether a good surgeon could repair the damage enough for her to continue to function; at least enough to be able to see someone. A psychiatrist.

Grace smiled down at him, her expression beatific. "Oh, yes," she breathed. "I can, my love; I can feel *everything*." She ran one ruined hand over her breast, and cried out – although whether in pain or rapture was unclear. Her breathing quickened, and she moved towards her husband, knife in hand. "Do *you* want to?"

Mike shuffled back as well as he was able, until he hit the wall in the hallway. Grace stood framed in the bathroom door, light spilling out and glistening on the juices that were escaping her quivering frame. "Do I want to what?"

Grace grinned, her perfectly capped teeth blazing in the dark ruin of her face. She raised the blade, watching it shine wetly before her, then traced it down her chest, watching raptly as a line of crimson followed the blade's progress. She dipped a finger in the wetness and touched it to her mouth. "Mmm." She moved closer still, her voice now heavy with desire.

Mike started to cry as she pointed the blade at him and whispered once more, "Do you want to feel?"

IN THE HOWLING OF THE WIND

The old man watched as the child pressed close to the window, staring wide-eyed at the falling snow – flakes large and small dancing in the moonlight. He shivered as a sudden draught swept into the room; the door swinging inward as if presaging the arrival of something wondrous.

It was nothing. "Just the wind," he muttered to himself.

The child turned towards him, his eyes full of questions; and the old man felt his spine turn to ice.

"What is it, Grandpa?"

"Nothing…it's nothing, child. Just the wind."

The boy stared at the door, and sighed as it swung shut once more. "Do you think they'll come?"

The old man nodded, clearing his throat as he gestured at the room – the gifts under the tinsel-laden tree, the mantel groaning with cards and pine garlands, complete with golden bells and red velvet bows. "Of course. It's Christmas Eve. Why wouldn't they come?"

The boy said nothing, just stared at his grandfather with an intensity he found unnerving.

The old man leaned forward, tried again. "They're your parents, Matthew, of course they'll come."

This time the boy responded. "How can you be sure?"

"They love you. You are…" he hesitated, suddenly unsure, then continued, "…their flesh. Their blood." He reached out to the boy, who skirted his grasp and hovered just out of reach. "Trust me. They'll be here."

The wind howled as if the skies themselves were in pain, and the boy's gaze shifted to the fireplace, where the wind whispered in sympathy.

"I don't like the sound the wind makes in the chimney."

"What do you mean?"

The boy smiled briefly at him, nervous; aware of how fanciful his words sounded. "It *cries*."

The old man laughed heartily at that. A little *too* heartily. "It's just air, Matthew. Just air." He sat back in his armchair with a sigh and gripped the armrests tightly, taking comfort in feeling the worn fabric under his fingers. On nights like this he drew strength from the feel of the fire warming his skin, the grooves his weight had worn in the chair over the years, the touch of cloth against his body. *This* was what counted, what was real…he cared nothing for what lay beyond the confines of his refuge.

Lights swept across the window suddenly, then were gone. Matthew ran back to the window and pressed his face to the glass. "Grandpa! It's them!" The bell stayed silent, and there were no voices at the door. The boy's smile faded as he surveyed the empty street.

The old man watched as the child raised his hand and laid it flat against the frozen pane as if he wanted to melt the ice with its warmth. He called the boy's name, softly, but he didn't answer. He almost didn't hear the boy's sob, muffled as it was by the sudden shriek of wind that battered the house, rattling the windows in their ageing frames.

"Matthew."

The boy said nothing.

"Matthew, come here… Please."

This time the boy came, reluctant, and the old man could see the pain etched on his face. He ached to stroke the child's cheek, hold him close – but that was impossible for a child like Matthew. All he could do was talk to him, and this he did willingly.

"You're a good boy, Matthew. And they love you, even now. If there's a way for them to get here – to get to you – they will."

The boy nodded, but his disbelief shone through. It was in the slump of his shoulders, the way his eyes slid away from his grandfather's, the sorrow on his face. He turned away, and went back to his puzzle, sitting hunched over it on the living room floor.

The old man loved his grandson, always had. Gazing at the forlorn figure bent over his jigsaw he offered up a silent prayer, *Please God, let them get through.*

The chiming of the clock on the mantel woke the old man up, and he heaved himself out of his chair, huffing. Moving around wasn't as easy as it used to be, he found. The clock said it was nine p.m., and the shadows flickering on the walls confirmed the day's passing. The fire crackled in the hearth, and Matthew was still working on his puzzle, his little face solemn but determined. It wasn't natural for a child to be so quiet, he mused. It didn't seem right, although he knew Matthew was perfectly happy – lost in his own little world, where he had always been happiest; never more so than now.

Wandering over to the window, he stared out at the poorly-lit street. Snow had drifted against the walls and hedges, he saw, the parked cars buried almost to the tops of their wheels. The snow on the road itself was pristine, no traffic had disturbed it – and it would be morning, probably, before the gritters reached this far out from town. He sensed the boy's eyes on him and turned, forcing a smile. "The snow's deep, lad, do you think they'll make it?"

Matthew regarded him in silence for a moment. His answer, when it came, was terse. "You're the one who said they would."

"Well, yes, but the snow…"

"You promised." The boy's tone brooked no argument, and the old man sighed, then nodded.

"I did, didn't I. And I meant it, Matthew. If they can make it, they will."

Matthew's smile was singularly humourless, and the old man flinched. "Remember what you said, Grandpa."

"About your parents?"

"About them…and about breaking promises."

The strength drained out of the old man's legs, and he fumbled himself back into his armchair. "What did I say, boy?"

Matthew's smile widened, baring his teeth; his eyes seemed to shine yellow in the firelight, and the old man cursed himself for a fool.

Matthew drew closer, his mouth close to the old man's ear. "You said you must never break a promise. You said God watches."

"God always watches, Matthew, you know that." His voice was thin, quavery, and the boy sniggered as he drew back.

"God's not the only one who watches, Grandpa."

He fought to quell the chill that rose in him at the boy's words. "What do you mean?"

"Others watch, too…" Matthew glanced around,

nervous again. "Sometimes I can almost see…"

The wind moaned and whispered in the trees, and the boy's attention was broken. Restless, he returned to the window, and the old man sighed with relief. Matthew had always been such a sunny little child. When had this solemn creature taken his place?

The wind sobbed and moaned in the eaves; this old house was far from well insulated, and it found its way through numerous cracks and gaps with ease. The old man turned his head to the sound – it seemed deeper, somehow, more sonorous. Was that a voice he could hear? The wind seemed to whisper to him, and he fancied he could smell something – a scent that was tantalisingly familiar, but he couldn't place it.

Not yet.

Music wafted down the stairs, a piano tinkling somewhere close by. Matthew stood, and this time his smile was genuine. "Listen, Grandpa. Listen!"

The old man took a step closer to the closed door, flinching as a gust of wind blew it open. The hall was empty, no sign of trespass – just dust motes dancing in the chill night air. Turning back to the boy, he asked, "I almost recognise it, don't you?" He moved towards the door, but hesitated at the threshold to the hall. It was dark out there, the shadows thick and somehow glutinous.

He sensed Matthew, standing just behind him, and moved to take the boy's hand. The boy moved back once more, and the old man sighed. He should have known better. Matthew had never liked to be touched, even before…

"Who is it, Grandpa?"

The boy was eager, but not so eager that he'd come close. The old man yearned for the warmth of a hug from his grandchild, but – as ever – he knew the child wouldn't allow it.

"I'm not sure, Matthew." He glanced back at the front door, dots of white peppering the blackened glass as the snow fell outside in the dark. It was firmly closed. "I didn't hear anyone come in, did you?"

Matthew looked at him strangely, and started up the stairs.

"Come back, boy!" His voice was harsher than he'd intended, and Matthew stopped at once.

The old man moved forward, climbed past Matthew slowly, then continued his ascent. The music faltered, just for a moment, and he froze; gesturing to Matthew to *be still*. He listened to his breath rasping in his throat, his heart stuttering in his chest – and finally the music began again. It was clearer now, and he thought he recognised it. *Für Elise*. His breath caught in his throat as the memories came thick and fast; how his daughter had loved that melody. One of the earliest tunes she had learnt when she was taking lessons, she had fallen in love with it and played it relentlessly, driving him to distraction even though he loved it. Now it floated down the stairs, bringing images of his beloved girl: Elise drawing, one foot curled beneath her as it always was; Elise at the piano, tongue poking between her lips as she concentrated on her lesson; Elise sleeping, hair spread across her pillow like a little angel…

He wiped a tear from his cheek, and took another step forward, only to freeze when the door at the top of the stairs opened and light spilled out, bathing him and Matthew in a golden glow.

A woman stood silhouetted in the doorway, her features indistinct in the light. Matthew made a move as if to step forward, arms outstretched…and the old man's heart leapt. "Matthew, no!"

Matthew turned to face him, his face wet with tears. "You said she wasn't here! You said we were waiting for them to come!"

"We are, boy, trust me!" Helpless in the face of the child's anger, he struggled for the words to make this right: a way to convince him of the truth.

Matthew's face was all the answer he needed, and it pained him to see so much anger on that sweet face.

The woman at the top of the stairs took a step forward, peering down the darkened hall. The old man stared at her, tears streaming down his face. Why wouldn't she look at them? What more did he have to do?

"Mark, is that you?"

As if summoned by his name, the front door blew open and snow blasted through the opening. A tall, dark-haired man rushed through and forced the door shut behind him. As the wind died he took his coat off, but first he shook the snow from his shoulders. He raised his eyes to the woman at the top of the stairs, and his face broke into a smile of such warmth that even the old man couldn't fail to be moved by it.

"Elise!" He stepped forward, raking a hand through the unruly mop that fell over his eyes. "Am I glad to be home! Have you seen the snow?"

The woman laughed, and started down the stairs towards him. "It's coming down fast now, isn't it."

As she reached the bottom he swept her into his arms, holding her tight. Her face was buried against his neck as he asked, "How is he? Is there any change?" Her body stiffened, and he knew the answer even before she shook her head

He held her tighter.

Matthew, sitting on a step about halfway up, turned to glare at his grandfather. "Who does he mean?"

The old man shook his head, unsure. "I...I don't know."

"You do, don't you! You *do* know who it is!" The boy ran down the stairs towards his parents, but stopped short of going to them. He turned to his grandfather suddenly, terrified. "But...when did she come in, Grandpa? I didn't hear her, did you?"

"No, Matthew, I didn't." He stared at the couple entwined in the hall, and gasped as the shadows grew deeper, swallowing them whole. They were alone once more. The boy whimpered and ran back to him, cowering by his side but not touching. "I didn't hear a thing."

"Where did they go? Did you see?"

The old man could only shake his head – the house had changed, somehow; the wind carried voices and sounds from things unseen, and the night outside was fierce.

They couldn't leave.

Midnight, and the old man woke to find the fire sputtering. Matthew was asleep on the rug before it, curled up in a ball. His beloved puzzle was gone.

The old man stared around the familiar room, wondering how things had changed, and why. Shadows flickered in the dying firelight, and with them, the room...*altered*. There was a painting over on the far wall that he didn't remember, had certainly not bought – it was too modern for his tastes, too *bright*. The television (how he hated the things, had always kept it hidden in a unit that looked like a wooden chest) was displayed proudly, and it was huge – not the smaller model he remembered. The ticking seemed to grow louder, and he turned to stare at the clock on the mantel. It was still there, calling him, but some of the ornaments up there were new, weren't they? There was a photo frame that was unfamiliar, with a bud vase beside it, now empty. He went and stared at the photo, felt the chill of the room sink into him. The figure that stared back was his own, a photo taken by his daughter Elise, on his seventieth birthday. For the life of him he couldn't remember when that had been, and wondered anew if he was going senile. He moved to the window and looked out at a wonderland; the ground was thickly carpeted with fresh snow and the sky was midnight blue, starlight making the snow glow cobalt-white.

There was another photograph on the windowsill, and he traced the outlines of that familiar face – feeling the chill pervade his body. Matthew. A happy, cheeky Matthew – not the quiet, untouchable shadow he had become. Next to this was a photograph of Elise with her husband, Mark; as yet untouched by the world's harsh reality. These pictures spoke of happy times, and he struggled to remember them…to remember his place in all this. And Matthew's.

He looked back at his chair, and froze. His beloved chair was gone, replaced by something newer, sleeker. He didn't like it. Yet when he closed his eyes and touched this…the familiar cloth sprouted beneath his fingers, only to vanish when he looked again. The smell of smoke made him cough, and for just a moment the heat in the room was intense – then the chill settled in once more.

And what of Matthew? He stared at the sleeping boy, wondering whether to wake him; he knew the child wouldn't react well. He rubbed his eyes, unsure of his vision suddenly – the boy appeared *dimmer*, somehow. Less there. He wondered how many more of these tricks the house would play on him before the night was over.

He stumbled into the hall, lost in this space that, once so familiar, now felt so strange. Music floated downstairs again, and he cried out in fear. Where was she? He made his way quickly up the stairs, eager to see his daughter, have her tell him what was happening.

Elise sat on the bed, clasping a picture in her hands, her face wet with tears. A bedside lamp made the tear tracking down her cheek glisten. The old man hovered in the doorway, unwilling suddenly to intrude on this, his daughter's grief. A door on the other side of the bedroom opened, and Mark appeared.

"Elise?"

She smiled up at him, put the photo back on the bedside table. Matthew laughed at her from it, caught in delight at some past party. "I'm sorry. I'm okay, really."

Mark nodded, sympathy evident as he asked, "Can I get you anything?"

She thought for a moment. "A tea would be nice, if that's okay?"

He grinned at her, then. "Should have known." He crossed to the bed, kissed her on the forehead. "Of course it is. I'll be back in a minute."

He brushed past the old man without acknowledgement, his face set. The good humour was purely for his daughter's benefit. What was wrong, he wondered? Was she ill? He moved closer, silent, unwilling to disturb her now she seemed to be resting.

She lay on the bed, eyes closed, and the old man became aware of the plaintive strains of *Für Elise* once more, the CD player beside the bed set low. He had named her for this song, over her mother's wishes. She had thought it too fanciful, instead of beautiful. He supposed it was lucky she'd loved the tune as much as he did.

He sensed movement beside him, and realised Matthew had joined him at his mother's bedside. The boy stared forlornly, and the old man was saddened to see how pale he was. Elise rolled over, and before he could think what to do, he found himself and the boy back out in the hall, just in time to sink deeper into the shadows as Mark returned.

The hall brightened for a moment as Mark went into the bedroom, then darkened again. Matthew and his grandfather stood just outside the door, listening, a little ashamed of themselves. Elise and Mark thought they were alone, and perhaps that was best – though neither of them could have said why.

Mark sat on the edge of the bed, a steaming mug of tea in his hand. He shook his wife gently. "Elise, wake up. Your tea."

She opened her eyes and stared blankly at him for a moment, then smiled and sat up, taking the cup. "I must have drifted off."

"Not surprising, love. You must be exhausted."

Her smile faded as she tried not to cry. "I'll rest when he wakes up."

Mark opened his mouth as if to speak…and then

closed it again. This was old ground, gone over too many times already. The wounds were fresh, just under the surface, and he had no wish to open them again.

The phone shrilled, and Elise dropped her cup.

Matthew sat on the hearth, his arms wrapped tightly around him. He stared up at his grandfather.

"Where did they go, Grandpa?"

"I don't know, boy." He was staring out of the window, at the tracks their car had left in the snow as it screeched out of the drive. "I don't know."

Matthew wasn't about to give up. "But it's late – the middle of the night. Why didn't they check I was alright, or take me with them?"

The old man could only shake his head. "I suppose because they knew I'd look after you." He sat down heavily, relieved to find the room back as he remembered. "But they should have told us, that's true."

The house was dark, and cold, but neither moved to turn a light on, or lay the fire.

Time passed, shadows fell. And the wind was screaming.

Elise stared at the shape in the bed before her, so pale and weak. She could barely take in the doctor's words. "He's been showing signs of waking, Mrs Banks. Very slight...but definitely there." A monitor went off again, and nurses bustled, clustering around their patient. He still hadn't moved. She felt a hand rest on her shoulder, and another snake round her waist. She leaned back – grateful for Mark's warmth. He kissed her hair.

"What do you think, Mark? Will he wake up?"

He sighed. "I don't know, darling. But God, I hope

so."

"It's been so long…" Elise's voice cracked, and she put a hand to her mouth; desperate to contain her grief.

Mark nodded. "I know."

They looked on, then, as the doctors worked; and they waited and watched, as they had for so long – forlorn in the hope that this time, maybe this time, hope would win.

Dawn was breaking through the living room window, its watery rays struggling to illuminate the cold and stark room, where Matthew and his grandfather sat waiting. As the room brightened, Matthew cried out – and his grandfather whirled towards him. The boy was…flickering. The old man watched in shock as the image of the lad faded out of sight. Then he was back, just for a moment…reaching out towards him. With a cry, he made a grab for his grandson's hand, desperate for the contact…and to keep Matthew with him.

Too late.

Elise was exhausted. Mark was by her side, and they leant on each other as they searched for some sign of the doctors' success. As dawn broke, Elise called her son's name, her voice shocked. Following the direction of her gaze, Mark saw his son open his eyes briefly, and smile at his mother.

"Matthew!" He was back, suddenly, and the old man slumped with relief. The boy was jittery, frightened…but he was here. "What happened, boy? Where did you go?"

"I don't know." The boy was staring around him, as if he were trying to fix his position, set it in stone. "It was bright...there was a bed...and my mother was there."

The old man wept. "Did she see you?"

"I think so." Matthew's voice shook with emotion, the first real feeling the old man had seen since...when, exactly? "She smiled...I *think* it was at me."

The boy began to fade again, and the old man moaned. "Don't leave me, Matthew. Don't leave me alone."

The boy flickered back into view and smiled. "Don't worry, Grandpa. I won't." He grasped his grandfather's wrist, and the old man cried out at the surge of feeling that shot up his arm.

They were back in that room, by the bed, but this time they were together. Matthew stared up at his grandfather, then at the figure in the bed, his face milk-white.

"Grandpa, look!"

The old man obeyed. "I don't understand, Matthew. How can this be?"

Matthew drew closer to the figure, traced the contours of its face, entranced. "I don't understand either. How can it be me, Grandpa?"

Back in the house. Alone. The old man groaned as he surveyed the living room he'd loved so much, and he remembered. The heat rose around him as he saw those flames lick the carpet and up the walls, the ember of coal that had caused this carnage glowing innocuously on the floor in the midst of it all.

He saw, again, the Christmas tree going up in flames, the smell of pine pervading the house as if it were no more than a scented candle. He groaned as he saw his beloved chair blacken, then burst into flames, the fumes causing the old man (he recognised himself, and started to cry) to scream in anguish as he rose to his feet and tried to put the flames out, calling out the name of the boy entrusted to his care while his parents were at a party. "Matthew! Matthew!"

He saw the child, huddled on the stairs, coughing; tears tracking through the grime on his face as he called in vain for his grandfather. He saw the hope in his eyes die as he realised no help was coming. Then he saw the boy slump to the floor as the smoke overcame him, eyes closed.

As he watched himself fall to the floor, flesh blackening as the flames licked at his body, he heard the front door as it broke under the force of the fireman's axe. He felt himself smothered – too late – by a blanket as he heard another man's voice call for oxygen: "There's a kid up here! Quick, bring oxygen – he's still alive!" He remembered the feeling of panic as he fought to stay alive. He'd been entrusted with the child; he had to look after his grandson!

Now, as the memories crashed in and he realised – too late – what had happened that fateful night, he heard Matthew calling him; and then he was back by the boy's bed, watching as he woke.

"Grandpa?"

Elise was crying, even as she smiled at the boy and shushed him, brushing his hair back off his face just like she had every night since the beginning. Mark watched his wife and son whilst trying not to show that he too wanted nothing more than to break down after the stress of the last months.

Matthew looked beyond them, his body frail and his

face wan – but he saw his grandfather. And he smiled.

The doctors were checking the boy over, this child that had hovered for so long in the between spaces, neither dead nor alive. Matthew took no notice. He looked at his grandfather, and he reached out his hand.

The old man reached for the boy's fingers, clasped his hand in his own even though he knew neither of them could really feel it. He tried to explain, to make it right.

"I was supposed to look after you, Matthew."

"You did, Grandpa. It wasn't your fault."

Elise frowned, worried. "What wasn't Grandpa's fault, Matthew?"

"The fire. He thinks he didn't look after me."

Elise shook her head. "The fire was no one's fault, darling. A fluke, that's all. Your grandfather would never intentionally let you get hurt."

Matthew nodded. "I know, but he thinks it was."

"He does?" Mark drew closer, leant over his son. "Can you remember the fire, son? Can you remember anything?" He exchanged glances with his wife, fearful of the answer.

Matthew shook his head. "No, nothing. I was coughing, then it was dark." His face brightened as he did, indeed, remember something. "I remember Grandpa, he's been with me."

"He has?" Eager to soothe the child, and close this chapter, his parents played along. They had no wish to lose him again if he was stressed, they just wanted to forget – and move on.

"All the time," Matthew continued. "He helped me with my puzzle while we waited."

"Waited?"

"For you to come home from the party."

Elise felt Mark's hand tighten on her shoulder. In the months since the party, while they'd buried her father and watched their son as he lay comatose, she'd blamed herself again and again for leaving them; for being out of the house when disaster struck. For leaving them alone. Had her father somehow managed to stay with Matthew, through all this? Had he stayed by his side?

Matthew giggled, and Elise fought to stay calm. "What's funny, sweetheart?"

Matthew's smile was warm, his delight genuine. "Grandpa. He says thank you for not blaming him, now he can go – find peace." Matthew's face fell. "He's leaving."

Mark cleared his throat, amazed at Matthew's words. "He needs to go to Heaven, son. He needs to rest."

"He died?"

Matthew's voice shook, but then the smile returned as his grandfather spoke. "Your place is here, Matthew, with your parents. I can leave you now you're back with them; it's where you belong."

"But where will you go, Grandpa? When will I see you again?"

"I'm going home, son. And I'll always be watching you, never fear."

The old man started to fade, and Matthew's face fell. He buried his face against his mother's chest, feeling her wrap her arms around him. His grandfather smiled, and nodded, and pointed out of the window, at the snow. "Go home, Matthew. It's Christmas, and your parents have everything ready, just waiting for you."

Matthew sniffed back a tear as his grandfather faded, and looked up at his parents. "It's Christmas?"

Elise nodded happily. "Yes, it is, Matthew.

Tomorrow…" She looked at the clock on the wall, "no, today, in fact."

Matthew grinned, then, and waved at what seemed, to everyone else, to be thin air. "Bye, Grandpa. Bye…and Happy Christmas!"

CAT AND MOUSE

She wondered afterwards why she hadn't seen him until it was too late; until he was right there, in her face. If she had seen him, *seen the knife*, she could have run. She could have screamed. She could have done *something*.

She shivered, a movement that made her moan at the pain it invoked. He'd tied her wrists to the bed too tight, her hands were already numb. She wished she could say the same of her wrists. Where was he?

The house was quiet, and she couldn't make out any unfamiliar sounds, try as she might. She turned her head to look at the clock. 11a.m. Damn. He had four and a half hours before she was expected at school to pick up Tim. He could do anything he liked to her in that time. He hadn't undressed her. At the moment, she didn't know whether that was a good or a bad thing. She heard the toilet flush, and lay still, her eyes closed. Footsteps came closer to the bed and then stopped. She willed herself to stay still. Christ, her head hurt. What had he hit her with?

She felt his breath against her face, quick and shallow. But he didn't touch her. When the breathing went away she risked opening her eyes slightly, certain he would be moving away. She gasped when he giggled delightedly, his ice blue eyes no more than an inch away from hers.

"I see you, mouse." He whispered the words, breath hot against her face, and then he kissed her. Hard. She felt as if she were going to gag, his tongue forced as far into her mouth as he could manage. She tasted Listerine, and tried to breathe, felt his teeth grating against hers. She would not kiss him back.

"Don't you want to play, mouse? Never mind, you will." He moved away, and she waited, sure there was more. Sure enough, he was back in an instant, teeth bared in a snarl. "We're going to have such fun!"

He grabbed her foot and forced her trainer off, then grabbed the other foot and repeated the action. She hadn't been wearing socks. She tried to kick him off, but he held her firmly and kissed and sucked each of her toes in turn. She felt sick. Even though she hated what he was doing to her, she had to admit the intensity of it was incredible. He started to bite her feet, a little too hard, and she shook her head, tried to pull away.

"No? Okay." He straddled her, stroked her face. "We can skip that part. Whatever you want."

"None of this is what I want."

"Ssshh. Of course you do, you're just mad at me. That's all right, though. That works." He kissed her eyes, her face, then kissed her on the lips once more, gently this time.

She lay quiet. She didn't think he would really hurt her. She just had to stay calm.

That was when he brought out the knife. Her eyes widened as he held it in front of her face, and she opened her mouth to scream. He clamped his hand over her mouth, his skin like ice, and proceeded to cut away her shirt and bra, exposing her upper body to the cold air. She whimpered as the point of the knife nicked the skin between her breasts, but she wouldn't scream. He pulled the remnants of fabric out from under her and threw them away, then took his hand away. A tear trickled down his cheek.

"I'm sorry, babe." Then his lips were there, licking at the scratch, tasting it, sucking it dry. He moved from there to her breasts, kneading one while he licked and sucked at the other. In spite of herself, Lucy felt herself getting wet. Her nipples were stiff and erect, and he was hungry for them. He raised his head to stare at her, grinning broadly. "I knew you'd want to play."

She forced a smile, not wanting him to see how angry she was. "My hands hurt. You tied them too tight." She tried to put just the right amount of wheedling in her voice, and smirked as he rushed to loosen them.

"I couldn't find what you did with the handcuffs. Never mind, that should do it."

She didn't interrupt him again; just lay there and watched as he cut her jeans off. She wanted to see if Tom actually had the balls to carry this off. She didn't start to join in, though. This was obviously some sick little fantasy he had decided to act on; but it was so out of character she couldn't believe he'd actually be able to go through with it.

She almost laughed at what he did next. Ever methodical, he stood up and undressed, folding each item neatly and laying it on the chair by the window. He had always been obsessive about keeping in shape, and she felt the familiar warmth start to flood through her as she stared at him. Smiling, he came towards the bed once more, and forcing them apart, knelt between her legs.

"You're going to love this, sweetheart. You're going to be begging for more."

She said nothing, just smiled at him. Let him play his little game. She had a feeling that he was stalling, but that didn't matter. His head dipped between her legs and she gasped as his tongue expertly went to work, gave herself up to the waves of sensation.

Inevitably, he tired of his efforts, and she opened her eyes to see him kneeling before her, desperately trying to revive his sagging erection.

"What's the matter, lover? Something not working for you?"

Shaking his head, he reached back and untied her wrists. "It's no use. I thought it might spice things up, for you, if we tried it like this, but…"

Pulling herself upright, she pushed him back on the bed and straddled him. She slapped him around the face, hard. "But Little Tom needed some help?" She grinned at him, feeling his erection stiffen against her buttocks. Raising herself, she guided him into her and sat back down, holding him still. She traced a line down his chest with her fingernail.

"What have I told you before, Tom?"

"You're the mistress." She felt him swell even more, and slapped him again, began to rock. She scratched his chest, hard, and smiled as he bucked.

"What?"

"You're the mistress. You're the cat, not the mouse."

She smiled, and leant in to kiss him. "That's better."

LISTEN...

Children walk hand in hand with danger.

That's the first thing you have to understand. What adults see as fraught with peril – a cup of coffee or a just-boiled kettle left carelessly on a kitchen counter's edge, the panes of a glass door just at the right height to break into a million splinters when you run into them, running along the top of a brick wall in the garden that overlooks a rockery several feet below – children see as exciting, with no thought of the mishaps that may occur. Perhaps this is what keeps them safe, this lack of fear, lack of care. Perhaps too much caution is what causes danger to become actual harm, tempted into being by fear itself.

There was certainly no thought of danger as the children scampered for seats in the front row that Saturday morning, sunlight beaming through the windows of the children's section of the library onto the head of the Storyteller. Brian ran faster than just about any of the kids there. He'd been waiting for this all week, ever since he'd seen the poster for today's event last Saturday when his mom dropped him off at the library for the morning, as she always did on the way to her waitressing shift. He loved stories, made his mom read to him every night, even though she said that he was too old now. He was nine. Brian didn't see why that was too old, just because he could read them himself. He didn't stop enjoying listening just because he was nine, any more than he'd stopped enjoying playing ball with his dad on a

Sunday when he came over. What difference did being nine make? He reached his favourite spot, in the centre of the group, a few rows back from the front. Far enough back not to stand out, far enough forward to be able to see and hear clearly. Perfect.

The Storyteller looked, to them, like the oldest man in the *world*, his hair all shiny and backlit by the sun so it looked as if there was a halo around his head. He was leaning against the librarian's desk, arms folded, a tiny smile etched on to his face like he was everyone's favourite grandfather. He looked down at the eager faces, pink with excitement, and the smile stretched, just a tiny bit. The room hushed slowly, as latecomers straggled in and sat behind their peers, begging them to budge up, "*Please*, we can't *see!*" The Storyteller was a wise man, used to the ways of children, and he waited patiently for them to settle.

Finally, there was quiet. The air in the room seemed to still, as if waiting for the magic to begin, exhaled on the mist of the Storyteller's breath. And so he began. He leaned forward, rested his hands on his knees, and looked at each child in turn – until they were squirming with excitement, desperate to hear what he had to tell.

"Listen," he said. "Can you hear something?" All the children strained to catch what the Storyteller was bringing to their attention. They couldn't hear a thing. Even the man and woman standing by the door at the back, loathe to leave their daughter till they were sure she was happy to be left, held their breath. The air was laden with anticipation. The Storyteller grinned, and held his hands aloft as if they encompassed the whole world in their span. "Exactly," he said. "In the beginning there was nothing, nothing at all."

He could say anything from this point on, and they'd lap it up. He could see it in the awe on their faces; hear it in the shallowness of their breathing, as if they were afraid of not hearing properly should they breathe too loud. This was *his* time; this was what he lived for. So he relaxed and began to enjoy himself, secure in the knowledge of their capture.

"Then came the wind," he said, and the children instinctively moved closer together as the room seemed to fill with whispers borne on the breeze, the air as full of sound as it had been of silence only moments before. Some of these whispers seemed to soothe, some caused disquiet, and more than one child glanced over his or her shoulder quickly, as if fearful of what they might find there. One little boy stood out. He sat straight, head high, and looked around slower than the rest, aware that things might not be quite what they seemed. He wasn't scared, not yet, just careful – he wanted to see where all this was going. The Storyteller saw him, and nodded to himself. There was one here more awake than the others. That was to the good, he thought. That made things *interesting*. "The wind was full of the noise of animals, and of men, of howling and screaming and roaring louder than you could ever imagine," he continued, "and there was such turmoil in the air it darkened as if night itself were coming – does anyone know why?"

One little girl timidly put her hand up a little, then snatched it back down again. But it was too late, he'd seen her. "Do *you* know why, honey?"

"Is…is it because they didn't have anywhere to rest?" Her hands were kneading each other in her lap, now, the knuckles white. What if she were wrong? A dim voice in the back of her mind not unlike her mother's whispered,

"*There might be consequences.*" She looked behind her for her parents but, thinking her happy, they'd departed till this was over.

Again he flashed his teeth, but you couldn't really call what he did a smile. There was no kindness in it, no joy. "That's right, honey. It's because the land wasn't there yet, or the water. Just the wind."

"But how…?"

"*Ssh*, and I'll tell you." The little boy who'd dared voice his question sank back, frightened though he didn't know why. Not yet. He looked at the floor, unwilling to say any more, or risk a peek. The air sounded like there were *things* in it… "The wind was full of possibility, you see. That's what could be heard…as if it were the breath of God himself, willing everything into being." He looked around at his audience, his face a little stern. "Do you see how that could be?"

The children nodded. *Almost* as one. *Yessir, they could,* that nod said. *We can see anything you want us to, just don't get mad.* One little boy, the *more awake* little boy – Brian – didn't see, but he wasn't stupid enough to say so. Looking around, he saw that neither were the others. All the children knew that danger was here, but most of them still thought it was only in their head. If he was to make a mistake, Brian thought, it wouldn't be that one. The wind sighed again, and a boy to his left flinched. He rubbed at his neck absentmindedly, and Brian saw that his hand came away a little bloody. This wind had *teeth*. He turned his gaze back to the Storyteller, lest he realise that Brian saw. And worse, that he was beginning to realise what it was that Brian could see.

"That's right, children. The wind was the sound of God's Creation, and it filled the void in a *second*."

"Filled it with what?" This from a moppet in the front row, all honey coloured curls and dimples, spellbound by his story and unaware of what was going on all around her. This question met with the Storyteller's approval, and he leaned closer to her, his face a mask of kindliness and good humour.

"Why, with *us*, honey. With people, and with the land for them to live on, and the beasts of the air, water and earth for people to eat. God made us, and it was all good." The children nodded sagely, realising that this was starting to sound a lot more familiar now God was part of the equation. Hadn't their moms and dads and Sunday School teachers taught them that God made the world in seven days? They were back on home ground now, and all thoughts of danger – of things not being *right* – receded.

"Truth to tell, children," he went on, "not *everything* was good. How could it be? For everything good there's something bad, we all know that, don't we?" Again the children nodded, images of apples and Eve and the devil dressed up as a snake running through their minds. Brian's mind, though, swam deeper waters.

"You know the stories your parents protect you from?" Smaller nods now, glances to the right and to the left, seeking reassurance where it could not possibly be found. "Sure you do," he said. His voice seemed rougher now, harder edged, though his words still seemed to reassure. "You know, the tales about vampires, and werewolves, and ghosts..." The Storyteller smiled, and this time there *was* humour there, Brian saw. This time he was delighted, and what made him so happy was the fear on the children's faces, the sudden dawning of the notion that now they were in uncharted territory, a land so far from what they knew they might never find their way back, and they were scared. Brian could see some of the smaller kids looking to the door, hope that their mom or their dad had come back for them written across their faces for all to see – because then it would be over, then they could go home. The story would become the stuff of nightmares, and in time it would fade – *but not if the Storyteller could help it.*

The Storyteller stood, and started to prowl. "Where do you think all those stories come from? Can anyone tell me?" No one spoke, and Brian saw that the Storyteller really didn't want anyone to interrupt. He was getting into the *swing* of it now, he was on a roll – he reminded Brian of a preacher he had seen on TV, asking people did they want to be 'saved', and to 'praise Jesus'. A 'holy-roller', his mom had called him – but only after calling him something else that Brian had got into trouble for asking her to explain. "They are around because they're *true*, kids, just like we're around – they're the opposite of God's creation, and they seek to destroy us."

"No!" This was from a little boy at the back, and when Brian turned he saw that the boy's face was wet with tears. As he stood to run to the door for his mom everyone saw the wet patch on his pants. They started to laugh, nervously at first, then louder and louder till they were almost hysterical – and Brian realised that was out of fear too. The laughter allowed them to let the fear out, in this shrill cacophony of noise that sounded so much like screaming that Brian couldn't see any humour in it – didn't find it funny *at all*. The little boy stood by the closed door; his back pressed tight against it, and knuckled his face dry. "I want my mommy," he whispered. "I want to go *home*."

53

"And you will, son, don't worry." The Storyteller had made his way all the way to the back of the crowd without making a sound, getting behind the children somehow, though Brian couldn't see how he'd done it so fast, nor so *quietly*. "There's a happy ending, don't you worry. No need to be so scared." He placed his hand on the boy's shoulder and turned him firmly away from the door. Then he took his hand (he had to work at that, the little boy didn't want to hold his hand, didn't want anything to do with him, that was coming across loud and clear) and led him to the front, sat him in the middle right in front of him, where he could see him all the time. The kids already there shuffled aside nervously, eager to make room, to get away from any chance the Storyteller might touch them. *As if he were sick*, Brian thought. *As if they thought they might get infected.* All the fight seemed to have gone out of the boy, Brian saw, his eyes were dull and his face was slack with fear. When he sat down he put his thumb in his mouth and started to rock, without even knowing or caring whether anyone could see.

The Storyteller sat on the edge of the desk once more, and surveyed the children sitting in front of him. They were a subdued bunch now, for the most part, all wide eyes and fidgeting. He waited for them to calm themselves, so he'd have their full attention when he started again. Things were about to get even more interesting.

The air had quieted a little, but it was still too full of hisses and whispers for the kids to be truly calm. That small boy had been right, Brian thought, there were *things* in it. He let his mind roam, and tried to keep himself calm, as free of thought as possible so he could just *listen*. This was a trick he'd learned whilst listening to his mom's voice every night, as she read to him. Didn't matter what the story was – *Hansel and Gretel, Where The Wild Things Are, We're Going On A Bear Hunt…* it made the stories come alive in a way that just listening never could. When he stilled his mind like that, and let it wash over him, his mom's voice faded and changed until it was overtaken by all the characters' voices, their *real* voices. His bedroom faded and he'd find himself walking through the forest, or sitting in the boat, or running from the bear. He became aware that the air was a little darker where the noises were loudest, and he could see the first signs of shadows, of things moving amongst the children. Here and there a child would flinch then look round, quick, as if trying hard to see who had pinched him, or nipped at him. The air around the Storyteller, though, was clear. The shadows grew clearer, and now Brian could see figures – creatures from his nightmares solidifying as they moved towards him, only to pull back when they got within a few feet. Brian could also see the reason they retreated. There was a glow emanating from the Storyteller. It was a hateful glow, all slimy and greeny-yellow, like radiation in those old sci-fi movies his dad let him watch when his mom was out for the night with her friends, or visiting Grandma, and he came over to babysit. The creatures flinched away from that glow, as if it could hurt them. Or worse.

Looking round the room, Brian tried to see if anyone else was glowing like that, but no one was. No one could see the shadows, or the figures that lurked within them, either. He was the only one. The shadows roiled around the room, and Brian thought he could hear more than just monstrous howls and screams in it. He thought he could hear sighs, and even tears. He saw the Storyteller looking at him, and fought to appear as upset as the rest of the kids, yet still obviously wanting to hear more.

The Storyteller examined Brian's earnest expression for a moment, then nodded. The boy was a little more awake than the others, true, but he didn't think he could see clearly. Not yet, anyway. He allowed himself to feel a little of what was seeping towards him from the children, and shivered slightly at the surge of energy that even the littlest piece of the whole granted him. This was going to be a *feast*, by the time he was finished. He wouldn't need to feed again for quite some time, he was sure. Time enough for the tale of today's adventure to die down, and be added to his repertoire. He glanced down at the little boy who'd tried to escape, and could see that his spirit was broken. If all went well, then this little fellow was going to be with him for a long time. A *long* time. The boy his parents would be taking home would be missing something vital. And all they'd know was that he seemed to have withdrawn into himself, though they'd never know why. Doctors and psychiatrists would be called, he was sure – it had happened before. A personality disorder would be diagnosed, then the kid would be classed as 'special needs', allowed to be as quiet as he wanted, so as not to upset him further. And the Storyteller would be one soul richer, with no one the wiser, unless they caught sight of him in the shadows that surrounded his tales, and very few could ever do that – the ones that did could be added to his following, easily enough, they tasted the sweetest. He took a deep breath, and the children hushed in an instant.

"Now, where we? Ah yes, I remember. I was telling you that all the bad stories are true, when our young friend here," he paused to smile benignly at the lad, who remained unaware of anything outside his own mind, "got scared. Boy, did he, huh?" There was a little ripple of laughter now; they were starting to relax, though not by much. "And I meant it, you should understand that, but perhaps not the way he thought I did. Of course there aren't vampires outside your window, hanging from the lintel trying to get you to invite them in; and of course there are no werewolves, howling at the moon every time it's full and looking for fresh meat." There was no laughter now, nervous or otherwise. "What is true, though, kids," and here he paused for effect, and searched their faces with all the seriousness of a preacher, "is that *fear* exists, *fear* is real and it's out there even as it walks among us, and that's where all these stories come from. Do you see the difference?" Again, they all nodded, heads bobbing up and down eagerly as they sought to reassure the Storyteller that *yes they did, indeed they did, just tell us how to sleep tonight when we're alone in the dark and no one can help us.*

Brian risked a look around him, keeping his head low so that the Storyteller might not notice. *Might* not. The words he'd just heard had crystallised everything that had been running around in his head since this tale started – he knew what was going on now. He sensed one or two of the shadows in the room coalescing near him, while others – further away from him – stepped up their activities, forcing little yelps of fear from the children even as the shadows cringed themselves in fear of the Storyteller. Some of the kids were crying for their mothers now, very quietly, almost under their breath. They understood not to let the Storyteller hear too much, even though they didn't know why or how they knew. Brian tried to focus on the shadow nearest to him, and thought he saw teeth that were far too long in a thin, bony face with eyes like coal. A voice rumbled inside his head. 'Do not try to see us too clearly, my friend. We do not wish to be made to harm you.'

"Harm me?" The words were out before he could stop them, and even though he'd tried so hard to whisper he felt the Storyteller's rhythm falter as he sought to locate the source of this interruption. Tension built, and Brian held his breath as he fought to escape detection. Children started to grow restless, sensing something new, something changing, and the Storyteller turned his attention to them once more. He couldn't lose them now, so near the pay-off of his tale. The rhythm strengthened as he went back to telling the children how it was fear itself that made them afraid – that fear was a *real thing*, not just imagination. And it had teeth. He wasn't telling the whole truth, Brian knew. It wasn't fear that had teeth, it was *him*. Fear just held you prisoner, kept you in its grip, ready for him to feed.

'Silence, boy. He'll hear you. There is no need for words spoken out loud, you know. We are creatures of the mind; we can hear what you want to say without you saying it out loud for all to hear.'

The boy closed his eyes and tried again. 'Who…who are you?'

The creature sighed, a sound so full of loss and desperation that Brian felt tears start to form and had to fight not to shed them. 'We are…for want of a better term…what your films have called *creatures of the night*. We are the stuff of myth and legend, vampires and werewolves, shapeshifters and ghouls. Your…Storyteller, as he styles himself, has kidnapped us, and we want to go home.'

'Home?' Brian wondered where home would be for such creatures. Graveyards? Hell?

The vampire – that had to be what he was, Brian thought – smiled sadly, and shook his head. 'No, child. Our home is here,' he tapped his head. 'We belong in the imagination, not in the real world, forced to hurt those who dream us best so that the Storyteller's lust for pain might be sated.' He leaned closer to Brian, and became, as he did so, a little clearer.

All of a sudden Brian was scared – right down to the base of his spine, with the little hairs at the back of his neck all prickly, like when he watched scary movies – and he shrank back from the apparition before him.

The vampire smiled. 'You see? *That* is where we are supposed to live, in your imagination. That chill down your spine, that clenching of your gut, *that* is what feeds us. And we are happy with this, we need no more. Not for us the tastes of the flesh.' He smiled again, a crueller expression this time. 'Or even the taste *of* flesh.'

Brian sought to calm his mind, and tried his best to keep the fear out of it. He thought he made a pretty good job of it, considering he seemed to be in the middle of a conversation with an honest to God *vampire*. Even if they weren't actually talking. Not out loud, anyway. 'So what happened? What changed?'

Another voice spoke this time (it was easier to think of it as speaking, Brian found, it troubled him less than the alternative), and the vampire fell silent – content to leave this part of the tale for someone else. The newcomer was far more powerful, to look at him. He was tall, and broad, and muscles seemed to almost burst out of his shirt, along with hair. His voice was rough inside Brian's head, as though his throat was so sore from howling that speech of any kind, even imagined, was painful for him. '*He* did. The *Storyteller*, as he calls himself.' He virtually spat the name, and Brian understood a little of the pain these creatures had been forced to feel – and wanted rid of. 'He was as we are, once, a creature of imagination, no more.'

'Not real?'

'Not as you would understand it, no. Think of the fairy tales – the Storyteller started as one of these, much as the Pied Piper, or Rumpelstiltskin. He was…*made up*…by one of your human storytellers. For a while, he lived in tales and was happy with that – a device used to tell, and frame, a story.' He paused and stared bleakly at the Storyteller, who appeared distracted. 'Time grows short boy. You must listen well now, before we have to go. Before he makes us…'

'He cannot, if we are quick. Hurry!' The vampire was decidedly edgy, baring his teeth in a vague gesture of warning, though at what, Brian couldn't see.

'The point, child, is that he grew *greedy*…'

Brian felt as if his mind had split in two somehow. On one side, he was watching the Storyteller sniff the air, searching for the cause of his distraction – and he had a feeling he was narrowing in on them. And then? He didn't want to know what then. On the other side, he was listening intently to these creatures that seemed to want to help him, and – by helping him – all the other children.

'As a species, we are singular. We do not need food, as you understand it. We are content to live in the imagination, to hide there, in the shadows and recesses of the mind.' He sniffed the air, and licked his lips as if savouring the freshest meat before continuing. 'And the spaces in between what is, and what is not.' Again he sniffed the air, and Brian's nerves got the better of him.

'And then?'

The wolf/man – who seemed to be growing more *wolfish* by the second and far less human – lowered his gaze and stared into Brian's eyes. The boy couldn't look away from that pinprick gaze of baleful yellow. 'And then he learnt the trick we've worked hard to forget. The trick we thought we'd been successful in banning.'

'We? I thought you were *all* stories. Aren't you as old as each other?'

'No. Tales spawn tales; one word can give birth to a million, if it's the *right* word. Can you understand that?'

Brian nodded, sensing the rightness of what he was hearing. It *felt* true, even if he didn't completely understand how it worked.

'We...' he gestured to his companion, the vampire, himself, and a wraith-like figure of a sobbing woman that hovered silently nearby, 'we are the old ones. We are the first. Humans spoke of us and trembled, and we were content. People embellished the tales, over time, and other tales were born. This is the way of things, the natural order. This is how you humans tell what was, what is, and what *shall be*.'

Brian didn't understand. 'So how...?'

'I'm getting to that, boy. Be patient, *bide your time* and all will become clear. Humans started to tell the old tales, of us and our kind, but prefaced them with "Once upon a time..." or made them into fables, with a fable teller that was part of the story. *Do you see now what happened*?'

'This Storyteller...*our* storyteller, was one of those. He wasn't real.'

'Not in the sense you mean, no, he was thought rather

than flesh, word rather than deed. But he grew stronger each time the tales were told, until he became *flesh*…and with the flesh came the hunger. A hunger greater than you could ever imagine, making him *hunger incarnate*.'

Brian didn't understand everything he'd just heard, but he understood enough of it. He understood enough to make him mad. 'And he likes to chew on fear, is that it? A big, fat fearburger anytime he wants one, just by terrorising a few kids.'

No one spoke, even in his mind. The monsters – let's face it, Brian thought, that's what they really were, who were they kidding? – had the good grace to hang their heads, as if ashamed.

'He scares us too, Brian. It's not just the children anymore. How else could he make us hurt you? Why would we hurt you when you are the source of our *selves*, of our very *being*? He forces us to do his bidding so that he might scare the children more each time, and we get *nothing but the scraps from his table*!'

This last was spoken in a roar, as the wolf-creature struggled to retain its human aspect in spite of its rage. The Storyteller was aware of them now, Brian could feel it. And he was coming for them – one step at a time, so the other kids wouldn't see.

'You must forgive us, son.' The vampire was terrified, his teeth bared as he turned one way and then the other, sensing danger though he couldn't yet see where from. 'We're so *hungry*. And each time he tells his tales and makes us hurt your kind, one or more of you join our number, and thus we grow weaker, as there's less nourishment to go round – until finally his is the only tale left. *Do you see*?' Brian nodded, dumb now with the shock of what he was hearing. 'This is why we must destroy him! This is why you must help us, Brian. *Can't you see?'*

Brian could, though he didn't want to. He wanted his mother. He wanted to curl up at her knee as he had so many times, while she read to him of dragons and elves, of trolls and fairies and children who had their dearest wish – if it were a true and unselfish wish – made true. He couldn't have that any more though, not now – the time for that was past, and he had to put it aside. Now he had to be the one who told the tale, and held the power. He had to be strong, for all of them, so that no more kids ended up scared of their own shadow because on some level they understood *that it wasn't theirs at all – and that it could bite.*

The Storyteller was staring at him, he knew it. He couldn't bring himself to look just yet, but he could tell by the way the skin on the back of his neck was crawling, and by the way the creatures that had tried so hard to get through to him were cringing even as they tried to make him see. Looking around, he saw that a space had opened up all around him, as the children, too, had shuffled a little away from him, leaving him alone, and in plain sight. He didn't have long, but what could he do? He was shaking, and he could feel the fear eating away at the edges of his brain – it wouldn't take much for him to lose it, and end up as one of the Storyteller's acolytes, doomed to follow him and collect the fear from children just like him. It wasn't fair! He wanted to yell it at the creatures, at the Storyteller, to make them see what they were doing to him. He was just a *kid*, for Chrissakes! He sensed, rather than saw, the creatures around him start to dwindle, their disappointment in him palpable. He looked at the little boy all the way in the front, still rocking, still unaware of anything except his fear. And all of a sudden he understood what to do.

'So let me get this straight. This guy is just a story?'

'In essence, yes. Or he was. I'm not altogether sure that's all he is now.'

Brian looked at the Storyteller with new eyes, and now he didn't look quite so awful. The yellowy-green glow had dimmed a little, and to Brian's eyes, the Storyteller didn't look quite so solid. He looked as if he wasn't entirely *there*, in the library with all the little kids who wanted their moms, wanted to go home because this was too scary. He looked at the Storyteller, and he looked at the monsters – the vampire, the werewolf, the ghost and the ghoul, and all the other shadows milling around (they'd stopped hurting kids, he saw, maybe the Storyteller knew what was coming) – and he felt power begin to rise in him. He could *feel* it – clean and pure and pulsing right through him. He closed his eyes and thought about that, thought about the power – and realised it had a colour he could see. It was blue, clear and bright as the sky, and it was all his. The blue pulsed out from him, spreading around the room, and he saw the Storyteller's sickly greeny-yellow aura begin to fade under such brightness. He saw the other kids start to brighten in response to it, becoming more alert, though they couldn't have understood why this was happening. Even the little kid all the way in the front stopped rocking, and took his thumb from his mouth. Brian thought he heard him say, "Mommy?" The monsters had tuned towards him now, Brian saw. They were waiting. There was an air of restlessness in the room, like a fresh breeze on a baking hot day. Still, Brian wasn't sure. He turned to the vampire, the wolfman, and the ghost – the oldest of the tales. 'So if he's just a story who forgot that's what he is, I can fix it, right?'

'That's what we hope for, Brian. That is our fondest wish.'

Brian felt the blue glow starting to build, even as the fear left him. 'So what I have to do is...*un*tell him? Make him back into a story, a ...what did you call it? A...device?'

'If you can, yes.'

'If he lets you.'

'Please, Brian, try...' This last was the ghost, and she was fading even as he looked at her. He was running out of time, he knew, so he took a deep breath, and got ready.

He stood up, and took control.

"Hey!" All the kids turned around to watch him, and the Storyteller managed to look outraged and flat out scared all at the same time – a mixture Brian hadn't thought possible up until now.

"Shh, boy, we're not finished the story." The poisonous yellow glow was fading, barely showing around the Storyteller now.

"Oh yes we are. We don't want to hear the rest of your story. It's mean."

Simple words, simply spoken, yet they broke the dam of fear that the Storyteller and his prisoners had fought so hard to instil, and the children were starting to break free. And as they did, so did the monsters. Brian looked at them all staring up at him, and he looked beyond them to the creatures that had materialised behind the Storyteller. They were standing eagerly behind him, the hunger shining bright and fierce in their eyes. He thought, though, that he was probably the only one here who *could* see them, because no one seemed scared, or worried, about them at all. Not even the Storyteller, though he soon would. Brian's time was coming, it was nearly here.

Brian took a deep breath, and let all that clear blue light flood through him, and started to speak. "Want to hear a proper story?"

"Yeah!" The cry was unanimous, and the Storyteller quailed at the sound of it, *diminished*. Brian stood tall and proud, and puffed his chest out to *throw* the words right to the back of the library, the way he'd been taught in class. He wanted everyone to hear him, especially the Storyteller's creatures.

"Once upon a time a mother told her son a story, except she wanted to make it sound all important, she wanted it to carry a lesson. So she started the story with 'Once there was a storyteller...' which of course made him real inside the story."

All the children nodded in agreement, it seemed perfectly logical to them that what was in a story was real inside that story. Just like all the really good stories start with "'Once upon a time...'

"The boy told his friends the story, and his friends told their friends the story, and so it went on. And each time it was told, the storyteller got to be a stronger *piece* of the story. Do you see how that happened?"

As one, the children nodded their understanding. Everyone knows that once a story's told a certain way, that version of it is out there, it's set in stone, almost – the foundation for all future versions.

"No. No, stop it. Stop it at once..." The rest of the Storyteller's words were muffled by the giant paw that clapped itself over his mouth, though no one other than Brian could see it, of course. The children were lost in his story of how a story got real, and hadn't even heard the

Storyteller's latest outcry. Brian had a suspicion that that might have been because his voice was growing a little weaker every minute.

"The problem with that was…well, can you guess what the problem with that was?"

A hand went up, and Brian was happy to see that it was the little boy that the Storyteller had dragged all the way to the front.

"I think *I* can."

Brian nodded his encouragement and smiled, and the little boy carried on, stronger now. "The storyteller forgot he was just a story, didn't he?"

"That's right," Brian said, and the little boy blushed, delighted that he'd got it right, and that this story was nowhere near as scary as the one the bad man had been telling. All thought of the Storyteller being anything other than the Bad Man was gone, as was the power he'd held. "The Storyteller got very strong, but forgot he wasn't real. He didn't see that if he was real he'd eat regular food like real people; he just knew that fear made him stronger, stronger than the other stories – the ones our moms protect us from. I don't need to say what they are, do I?"

The children were unanimous on this one. *Nope, you don't need to say another word, we get it.*

Brian saw that the creatures had solidified even more, surely someone would see them soon? He looked the vampire square in the eyes and heard its voice in his head: 'No one will see us, Brian, except you. You are the new Storyteller for these children; you are all the voice we need.'

"Good, 'cause I don't like to hear them any more than *you* do, believe me." Children and monsters alike laughed at that, and Brian thought that they sounded about the same. "The other stories, though, they didn't forget. The Storyteller held them prisoner, 'cause he was stronger than they were, and he made them live his stories, scare the children badly so there'd be more fear to feed on. He was a Bad Man, all right. A really Bad Man." His voice cracked, and he was surprised to find he was near tears, sorrow for the plight of the creatures that had been forced to hurt those that had dreamed them into existence (their *Gods*, in a way) making his eyes tear up and his throat all scratchy. "So…do you know what the older stories did?"

"Noo!!!" This was the Storyteller, aghast that he'd been so caught up in Brian's story that he hadn't realised he was hearing the tale of his own ending, and Brian's beginning. He made as if to part the children like a wave, so he could bear down on Brian and stop him before things went too far, before he lost control. Too late. A thin, bony hand clamped itself on the Storyteller's shoulder, the fingers digging in deep – a thin ribbon of blood (*black like ink*, Brian thought) drawing a dark line down his chest. On the other side, the werewolf was growling into his ear, or… was he chewing on it? Brian didn't want to look too close – that wasn't a story he wanted to be telling in years to come. Not to kids, anyway. Kids deserved so much better than that.

"The older stories waited until they found a special kid. One who dreamed brighter than most, and remembered his dreams. One who would *believe*."

"Then what?" This from the little moppet who'd been so scared earlier, honey curls bobbing with excitement as she waited to hear the ending. This story was going to end right, she could tell. This story was going to be *awesome.*

Brian smiled, and the light seemed to stream from him, making the library a brighter, warmer place than it had been all morning while they listened to the Storyteller. "Then they told him a story, of how it had all happened and how it had all gone wrong. And the boy believed them, and told the tale again – only this time he started it without the Storyteller, turned the story back to what it should have been in the first place. Which is… what?" Brian yelled this last, scared that the Storyteller was going to break free, scared that the monsters were wrong and his tale wouldn't be enough. It wouldn't work, and the Storyteller would have his soul, before moving onto fresh meat, and starting all over again. He waited, scarcely daring to breathe, he was so scared. Right here, right now, he wanted his mom. And more than that, he wanted his dad to be standing right behind her, backing her up as she defended her Brian. Tears pricked at his eyes, and he blinked hard, fighting them back.

There was a puff of yellowy-green smoke that reeked of rot, and a fading roar of monsters that had been sent back to the night, and to spaces between spaces, and that had taken their prey, still bleeding black ink, right back with them. There was one cry, loud enough to bring the parents running, eager to see why their kids were so excited.

"JUST A STORY!"

Brian did cry then, tears of relief streamed down his face as he saw his mother elbowing her way through the crowd of adults looking for their kids. She looked scared, like she always did when she couldn't control things, and she couldn't keep Brian safe in her orbit, had to let him go out into the world of bullies, and crime, and dads that couldn't stay because they loved booze more, and had let it win. He saw all of that and none of it in her face, because she would never have told her son what she was so scared of – that her son's innocence would be spoiled too young, and blight what remained of his childhood. He saw his mom, worried because she couldn't see him, and that was enough, even though on some level he surely sensed the rest.

He saw his mom, his world, arms extended and a smile spreading across her face as she saw him. And he ran to her.

PLUS ÇA CHANGE...

Ava walked along the length of Dr. Greg Templeton's office, carefully rearranging the books so that the spines sat at a uniform depth on the shelves – none sticking out of line by so much as a millimetre. "Nothing different," she routinely said on her visits. "Nothing can be different. Nothing can *change*."

The good doctor said nothing, merely watched as she traced the room's contours over and over in her relentless search for absolute symmetry. Finally, after a good fifteen minutes (this time; sadly, it was a vast improvement on the initial frantic forty minute routines), Ava relented and stood in the middle of his office, turning slowly one last time before nodding, once, and sitting down in the freshly polished (by Ava) black leather chair facing him across the desk.

Greg leaned forward. "Is it better now?" Not for the first time, he wondered if the fact his office was so sparsely decorated was what kept her coming back.

Ava nodded, just once, bird-bright eyes darting across his before her gaze dropped to her lap, where fingers kneaded themselves into endless, intricate, but resolutely repeated patterns. "It's the same."

"The same?"

Again the nod, just once. "Same as before. Has to be the same as before."

He waited, but Ava ventured nothing more; she just sat, eyes endlessly tracing the room and everything in it, in her mission to keep anything from changing. Going

71

through his notes, Greg thought back to when she'd first slouched into his office. It hadn't been voluntary. The police had taken her into custody after being called to the local supermarket – the manager had got fed up with her re-arranging the shelves, hour after hour, until every tin faced forward a set number of millimetres from the front of the shelf, every bottle did the same. In short, the whole store was laid out with regimental neatness. She had become quite violent when customers ruined her perfection by having the audacity to take things off the shelves and actually attempt to buy them. It had taken three policemen to escort her off the premises and into the waiting police van.

The court had committed her to hospital for evaluation (a mandatory seventy-two hour hold, long since past), and she had done the same there: relentlessly tidying both her own bay and other patients'. The nurses had watched, bemused, but only restrained her when she started trying to 'fix' their filing system.

And so here she sat – legs crossed demurely at the ankle, right over left as always; hands restrained in her lap, kneading themselves into a frenzy; charcoal eyes staring at him, full of hope that he held the answer. The key.

He didn't.

Ava twisted, suddenly, staring round at the shelves to the rear of his office.

Greg followed her gaze, but saw nothing that might have attracted her attention. The shelves stared blankly back, with no sign of anything having been disturbed. "Are you all right, Ava?" he asked.

She glanced very quickly back at him before directing her vision to the shelves again. Her answer, when it came, was thrown over her shoulder. "Did you hear something?"

"Hear what?" he said. "It seems pretty quiet."

She turned to him properly then, slowly fastening her gaze on him as she answered: "It does, doesn't it." She was clearly fighting the urge to turn back and examine the shelves once more. "I wonder why that is?"

He had no answer to that. The room looked as it always did, he hadn't heard a noise – yet clearly Ava was scared. Greg found himself listening, head cocked to one side, ready for some sign that his patient had heard something, after all. There was nothing. He caught sight of the clock, then; 4.54p.m. "I'm sorry, Ava, our time's up."

She said nothing, just stared around the office, eyes wide – as if that way she'd see more, might catch sight of anything that had changed.

He cleared his throat; tried again. "I'll see you next time?"

She nodded, then; just once. And scuttled out of the office before he could say anything else.

He watched as she went through her usual routine: first she placed an ear against the door and listened, then she grabbed the handle but didn't open the door yet – she just listened a bit longer, then finally she'd open the door – checking what lay beyond in both directions before setting foot outside the sanctity of his office. Then she was gone, the door shutting quietly but firmly behind her.

The next Tuesday saw Ava return. As usual, there came a tap at the door, and then it opened a crack. Greg saw an eye, peeking at him through the gap – just one eye, slate grey, regarding him with great seriousness.

He smiled. "Come in, Ava, please."

The door opened, and she sidled through before closing it behind her and leaning against the closed door as she listened, made sure there was no one creeping up behind her. She eyed the room with distrust, and the doctor sat back, knowing this could take a while. Her hair looked slightly dishevelled, as if she'd been running her fingers through it – a new habit? He saw a spot of something dark on her jacket sleeve and frowned. She was normally immaculate – perhaps whatever accident had caused this stain was what had made her so anxious? She gave no sign of having noticed the mark, just set about the business of checking his office for signs of change.

It took twenty minutes this time. She pored over all the books on the shelves, looking for any that might have been returned to the wrong slot or moved from the correct position, making sure they stayed in their regimented rows and weren't out of order. She wiped down the chair facing him and nodded – a tad apologetically, this time, he thought – before pulling it out the required number of inches so that she could sit down without having to go through the routine of cleaning it again (allowing it to venture too close to the desk before she sat meant it could be contaminated, although he didn't get quite how – he just knew she needed the chair to be far enough away from the desk that she could sit in it without further contact, after which she could pull it closer); then she went to the sculptures and paintings – examining them closely, her expression grim. Finally, she sat down.

"Everything okay, Ava?" he asked.

She shook her head, but said nothing, her eyes still darting around the room.

"No? What's wrong?"

She turned her attention back to him – slowly, clearly uncomfortable, before answering. "I'm not sure. But something's not right." Then she was off again, searching for the source of her disquiet.

He sought to reassure her. "I promise, Ava, that I haven't moved anything."

She shook her head. "No, that's not it. Nothing's moved." Her hand strayed to her hair, shaking slightly, but she forced it back into her lap – clasped it with the other hand, tight, ensuring no further escape.

"Then I don't understand," he said. "If everything's the same, then…"

"I didn't say *everything's* the same," she snapped. "I said nothing's moved. That's not the same thing at all!" Her breathing was fast, shallow – her eyes refused to rest on anything, glinting like the pavement when the sun comes out after a storm. She looked like a cornered animal.

He struggled to understand. "I'm sorry, Ava, but if nothing's moved, then what's different?"

She smiled, then, and for the first time he was scared. Because her expression seemed so alien, somehow full of threat – her normally placid features almost manic. "Hard to tell, isn't it?" Then she tipped the chair back and ran out of the room, laughing, leaving him staring after her, totally confused as to what had just happened.

She missed the appointment after that, and the next; but finally returned three weeks after her sudden exit. She tapped on the door, then entered and slammed it behind her before going through her usual routine of checking for sounds of anyone following, and commencing her regular rounds of the office.

Greg watched her carefully. Her grooming was immaculate once more, there was no trace of any blemish on her clothes – and she moved quietly but seriously round his office, calmly adjusting the odd book or knick-knack on a shelf. Finally she pulled out the black leather chair facing him, positioned it carefully, wiped it down and sat in it, leaning slightly against its back, hands folded sedately in her lap.

"Well," he said. "You seem calmer than you were on your last visit."

She permitted herself a small smile. "I do, don't I."

Greg nodded. "I'd say so. Are you feeling better?"

Again, that half-smile, her eyes clear and bright, dove-grey as they reflected the sunlight breaking through the window behind him. "I am," she said. "I feel much more… myself."

Greg watched her for a moment, unsure of how to respond. It was unusual for a patient to return to relative normality so – apparently – easily without some kind of treatment or counselling. Yet Ava seemed to have managed it all on her own. He saw a slight tic below her left eye, and wondered whether to comment, but thought better of it. Even if the calm was a façade, it wouldn't help to shatter that illusion this early in the session. He sat back, laying his pen on the desk atop her notes. Her eyes flicked down, then back, but not quite quickly enough to escape his notice. "So tell me," he said. "What have you been up to the last few weeks?"

"This and that," she said. "Nothing important."

Greg frowned. This vagueness was new, too; she normally detailed everything to the nth degree. "Nothing?"

She frowned, then. "Nothing I can remember, actually." The frown deepened as she considered this; as if she was trying to recall specifics. When she looked back up at him, her expression was troubled, her eyes the colour of a stormy sky. "I can't remember anything."

"That's not like you," he answered, and saw her eyes gleam for a moment before the mask fell again, and her usual placidity returned.

"Maybe it is," she said. "Maybe the real me is a bit more *relaxed* than the Ava you've known up to now."

The Ava you've known. Greg didn't like what that implied, and he was fairly sure she knew that, and was amused by it. He leaned forward, eager to press on, see what was at the bottom of all this. "Are you saying I *don't* know the real Ava?"

Again that smile, quickly stifled. "I'm saying that people... change. The face they show the world isn't always the real one." She giggled, then, but said no more.

The session went downhill after that; Greg tried to draw her out, find out where she'd been, what had set off her outburst on her previous visit – but she wouldn't be pushed.

As their time together drew to a close Ava stood, and for once leaned directly over Greg, smiling down at him. She was wearing perfume, something heavy and intoxicating. Another first. "Remember what I said, Doc; I don't like change."

"What's changed, Ava?" he asked.

She grinned, but Greg thought she looked as if that was the least funny question in the world.

"Nothing," she replied, her expression heavy with sorrow. "That's the problem. I thought..."

"Yes?" he prompted.

"I thought wrong," she hissed, and turned away. The door slammed moments later, and Greg belatedly realised she hadn't bothered with her usual routine before leaving.

As he approached his home later that evening, Greg reflected on the sudden change in Ava – and the way she'd been when he first saw her. There'd been nothing in her notes to indicate such a change might occur. Thinking about it, there hadn't been much detail in her notes at all – at least, not about her background.

He placed the key in the lock, smiling at the familiar creak as the door swung inward, signalling his return. He switched on the light and hung his coat on the hook just inside the door before heading for the kitchen. Five minutes later he was sitting in the living room, eyes closed, with a scotch in his hand and the news on the TV.

The newsreader was droning on about unexplained 'disturbances' in the local area over the last few weeks, and Greg felt something nameless roil to the surface of his mind. He opened his eyes and started to pay attention.

None of the incidents were related, as far as anyone knew – but Greg couldn't help himself. He studied the background footage showing as the newsreader's words washed over him. It took a few minutes, but then he saw her – a face in a crowd, or a glance over a shoulder as she walked away – but it was definitely Ava. And not *his* Ava – this one was a far freer, if darker, spirit. She had a swing to her walk and a bounce in her step; she laughed outright in at least two or three of the scenes being shown; and her clothes were so far removed from the neutral tones he'd known her to favour – here she was in reds and purples and oranges, determined to stand out; to excite attention.

Something snapped, outside his window. Greg muted the TV and listened for long moments – but nothing else disturbed the peace. A cat, he thought, or a fox, treading on a twig. His mind tried to whisper they'd be too light to make a twig crack like that, but he wouldn't listen.

Something crunched the gravel, and he was up and out of his chair in an instant, pulling the curtains back so hard they nearly came off the wall. Again, there was nothing, but that sense of having just missed something vital persisted. He saw no sign of movement, heard no further noise. Finally, he checked the lock and pulled the curtains tight, shutting out the night.

Unsettled, Greg went through the rooms, checking windows and their locks, pulling curtains closed wherever he went. When he was sure the house was secure, he approached the living room once more – stopping when he heard the TV. Hadn't he muted that? A gleam of buttery light spilled out onto the wooden floors, and Greg stood still, watching as a dark shadow walked across it, first one way and then back – slow and deliberate. His throat dried and he was cold – who was here? All was quiet once more, and finally he pushed the door open, watching as it swung inward, revealing his now-empty living room. The news had given way to the weather, and a too-jolly weatherman was predicting showers. "Not a day for doing the washing, ladies," he joked, and then was replaced by the music blaring over the end credits.

He must have hit the mute button again as he put the remote down, Greg reasoned. He couldn't see anything else out of place. He sat back down in his chair and reached absently for his glass, eager now for a drink to calm his nerves. It took him a moment to register the difference in weight, then he looked more carefully – he had no memory of having finished his drink, and yet there was the empty glass. He placed this back on the side-table and poured another drink, then picked the glass back up – he'd keep a closer hold on it this time. He downed one, then another, and then he was nodding – the TV blaring rubbish at him as his head dipped and his eyes welded themselves shut.

Morning. Sunlight poured through a crack in the curtains and hit him square in the eyes. Greg grunted and raised an arm, held it across his poor eyes. The TV was still on, and now it was the morning news.

"Shit," he groaned, and headed for the shower, shedding clothes as he went.

An hour later he was climbing the stairs to his office, out of breath and fighting a headache that threatened to force him to bed if he couldn't get rid of it.

At the top of the stairs, he slowed. The door was shut, his office seemed as it always did, and yet he was nervous. His receptionist glanced up and nodded, then bent to her work once more. She never had been the talkative sort.

Greg opened the door to his office and stared around its interior. The walls were bare, entire bookcases upended and their contents scattered on to the floor; pictures lay on the carpet, shards of glass crunched underfoot as he made his way to his desk, eager to check his computer.

The leather chair swivelled as he got closer, and he stopped – Ava, the *other* Ava, was sitting cross-legged before him, grinning widely. She leaned forward, eager to see his reaction.

"Well?" she asked.

"Well what?" He tried to make sense of this but couldn't – it didn't fit with what he knew of her.

"What's the matter, Doc?" she asked, and the smile widened. "You look a bit lost."

"What?" His mind was shrieking a warning, but he couldn't make any sense of what he was supposed to be frightened of. Why had she done this? It went against–

"Me." Now her smile disappeared, and in its place was a woman so cold and mannered that he wondered if he'd ever met the real Ava at all. She stood, and took a step forward, pretending not to notice Greg's corresponding step back. "I warned you about change, but you didn't listen."

"I-I know you d-don't like change," Greg stammered, "but what made you do…"

He gestured towards the carnage that had been his office, lost for words.

"You did," she said, and now the storm was closer. "I warned you things had to stay the same, but you didn't listen."

"I kept things the same," he said. "I don't know what else–"

"You see, that's the problem," she hissed. "It was never about the office. Christ! How anal do you think I am?" She took another step forward, and leaned into Greg, her breath hot now against his neck. "It was about *me* changing. I mustn't, you see, not unless you want this to happen."

Greg looked around the office, noticing now the writing scrawled on the walls. He tried to make out the words, but failed – he had a feeling they didn't really matter.

Ava walked across to the wall, trailed her finger along the same lines he'd just examined, and walked the length of the office; talking almost to herself, her voice a sing-song of lunacy. "I tried to be good, you see. I tried to be nice Ava."

She stared back at Greg, her expression grave. "Nice Ava likes order. She likes to be neat."

Greg gaped in disbelief as she bent to the floor and picked something up, then turned and moved towards him. She'd concealed whatever it was in her hand, hidden in the folds of her long cardigan, but he fancied he'd seen something glint. What was it?

Ava stopped a foot or so away from him, and her gaze when she regarded him was full of sorrow. "It was for the best, you see," she said. "Nice Ava likes you. Even *I* like you."

"I like *you*, Ava," he said, but she just shook her head.

"You like nice Ava, that's true." She moved closer again, and breathed in his scent. "But you're afraid of the real Ava, I can tell."

"Nice Ava isn't the real one?" he asked, eager to delay whatever fate she had in mind for him.

She shook her head. "No. Nice Ava is for when I need to play by the rules, let people think I'm safe. She's for when I don't want anyone to *see* me."

"And what happens when they see the real Ava?" Greg asked.

She sighed. "Well..." she said. "Then I have to stop them seeing. It's a shame things had to change this time," she went on. "I really liked you. We both did."

Her hand swept towards him, and Greg reacted instinctively, leaning back so that the shard of glass she held did no more than skim across his chest. A crimson line appeared in its wake, and he watched in amazement as the blood started to flow. There was no pain yet, he realised, just cold.

Time slowed, and he tried valiantly to move faster than the blade he sensed moving his way again – too late, this time. *It's shock,* he thought. *I'm slow because I'm in shock.* He was in trouble now, fear stealing the strength from his limbs so that he couldn't escape her. The blade flashed again, and this time the world went away – he felt the blood gushing from the wound in his neck, and was dead almost before he hit the carpet.

Ava stood staring down at the body lying before her. "It's too bad," she said. "Ava liked you. All the Avas liked you." Sirens wailed in the distance, looming closer, and she dropped the blade, then walked towards the office door, listening for a moment with her hand on the doorknob – before she walked out into the lobby to face the receptionist's screams.

IN TIMES OF WANT

Once in every generation, I come; whenever I am needed. It seems mankind can only go so long without making a mess of things.

Time and again I have been sent; time and again I have died. And for what? Not for man, that's for certain. I do it for my mother, the Earth. Every so often she must be restored, rescued from the privations forced on her by your petty voraciousness.

Of necessity, I am born each time into squalor and privation – love not the only thing in short supply. It seems I always grow in solitude, my 'siblings' sensing from an early age that I am different. Not like them, thank God. "She's strange," they say, "something's wrong with her." If only they knew.

In some ways I long to be like them, to be unaware, blissful in my ignorance. How I long to belong, to be accepted. To be loved. How peaceful it must be, in some ways, to live my life unaware of the true briefness of my span.

As I grow to maturity, I and those around me become more aware of the changes wrought by their handiwork; the failing crops, polluted waters, dying wildlife… all the detritus of a supposedly 'civilised' society.

Who are you trying to kid?

I watch my family as they struggle to wrest one more decent crop from the failing earth, one more good harvest. They can't. I watch the sky for signs of rain, coming to save me from what I know must happen.

It's no use.

All the time, I can feel the clock ticking, the earth dying – inch by inch.

When I am ten, my oldest brother marries. She is a healthy, smiling girl of seventeen from a nearby farm. Everybody welcomes it, saying maybe their luck will change now. Look at them. A girl of seventeen, and a 'man' of nineteen. He's scarcely more than a boy. Survival of the fittest?

Give me a break.

Within a year they will have another mouth to feed. A mewling pasty-faced baby desperate for milk its mother will by then be too scrawny and malnourished to provide.

And so it goes on.

Round and round it goes.

Generation after generation.

When I am fifteen, both of my sisters marry. Just like that – within six months of each other.

Both waltzing merrily off to the same fate, a lifetime of drudgery, struggling to raise families while their men struggle hopelessly to provide.

It's a farce. A constant battle in which no one can really win. Yet I still wish my life could be that simple.

So the seasons pass, one after the other. I feel them winding down like an old, tired clock. As I am, I suppose. The time grows near. My time. I can feel my body growing, changing, getting ready for its final cycle. I am not the only one that notices, it seems. The local boys start buzzing round, like bees at the proverbial honeypot. My father shoos them away, issuing dire warnings to me of what will happen should I get too friendly with them. As if I would.

It seems as if the heat this year is particularly intense, the air even more humid than usual – and yet there is no relief. No thunderstorms erupting out of the night air to cool and refresh. Not this time.

Listening to the radio with my parents in the evenings, we hear of famine, drought, all over the world. Tiny little pockets yet, I know. But soon…

Now. It's time. My sixteenth birthday. Soon the sign will be sent, and I must go. The local boys are still hovering, and this year it is viewed with more tolerance. It seems I'm old enough now. I look into my mother's mind and am amused to see she has started to muse once more of weddings, babies.

If only she knew.

Still, I must choose someone. One of these boring, coarse louts must be the one to initiate the final day. The 'coming', if you'll pardon the pun.

I watch them, and one by one they manage to put themselves out of the running. One remains. Shy and quiet, he had been content merely to stand back and watch the posturing of the others. He isn't eager to repeat their mistakes. Laughing at something particularly stupid one evening I catch his eye, and we share a smile. He'll do.

We strike up a friendship, he and I. An understanding begins to grow. We take long walks through the fields, charmingly innocent – at least at first.

One evening we come home to hear my father berating the world in general, the weather in particular. "If there's no rain soon," he says, "we are finished. It will be too late for the harvest, and we'll starve."

I take this as my sign.

As I say goodnight to my boyfriend (I've never liked

that expression – so sickeningly coy) I whisper "meet me by the old oak tonight. Midnight." He searches my face for confirmation of this, his dream come true – I have sensed his desire growing for weeks, although he has struggled manfully to behave in a seemly fashion. I smile convincingly, and he goes off happy. One night of joy will be mine, at least. Tomorrow belongs to mankind, once more. I can give them that much.

I stand by the tree at midnight, shivering. The air is cool, holding the promise of autumn. I hear rustling, and turn to see my suitor trying desperately to be quiet, and thus making far more noise than he normally would. We sit in the shelter of the tree, he and I, his arm comfortingly around my shoulders. One hand slips lower to caress my breast, and my breathing quickens. Turning to him, I look deep into his eyes, hopelessly clear and completely without artifice. He's mine, it's that simple.

We kiss, and all is lost. I surrender myself to feelings, the tides of passion rising fast in us both. Dimly, I am aware of being penetrated, although in truth I barely feel it, so lost am I in the currents we generate in the earth below us and in the air above. Truly, this is my time.

At last, when all is done and we lie spent in each other's arms, I cry; for I know my time here is done. My lover tries to comfort me with his protestations of undying love and promises of matrimony – never knowing he's only making things harder; knowing as I do that this is my last night on earth.

He will marry some other girl, and live as his kind has done for more generations than I care to remember. And he will be happy; at least for the most part. He will dream of me, now and then, but that's all. Of what might have been. I say my goodbyes and we each make our separate ways home, to our narrow beds where we lie aching and alone. I fall asleep crying. I would have liked to stay a little longer, just this once.

I feel the sun's hesitant call as it rises. Even the sun is reluctant to call me away, knowing today is the day.

The sun warms me, and I feel my pulse quickening in response. Every cell in my body seems supercharged – absorbing energy in an animalistic version of photosynthesis. My senses are preternaturally alert. I can feel the new life flowing within me – my lover's legacy; more important than he will ever know.

Dust motes dance in the thin beam of sunlight piercing my bedroom's curtains – time to go. I have a long way to go before I can begin.

I dress quickly, after sluicing myself down with cold water, and pause in my parents' doorway, fixing their faces in my mind's eye. My memory will live on, intact, from incarnation to incarnation – knowledge of what I am and what my task is.

Ready for the next time.

They were good people, my parents. They tried hard to do what was right for us, their children. Their future.

I am careful not to wake them as I leave. Even as I go out the door, I am painfully aware that their grieving will be mercifully short-lived. My fate is to be written off as a runaway, one of those myriad hopefuls who flee their lives, mundane or horrific, each year, seduced by bright lights or a safer future, however mythical such futures might be. For most of them, the brightest light they will encounter will be the one above the autopsy table. My parents will write me off as ungrateful, uncaring of their efforts on my behalf, and consign my memory to some deep corner of their minds, hidden away like some shameful secret. I suppose that's exactly what I will be.

If only I could tell them.

I strike out into the bush, raising a little cloud of dust as I go… the earth is so dry. The clouds are already gathering, aware of my imminent arrival. They are hundreds of miles away at the moment, racing to meet me at the appointed time. On I walk, mile after mile. The sun is high now, almost at its zenith. The first breeze, cool as silk, caresses my sweat-streaked face, lifting my skirt almost coyly, eager to feel. Refreshed, I push on. Almost there now. Not far to go.

The wind blows stronger now. Clouds rush towards me and darken, imminent rainfall promised in their every gust.

Help me.

Noon. The sun has reached its peak, and the winds whip round me in frenzied circles, eager for release.

It's time.

Once again, I am the eye of the storm. I shed my clothes and stand naked – ready to meet my fate. Behold, I am life! Feed on me, and renew.

I raise my arms in a gesture of greeting, acknowledging the elements and the power they hold. I am ready.

The wind stills suddenly, all is quiet. The animals are skulking in their holes, even the birds have found shelter. I can hear nothing. The air itself is holding its breath, the calm before the storm.

Wind, rushing at me, lifting me high in its embrace. I see the ground, rushing away from me at a dizzying speed.

I am life – beware.

Now the transformation begins – an incredible,

intoxicating sensation. Cells spinning apart, transmuting – fireflies on the wings of the wind – motes of me dancing with the rain; falling to the parched earth, eager and waiting for my seed.

My life.

To the far reaches of the earth the winds carry me, supporting what's left of my flagging body, far less substantial now than it was before. I feel cells dancing off to join the festival of life. Everywhere I pass, the rains come, sudden and intense. Flooding, refreshing, *replenishing* the earth.

Farmers drop to their knees beneath me, and give thanks to their Gods.

They should be thanking me!

Children run out and play, eager to stamp in the life-giving puddles while their mothers smile indulgently, pleased for the respite, however momentary it might prove to be. I raise my hands in supplication to my Mother and she hears me, pleased with my sacrifice. A rainbow appears in the sky, my reward, my welcome – and the children laugh and clap, happy with my benediction.

The earth breathes a sigh of relief as I pass over, cracked gullies and arid plains unclench themselves and relax as they are covered with the tears of my joy.

Life goes on.

All across the world satellites crackle and reports are given of freak weather conditions – a deluge, worldwide.

Not quite.

Gentler am I than any deluge, falling most where need is greatest. Where there is no real need, no more than a gentle shower. I waste none of my flesh on places already bountiful. There isn't enough to spare for that.

I go where I am needed, where I will make the difference between life – however hard – and a slow, undignified death. Children, with bellies swollen by starvation bearing a single malignant child. Death.

As I pass over these stricken places I add my tears to the falling rain – a spark of life, hope, in each one. I pray they fall on fertile ground.

I can feel the earth give thanks, even as it flexes and sighs with relief. Seeds germinate; the crops will not fail this year.

"It's a miracle," they say, and I smile, hearing my name on their lips at last.

I am Miracle, writ large. I die again and again to bring life, refreshing the earth and its myriad life forms once more.

For ever and ever, time and again, that the world might not end.

Amen.

THE UNQUIET BONES

Alex watched her breath plume out in ragged bursts from between her clenched teeth as she stamped her feet to keep warm. "I can't believe I let you talk me into this!" she hissed.

Mark at least had the good grace to look embarrassed as he muttered, "Well, *I* didn't know the bloody car was going to break down, did I?"

He continued ferreting around under the bonnet and clunking noises ensued, but Alex had the distinct impression he was just banging a wrench against the side or something. He'd never boasted of his mechanical prowess before, and God knew men – in her experience – did like to bang on about such things if they were good at them.

She shivered again as the wind forced its way into the gaps in her clothes, bathing her in icy air. She crossed her legs as the chill made her desperate to pee, and stared up at the building looming over them. Alex moaned, and yelled at Mark again. "I know, but did it have to be here?"

'Here' was officially the Middle of Nowhere, she'd decided; capital of Arse End of the Universe. She tilted her head back and held a hand over her eyes to keep out the rain; it was hard to gauge how high this thing was in the half-light. She was standing in front of a huge, crumbling stone… what? Monastery, hospital?… about five miles outside the nearest small town. And it had taken them about a minute and a half to drive through that – she couldn't even remember its name. Silently, she once more cursed the whim that had made them up sticks and head out on this abortion of a road trip. What in God's name had they been thinking?

Mark finally admitted defeat and slammed the bonnet down, swearing under his breath as he locked the car and walked across the road to join her, wrapping his arms across his chest in his own feeble attempt to keep warm. "Sorry, love. We're stuck here for now." He squinted up at the forbidding walls ahead of them. "Think they have a phone we could use?"

"You know what, at the moment I'll be happy if they just have a loo I could use." She groaned again, now hopping from foot to foot in her discomfort.

Mark grinned. "If you're desperate we could always find a bush. I could stand guard."

Alex snorted. "If you think I'm baring my behind to the elements you've got another think coming, mate."

"Had a feeling you'd say that." He grinned, then took her hand and pulled her close, wrapping his arm around her shoulders in an effort to impart some heat. "Come on, we won't know if we don't knock." He grabbed the round iron knocker hanging from the dark wooden beams that made up the door and swung, hitting the door hard. *CLANG*. Again. *CLANG*. They waited for a few moments, but heard nothing, so he swung the knocker again. *CLANG!*

This time someone heard them – or chose to admit it, realising they weren't going away any time soon. A light flickered in an upstairs window, and they heard the distant sounds of doors slamming, someone walking down a flight of obviously uncarpeted stairs.

Alex chanced a sideways peep at Mark, who

steadfastly refused to meet her eye – he kept his gaze firmly on the doorway, jaw set. He was every bit as nervous as her, she realised. Alex moved closer to him, and was relieved to feel his answering squeeze. "If a guy wearing a creepy butler's costume, or suspenders and a basque answers the door, I'm gone." She heard Mark's muffled snort, and smiled. At least she'd managed to ease his nerves a little, even if it didn't last.

There came the sound of bolts being drawn back, hinges starting to creak – then the door swung slowly back. All was dark within. Alex and Mark stood motionless for a moment, unsure of their reception.

Mark cleared his throat. "Hello?"

A hand appeared on the door, ready to pull it further open, and Alex gasped. She saw the strain on the hand as its owner heaved the dead weight of all that wood further back, and understood then how old – how solid – this place really was.

The hand's owner appeared then, and Alex saw that this was indeed a monastery. The man who stood before them looked to be middle-aged (she'd guess around fifty), with thick, powerful arms and upper body – that much was visible even through his woollen monk's robes. A scar bisected his face, tracing a jagged line from his left brow down to his right jaw-line. One eye stared blindly outward; the other was currently shining with amusement at his visitors. Alex realised she was standing with her mouth open and shut it with a snap, not wanting to appear rude. She felt Mark stir, clear his throat, and knew he must have had a similar reaction.

The stranger spoke, his voice deep and lyrical. "Can I help you?"

Alex nodded. "Please." She gestured back at the car.

94

"Our car broke down. Do you have a phone we could use, to call a garage? We'd really appreciate it."

He stared at them for what felt like forever before nodding. "Of course." Holding the door even wider, he added, "Come in."

They hesitated, just for a moment – until a gust of wind almost took Alex's feet away from under her. Alex grabbed Mark's hand, and together they walked forward into a narrow, deserted yard. Looking back at the door they'd just passed through, Alex could see now that the building was so close to the wall, and the wall itself was so high, that in the dark they hadn't realised there was a yard at all. A light blinked fitfully across the way, just inside what must be the front door. Shadows obscured the glow for a moment, then it returned, guttering in the wind – it was a candle. Had there been a power cut?

They followed the monk across the yard, and rain battered them as if trying to force them back. The sky was gunmetal black, thunder growling in the near distance. *Jesus*, thought Alex. *All we need is lightning and we're in a horror movie!*

They passed through the door on the far side, and found themselves standing in a large, stone-flagged hall. Footsteps echoed somewhere above their heads, and candles flickered in sconces on the panelled walls – dancing in the wind that had found its way inside, even here. Alex shivered. Where were the radiators, the electric lights?

On cue, the monk apologised for the chill. "I'm afraid we're a bit out of touch with things out here. When there's a storm, the power is the first thing that goes. The phone is in here, though," he gestured to an alcove off to their right. "It *should* still be working. It takes something extraordinary to put that out of action as well."

Mark went over to the alcove and picked up the black, Bakelite phone he found there.

They really weren't kidding about being out of touch, Alex saw.

Mark listened for a moment, then smiled at Alex and nodded. There was a ring tone after all.

She closed her eyes and muttered "Thank God." When she opened them again she saw the monk staring at her, his expression quizzical.

"Did you doubt it would be working, Miss?" he asked, his tone amused.

"It crossed my mind," she admitted. "You know, the weather…"

"Of course." He smiled, but there was something off-kilter about it. The monk was staring at her as if he'd seen a ghost.

She smiled, embarrassed, and looked at Mark, willing him to turn and see her; rescue her. At that moment he put the phone down and turned, smiling, then gave her the thumbs up.

She grinned. "They're coming?"

"They are," he said. "Should be here by morning at the latest."

Alex's heart sank. "By morning? Why so long?"

"Something about a bridge crumbling," Mark said. "Traffic's a bitch, apparently. Nothing's getting through." He remembered the monk's presence and coughed, guilty. "Sorry, Father; I er… I forgot you were there."

The monk's gaze was flinty, his disapproval palpable. "Obviously. And it's Brother, I'm no *priest*." He almost spat the word, and Alex wondered again what this place was. "Brother Saul."

"Well I'm sorry, Brother Saul," Mark went on. "I should have been more careful."

The monk nodded. "You should indeed, but no matter." He pushed a door at the far end of the hall open, and invited them inside. "It looks as if you'll have to wait for quite some time. You'll be more comfortable in here."

They walked through, and found themselves in what looked like a library – shelves of leather-bound books lined the walls, and big old, wing-backed chairs situated facing each other in front of a roaring log fire. Further back were more chairs dotted here and there, small tables set beside them. Similar tables stood beside each of the chairs by the fire. Alex relaxed as the warmth started to sink into her, feeling coming back to her numbed fingers and toes. But the need to pee reasserted itself with a vengeance, and Alex moaned. "I'm sorry, F... Brother. Is there a bathroom I could use, please?"

He nodded, gesturing back into the hall. "Go out and turn left; it's the door at the far end of the corridor."

Alex put her head out into the hall and looked to her left and right; no one else seemed to be around. Brother Saul's voice boomed from just behind her, and she jumped, emitting a shrill yelp before she could stop herself.

"Would you like me to show you the way?"

She could see Mark smirking in the background, and her embarrassment quickly became stubbornness. "No thank you, Brother, I'll be fine." She peered out into the darkness again. "It's not far." Alex walked into the hall, and started towards the bathroom.

She almost stopped and went back when the light began to fail as she made her way further from the library. In the darkness, this hall seemed to go on forever, and it was so cold. She shivered and moved closer to the wall, ran her fingers gently over the brickwork – it was okay, she reasoned. If all else failed, she could feel her way along the wall until she reached the end.

The bricks were irregular in size, and dust kissed her fingertips as she brushed them across their surface. At intervals, she felt inexplicable bumps in the brickwork, and tried to trace the shape – these things didn't feel as if they were made of brick at all; they were smoother, rounded at the edges but of varying shapes. She hissed as the pointed end of one such piece scratched her finger, drawing her hand back to suck at the wound. Salty liquid filled her mouth, and she felt slightly sick. She rushed down the hall to the loo and told herself she hadn't really felt whatever it was move, twisting as it tried to get loose, eager for more.

Mark tried to think of something to say. Ever since Alex had left to go to the loo (*What was keeping her*, he wondered? She'd been ages.), Brother Saul had said nothing, just stood staring at the door, waiting for her return – leaving Mark to wait awkwardly in front of the fire.

He stared round the room, searching blindly for inspiration. Turning to face the fire, he saw a painting above the mantel and groaned. *Best way to ruin a painting*, he thought, *putting it there*. He leaned closer and examined the picture in more detail – the building in the background looked remarkably like this one, and the foreground was the yard they'd walked through. Only this must have been long ago, as someone had lit a bonfire in its confines, and a post rose from the flames. The picture was dark, damaged by years of soot and smoke, and it took Mark a moment to realise that a figure was tied to that post, above the conflagration. A woman. What the...?

"'Thou shalt not suffer a witch to live.' It says that in the bible."

Brother Saul again. The man was like smoke himself; he made next to no noise as he walked. Mark found himself idly wondering whether the monks wore shoes, then realised it was irrelevant. He should still have heard the slap of the man's feet against the wooden floor. Mark cleared his throat. "It must be very old, then, this picture?"

"Why do you say that?" Saul asked.

"Well, the witch trials were what, two – three hundred years ago?"

The monk nodded. "True, they were." He moved back to the door, watching for Alex. "But witches still exist, even today. We must always guard against evil."

Mark stared. The man couldn't be serious. And even if he was deluded enough to believe that, it was hardly legal anymore to burn suspects! "B-But still..." he stammered.

The monk turned to face Mark once more, his face alight with zeal. "The picture is old, my son; forgive me. You must permit me a small joke."

Mark sagged with relief. "Of course. I have to admit, you had me going for a minute there."

The monk nodded. "I know. But I did not lie. The picture may be old, but evil is older still. And it's here."

"What?" All warmth had been sucked out of the room, Mark was sure. He felt as if he'd been doused in ice water. Unnerved, he couldn't help looking over his shoulder at the painting, convinced that the woman – for it *was* a woman, he was sure of that – had moved, and was looking at him.

The monk roared with laughter. "I mean it's still in the world, today." He sobered in an instant, and his face became melancholy as he considered the world's fate. "I want no part of it, and neither do my brethren." He pointed to the walls. "It's why we lock ourselves away, and stay apart from all things outside – so that we can better keep ourselves pure, and pray for humanity's salvation."

Alex chose that moment to walk back in, still sucking a finger – her face a sickly white. She headed straight for Mark, and he saw her sway slightly as he moved to meet her, to hold her. He enfolded her in his arms, mindless of the monk's presence; felt her shaking against him.

"Are you alright?" he asked, worried at how frail she seemed.

Alex nodded, head against his chest. "I think so. I just cut my finger; there was something sharp on the wall." Her voice grew small as she went on, "You know I don't like blood."

Brother Saul was there in an instant. "You were cut? Let me see." He grabbed her hand, examining her finger. The firelight illuminated a faint tracery of white lines on her arm, and Saul hissed. "What is this?"

Alex drew it back, embarrassed and a little frightened. "It's fine, Brother. Please don't worry." She drew a tissue out of her jacket pocket and wrapped it around her finger, burying her hand in her pocket. "What are the things embedded in the bricks out there?"

Saul stood back, and didn't answer for a moment. His eyes strayed to the picture behind Mark, then quickly away as he felt Mark watching. "They are part of this place's history, that's all."

"Yes, but what are they?" Alex persisted.

"They are bones."

Mark was aghast. "Bones? In the walls? What kind of bones?"

This time Saul looked directly at him. "Human." He pushed Alex, gently, towards the fire. "Please, warm yourself. I will arrange for some food, a hot drink…"

Alex cried out as he urged her back, her face a rictus of fear. She launched herself from the fireplace and curled up in one of the chairs, shaking.

Saul made as if to touch her again, comfort her, but Mark stepped in front of him. "It's nothing. She just…" He turned to look at Alex, and she nodded her consent. He turned back to Saul and continued, "She just has a problem with fire, that's all. Alex was burned as a baby, still has the scars. You saw them, remember?"

Saul stiffened. He looked at Alex closely, then back at the painting again. His lips moved silently in prayer as he made the sign of the cross. "I'm sorry, I had no idea." The monk bowed and turned to leave. "I'll get the food, you must be hungry."

"I'm sorry, Brother," Alex said. "I didn't mean to make you uncomfortable."

Saul smiled at her for a moment, then his face hardened as his gaze was drawn back to the picture once more. "No matter, child. I'm sorry I scared you." He nodded once more, and was gone.

Alex stared up at Mark, her voice plaintive. "What do you think that was all about?"

"Christ knows," he answered. "The man's insane. I asked about that picture and he told me it was the burning of a witch."

"Charming," Alex commented, staring up at the thing.

"Tell me about it. When I said it must be quite old, he asked me why, said witches still exist."

"Jesus!"

Alex rubbed her eyes, and Mark watched as she drew her feet up under her; something she always did when she felt vulnerable. He wondered if she knew that was when she did it. Mark knelt in front of her, pulled her hand towards him, unwrapped the tissue. Her finger had stopped bleeding, but there were irregular punctures along its length – ugly wounds, deep and jagged. "He said it was a bone that did this, didn't he?"

"So he claimed," Alex answered. "Although it's really old anyway, so hopefully I won't need a tetanus shot. You know, only old bugs not nasty fresh ones?"

Her feeble attempt at humour did nothing to make Mark smile. He kissed her fingers, his face serious. "I'm not sure it works like that," he said. "We'll have to keep an eye on it."

"Don't worry, love," she said. "It doesn't hurt that much. I feel a bit stupid, really."

"Why?"

"Because just before it cut me, I could have sworn I felt the thing move."

Mark laughed. "Must be the weather. We're giving each other the heebie-jeebies. Next you're going to say it bit you."

She nodded, then made room for him on the big old chair. She snuggled into Mark as he sat down, but said nothing – just stared at the flames, grateful for the warmth. Her finger throbbed, and she rubbed it without thinking, which only made the pain spread to her wrist.

She cradled her hand against her chest and closed her eyes; exhausted. In the morning the car would be fixed and they could go on with their journey – find a place to settle down. That was what this whole trip was about, after all: finding somewhere that was theirs, where they could start anew.

Standing with his back against the kitchen door, Brother Saul shook as he closed his eyes and prayed. "Please God, not now," he whispered. "We've been so careful. Please…" The wind howled and sobbed, and the monastery groaned in sympathy as it tried to hold firm against the night's onslaught. In the hall, dust fell to the floor as things best left unseen started to stir, eager to break free…

By the time Saul made it back to the library with a tray of sandwiches and cups of tea, Mark and Alex had dozed off in the chair. Saul set the tray down on the small table beside their chair and stood over them, examining Alex's face. It seemed ordinary enough, although pretty, certainly, but was it familiar? He wasn't sure.

Something made him turn. He saw the flames were starting to die down – creating eerie shadows that capered and swept across the room before scurrying into the deeper darkness at its edges. He walked across to the painting, examined it. Was the woman's face turned slightly more to the front? He must be getting senile in his old age, Saul chided himself. As if paintings could move. A noise behind him made him jump and he turned, suddenly scared.

Alex smiled up at him, eyes bleary. "Thank you for the food, Brother. And for the tea." She straightened in her seat and Mark, too, started to stir. She reached for a cup and held it in both hands, comforted by its warmth. Alex took a sip, sighed, and looked at the brother once more. "What's the matter? You look…"

"I was just surprised, child," he said, smiling, and forced himself to relax. What could she know of this place's history, its shame? "No need to worry yourself."

She smiled again, happy enough for now to accept what he said at face value. Alex yawned, and Mark sat up, stretching, smiling as she handed him the second cup of tea. He looked at Saul and nodded his thanks, but said nothing.

Saul knew he had scared the young man, and part of him rejoiced. He needed to be scared. This modern generation (he forgot, sometimes, that he was only fifty-four himself) knew nothing of the old ways other than what they saw in films – they took nothing seriously except the pursuit of pleasure, not realising that there was always a price to be paid, and it was people like him who paid it, so that they could remain blissful in their ignorance. Saul had questions, many of them – but wasn't sure yet how to proceed.

As if reading his mind, Alex grinned up at him. "Was there something you wanted to know?"

He had the grace to look embarrassed. "Yes. I was just wondering where you'd come from, how far you'd travelled." He saw the fear that flashed across Mark's face, and realised he'd hit a nerve. But how? He hastened to reassure them. "It's just you seem so tired…"

"It's all right, Brother," Alex said. "We've come quite a way – from the Peak District, in fact."

"A long way to travel, especially in this weather," Saul ventured.

"Yes, it is, I suppose." She stared at Mark for a moment before continuing, but he was refusing to be drawn into the conversation, staring down at the floor, his face sullen. "Truth is we're fed up with things where we live; we wanted to start somewhere new. This was... something of a tour, looking for a place that felt like we might be able to call it home."

Saul smiled, even as he felt the sweat greasing his back. "And have you found somewhere like that?" *Please God, no,* his mind whispered. *Not here. Not now.*

Alex shook her head. "Not yet. We're not even sure where we are at the moment; the rain came down so fast and we took a wrong turn just past Bodmin..."

Saul sighed. "You're just outside Perranporth, not far from Newquay. A small place, but we like it."

Alex thought for a moment. "We've still got a bit further to go to hit Land's End, though, haven't we?"

"A bit further, yes. You should be able to reach it tomorrow, if your car's fixed."

"Good." Alex smiled at Mark, happier now than she'd appeared since arriving here. "That's good, isn't it? I've always wanted to see Land's End."

"Yeah, great." Mark's expression belied his words, but he said nothing more. The wind screamed down the chimney, and somewhere a door slammed, making them jump.

Saul flinched, too, but was careful not to let any trace of his disquiet show. Blood had been spilled. All he could do for now was pray that nothing had woken. "Old building," he said. "Nothing to worry about, just the storm." He headed towards the door, intent on finding the source of the disturbance. "Please excuse me," he asked as he walked through the door. "I have some tasks to attend to." Then he was gone.

Alex gazed thoughtfully at the fire, her hand throbbing with a cold fire that was surprising in its intensity. *Maybe I did get tetanus after all*, she thought, then shook her head. She stared up at the painting, and as soon as she gazed on the woman's face (for it was a woman, she could see that clearly now), the pain in her hand started to scream. She flinched, and looked away.

"Where do you think he's gone?" The voice that grated in her ear seemed foreign somehow, its cadence unfamiliar. Alex turned her head slowly, scared of who she might see – and relaxed visibly when it was Mark.

He frowned, worried about Alex. She was pale, yet her cheeks were flushed – she looked sweaty and sick. He noted how she was cradling her hand and wondered if she'd been right after all; could it be infected? He reached for it, gently, and was quick to reassure her when she whimpered in pain. "I won't hurt it, I promise. I just want to see…" He was unwrapping the handkerchief she had round it as he spoke, and as he unwrapped the final layer his eyes widened in disbelief. "Christ, Alex…"

She snatched her hand back, buried it in her armpit, even as the pain forced a howl of protest from her lips. "Ooww!"

Mark coaxed it loose once more. "You have to let me see, Alex, I'll get some water to clean it or something."

This time she let him. Her hand was swollen, the flesh around the bite (it really was a bite, he saw, there were actual teeth marks there, and the punctures went almost to the bone) had turned an angry purplish red colour, with veins of infection snaking their way up to her wrist and even beyond. He saw with an almost detached curiosity that these veins followed the spidery thin scars that were the only legacy of the burns she'd incurred as a child.

"How bad is it?" Alex's voice was thin, quavery, and Mark was touched to see that she'd closed her eyes, unwilling to see the evidence of her hand's injury.

"It's pretty bad," he muttered. Mark touched the flesh, and winced. "Blimey, Alex, it's baking!" He laid her hand gently on her lap and stood, unconsciously wiping his own hands on his trouser legs. "I'd better find Brother Saul, see if I can get something to clean it with, dress it." He made for the door. "Just sit tight, okay? I won't be long."

The door slammed behind him and she was alone, hand throbbing in time with the rise and fall of the flames, or so it seemed. She sank back into the chair, mesmerised, all thought banished bar the knowledge of her pain.

Mark found himself back in a dark hall, with no idea of where to go. He heard footsteps off to his left, somewhere in the depths of the building, and turned in that direction. Even if it wasn't the kitchen, someone was there, he reasoned. Someone who could help.

Some minutes later he was forced to admit that he'd been wrong. There was no one in sight, and all sounds had ceased. He found himself approaching a turn in the corridor, and paused. "Hello?" No response. He edged a few steps further forward and peered round the corner into the blackness. "Hello?"

This time he heard a whisper, quickly stifled. He heard rustling, close by, and he cried out as he stepped quickly back. His foot crunched on something brittle and he felt, rather than heard, the resultant hiss as something skittered away into the depths of the corridor. He turned and knelt, traced the contour of the flagstone with his fingertips. The dust felt curiously textured, large granules of something solid amidst the usual detritus that made up dust – dead skin and fluff of varying kinds. He brought his fingers up and examined them closely – the granules were chalky white in colour, curiously hard looking. He rubbed his fingers together, feeling the coarseness of the grain, then looked down – his eyes happening upon a larger fragment still. He picked this piece up and stared closely at it. Was that… bone? His mind tried to whisper that it couldn't be, but he knew now what he held in his hand. A parchment yellow fragment of some long dead bone; but from what?

A dry, cracking sound echoed just behind him and he whirled, ready to face whatever this thing was. Again, he saw nothing – but he heard the dry, creaking sound of it edging back into the night.

"Can I help you?"

The voice was high and nervous, even more so when Mark yelped and jumped at its sound. He fought to regain control of himself as he took in the figure standing before him. It was another monk, younger than him this time; he looked to be barely out of his teens. Tall and thin, his habit seemed to swamp him, leaving only his bony hands and feet showing outside its folds. "Who the hell are *you*?" Mark croaked.

Saul's voice grated behind him, frightening Mark again. "This is Brother Peter, one of our newer members." Saul sighed. "In fact, Peter is our only new novitiate for some time. It's a more secular world these days."

Peter nodded. "I'm sorry if I frightened you."

"That's okay," Mark said. "It's just it was dark, and there was something..."

"What?" Saul's voice had sharpened, and he stared at the floor as if terrified.

"I don't know, now," Mark admitted. "It was probably only a mouse or something, it's just it sounded—"

"Yes?" Peter prompted.

"It was... dry. Like a cricket, or a locust or something. Or..." He stared at the two men, aware he sounded like a lunatic. "...or bone," he finished.

"Bone?" Saul was trying hard not to smirk, but he was desperate not to show this as he went on. "I'm sure you must be mistaken."

Mark heard a stifled giggle from behind, and sighed. This day just kept getting worse and worse. "I'm sure that's it. Anyway, I wondered if you had a first aid kit?"

"Why? What's wrong?"

Saul's face was creased with concern, Mark saw, and tried not to let that fact sink any deeper into him than his own worry already had. "It's Alex; it looks to me as if her finger's infected."

The monk looked blank.

"You know, from the cut she got earlier?"

Saul pushed past, then, heading left instead of the direction Mark had briefly considered. "Come with me," he shouted, already halfway down a corridor.

Mark rushed to keep up, barely noticing Peter's disappearance. Saul had pushed a door halfway down the corridor on the right-hand side open, and marched straight in. Mark followed, finding himself in what looked like a doctor's surgery. He stopped and stared at the modern equipment, at odds with the surroundings.

Saul looked up, his expression amused. "What? You think because we're monks we live in the dark ages?" He was rummaging around in a chrome and glass cabinet as he spoke, gathering supplies – a bowl, a bottle of what looked like antiseptic, cotton wool, dressings... he handed this to Mark and gestured at a sink in the far corner. "Fill that with warm water, would you?" He slammed the cabinet shut and locked it as Mark did his bidding, then they were off again, racing down the corridor towards the library.... and Alex.

To Mark, it seemed as if the darkness actually cowered away from them as they burst through the library door. Shadows seemed to roil backwards, and he heard hissing – then felt a little ashamed at his own nerves as he realised it must be the coals from the fire, hissing as they released some errant hint of gas or moisture from their depths. Alex was still in the chair, her form oddly wasted in the half-light from the fire; she looked.... *different*, somehow, although Mark couldn't have said why; at least, not then.

She struggled to sit up as they approached her, and they could see the damage the fever had visited upon her. Alex's face was thin and wan, her expression harried. Beads of sweat stood proud on her forehead, and her skin had a sickly yellow sheen that spoke of the infection that seemed to have raced through her body. Mark was shocked to see the thin, spidery purple lines were now erupting from the neck of her jumper, scoring faint lines upwards as she struggled to keep some semblance of herself.

"What is it? What's wrong?" Alex whispered, her

voice as insubstantial as the smoke disappearing up the chimney, drawn by the storm's force.

"Nothing, love," Mark answered as he sat by her side, placed the bowl of water upon the small side table there. He nodded his thanks as Saul placed the cotton wool beside him, opening the small bottle to pour some of its foul smelling contents into the water.

"Antiseptic," Saul explained, in answer to Mark's unspoken question.

Alex was muttering, slumped back in the chair once more now she realised who was with her. Her eyes were half-open and she seemed to be speaking with someone, although no one else was near.

"Who are you talking to, love?" Mark asked.

"Secret..." she whispered.

"A secret?"

Alex nodded. "Mustn't tell. She'll leave if I tell."

Saul stiffened. Fighting to keep his voice level he asked, "Who will leave, child?"

The voice that came from Alex's mouth was different now, its tone harsher, its cadence more formal. *"You would have me believe you don't know, Saul?"* She laughed – a harsh, crazed sound that was at odds with Alex's semi-comatose state. *"Be careful what you ask."*

Saul said no more, simply crossed himself and started to pray, casting glances at the painting as he did so.

Mark followed Saul's gaze, and told himself, afterwards, that he couldn't be seeing what he thought. Couldn't be staring into the face of the blaze's victim. She was looking straight at him, her expression one of joy – and hate.

He shivered. There was a grating noise, and dust showered the floor before the fireplace, although he couldn't see where it came from.

"Don't look at it!" Saul pushed forward and took hold of the painting, pulling it from the wall and casting it into the flames. The wind screamed, and the fumes pouring off the painting as it was consumed were sucked straight upward. The canvas shrivelled up and burned to a crisp, the frame's embers joining the coals as they glowed with a fierce heat. Then the wind seemed to funnel straight back down the chimney and into the library, hitting Saul full force and throwing him back across the room. He slammed into the wall, and Mark saw the light go out in his eyes as blood erupted from the split on his scalp, pouring down his face. His body went limp and slid down the wall, landing in a heap on the stone floor. The wind vanished as quickly as it had come, and all was still once more.

Alex screamed; Mark whirled round.

"Alex?" She'd fallen forward, over the arm of the chair, and Mark brushed the hair back from her forehead as he eased her back in the chair so that she was more comfortable. She was unconscious now, moaning in her sleep. The first faint traces of purple could be seen on her jaw-line, creeping ever upwards.

Saul's body moved. Mark watched in horror as the mound of cloth squirmed, giving the monk the semblance of sentience once more. Something wet ripped, and a pool of dark fluid welled around the body. Mark moaned.

Still the body moved, accompanied by sucking sounds, and Mark's feet failed him as he saw what looked like the monk's hand – bloody still, but just bone now – inch away from the light, eager for the dark recesses of the room.

The movement stopped, and Mark realised he was

sitting on the library floor in a pool of his own fluid. He'd wet himself.

"*Soon*," Alex muttered, in that voice that was so unlike her natural one; and Mark cried out as if he'd been struck.

What was going on in this place?

The stones creaked and moaned, bewailing the ruin that was coming for them all – long years had they held the monks' secrets, and in all that time their inhabitants had been left alone. Now the Beast was awake, and would destroy them all.

Now that she was back.

Down the halls things crept, woken from their slumber by the painting's destruction. Held fast for so long, encased in stone, they inched their way towards the library where they sensed their rebirth was imminent. Somewhere deep within the building's heart, something rejoiced.

Peter huddled in his bed, covers pulled over him. He prayed for redemption, and for the Good Lord to deliver them all this night. He sobbed as he prayed, words almost unintelligible in his fear. "Dear Lord, protect us from the Beast, help us to protect the innocent; to hold them safe from harm..."

Something laughed in the darkness. *"You'll need more than prayers this night, boy!"*

Peter screamed as a mist enveloped him, the ice of its breath freezing his own. He felt himself squeezed tight as the creature's embrace grew stronger, and was still aware when his bones started to crack under the pressure; when blood bubbled up in his lungs as splinters from his ribs pierced them over and over; as his heart ruptured and its beat faltered to a stop, blood erupting from a mouth that breathed its last.

The creature sighed in delight, and rose from the body in a mist now crimson with gore. Features could be discerned, if only dimly; slivers of flesh and bone more solid here and there among the mist.

"Soon," it said.

Mark crouched on the library floor, listening to the sounds of destruction that raged around him. He whimpered as things skittered behind the skirting boards, watching clouds of dust as they fell from the ceiling and out of gaps in the walls; gaps that seemed to be growing wider by the second.

"Mark?" The voice was weak, but it was undeniably Alex. *Thank God*, Mark thought, as he faced her.

She was even frailer now, if that were possible. Skin and bone. He quailed at that; felt ashamed for recoiling, even if only slightly.

Her brow creased, and she fought to push herself into a more upright position. "I had the strangest dreams…"

Mark went to help her, shocked at how light she was. Her bones felt like twigs under her clothes, flesh stretched thin across them – almost wasted away. "You did?"

"There was a woman; at least I think it was a woman. She seemed to know me…"

"Any idea who she was, love?" Mark had an idea this question was more important than they yet realised, and was half afraid of the answer.

"No," Alex said, voice full of regret. "But I get the feeling I really should. There's something so familiar…"

114

Her voice tailed off, and she stared into the flames, all concentration on them now.

Mark stared at the painting, inexplicably back on the wall, undamaged, wondering what it was that had frightened Saul so badly the last time he'd gazed at this. It took a moment for that knowledge to sink in. The woman was gone. The poor soul who'd been burnt at the stake wasn't tied to the pole in the middle of the fire any more. He moved closer, saw that the ropes were still there, looped around the pole's base – and the flames were licking hungrily at the twigs and branches piled high around it. But the woman (*witch?*) was now nowhere to be seen.

"*Remember...*" The word was little more than a whisper, but Mark spun round as if possessed.

No one was there. Alex was watching him, eyes hooded, a half-smile on her lips.

"Alex? Did you hear that?"

She sighed, then looked up at him – with someone else's eyes. Mark shuddered as he realised Alex wasn't with him anymore, the creature had taken her place. "*Alex is... elsewhere, for the moment.*"

Mark fought to keep calm, keep this – thing – talking while he figured out how to help Alex, get her back where she belonged. Far away from this God-forsaken place.

The creature inhabiting his girlfriend laughed at that. "*You are right, boy. God forsook this place many years ago.*"

"Why?"

The creature sat forward, Alex sneered as it growled at him. "*It would be better to say* He *forsook* me. He *let them burn me, as a witch, let them damn my soul.*"

Mark cringed. "You're a witch?"

The creature inside Alex shook her head. *"Not then, no. I was just… different. I had some skill in healing, a sixth sense… the monks* believed *I was evil."*

"And they burned you? For that?"

It nodded once more. *"It is as you say. They burned me, for that."*

Like a puppet, Alex's body lurched upright, then jerked around the library, examining shelves and walls with eyes that should have been sightless, but somehow saw even though Alex herself didn't. Couldn't. Not with that thing in control. Something rapped on the door and it flew open, the wind it admitted soughing through the room in an instant; the fire dimming under its assault. Alex traced the mantel with her wounded hand, leaving a trail of blood along the stone. There was a crash as the mantel broke free and fell to the floor; releasing what it had held prisoner for so long – the eyes in that skull glowed with a fire that spoke of its desire to hurt, to seek revenge. Alex moved into the centre of the room, still controlled by the… thing that walked in her flesh.

Mark shivered, and the thing laughed with Alex's mouth, her features still blank and unknowing. *"But oh, the things I learned after they'd burned my body."*

Something was crawling towards her, he saw; the floor seemed to be covered with creatures Mark couldn't put a name to – even if he'd wanted to. The light flared a little brighter, and he shivered as he realised the creatures were something else entirely, not even alive. Bones inched their way along the stones, clacking their progress towards this beast. Some were ancient, by the look of them, resembling the thing that had bitten Alex. Small clouds of dust rose from the midst of these, as the bones shook off the remnants of their erstwhile prisons, eager for a *newer*, wetter home. Others... were harder to look at, dripping with the fluids that had erupted from their vessels as they were ripped free; flaps of flesh hanging from them as they crawled, sweeping the stones into a bloody mat that heralded the coming of a new mistress here, in this place.

The creature laughed when it saw Mark's expression. *"Don't be so squeamish. I won't always inhabit this, your partner."*

Hope dawned in Mark's eyes. "You mean, you'll let her go?"

"Of course. I have no wish to hurt my daughter, my only flesh."

"What?"

Realisation began to dawn as Mark stared at Alex's body, inhabited now by a much crueller mistress. He saw the spider-thin scars she'd had since infancy, legacies of a fire, she'd said. Mark looked again at this creature within her; its features now superimposed over those he loved and knew so well   eerily similar, he could see.

Mark stared at the painting once more, then turned back to Alex. "But the fire..."

"You should have listened to Saul, boy. Evil didn't end with the burnings long ago; it still persists." The creature smiled, and looked down at her daughter's form, relishing the blue fire that rippled up and down its length. *"Saul himself set the fire that damned me, picked my daughter from the fire that birthed her, when I went into labour because of the pain."*

Mark stared. "You were *pregnant* when they set the fire?"

She nodded. *"Now who was evil, and who maligned?*

He hid her! He stole her from me; hid her where he thought I'd never see!" Keening, she lifted her arms and allowed herself to float free of Alex, who collapsed on the floor at her feet. Mark rushed to her, pulled her clear, and cradled her in his arms as he sank to the ground. Bones chattered as they approached. Mark watched in fascination as, one by one, they were swept up into the maelstrom that had been Alex's mother, once upon a time. Now her form was clearer, denser; the bones and gobbets of flesh that clung to them gave her solidity, bringing her nearer in flesh… bringing her properly into their presence. To her daughter.

"Give her to me!" it roared, and reached for Alex.

Mark shook his head, too frightened now to speak. He pulled Alex tighter, and groaned as he felt the scratches of bones not yet absorbed by the Beast. He brushed them off as best he could, from himself and Alex, struggling to remember how to pray. "Dear God," he started, and the Beast screamed.

"Do not try to escape, she's mine! Your God can't help you now, this place belongs to me!" She howled once more, and dust fell from the walls. A crack appeared in the floor by its feet, snaking its way towards them.

Mark began to cry – then stood tall once more, determined to defend Alex even to his own death. *"You can't have her,"* he said, and made the sign of the cross, and the walls themselves shuddered.

The creature hissed, and gestured at Mark. Unseen things plucked at his clothes, and he batted them away, unconcerned. Then he glanced at Alex, and his gaze hardened as he sighed, turning to face the Beast.

"You can't have her," he repeated. *"She's beyond your reach now."*

"No!" The Beast shook its head, and Mark flinched as something – flesh, bloody bone, he wasn't sure which – struck his cheek. It hissed as it burned its way down to his neck, but he barely noticed.

Mark gestured, and the fire blew towards the Beast in a great cloud of destruction... to no effect. The Beast seemed to feed on its flames, bones knitting together and flesh growing more solid in its warmth.

Alex moaned; Mark tightened his grasp on her. He could feel the heat snaking through her body; see its evidence in the traceries of her scars – growing redder and more livid by the moment.

She opened her eyes, then, and Mark nearly dropped her – fire blazed in each pupil, no trace of his Alex remaining. She forced herself upright, and when she laid a hand on his arm to pull his grip loose, he nearly screamed. The heat was unbearable.

"Alex!"

"What, love?" Her words were soft, kind, but her actions belied them. She pushed him back, smiling as the flesh on his arm hissed and sizzled – as she stood she turned her gaze on the Beast that stood in the remnants of the fire, triumphant.

Mark fell back as Alex released him, and as he hit the floor he saw what was left of Saul dangling from the Beast's grip, the creature almost solid now, a myriad of bones (both hers originally, he guessed, as well as from her victims tonight) – fixing themselves in their allotted space on her dreadful frame. She stood before them clad only in a robe of smoke, and the smell was awful – a mixture of charred flesh, fresh blood... and decay.

Mark lay there, choking for breath, but couldn't move as the Beast gestured and his beloved Alex began to move forward. As she drew closer, a weird metamorphosis seemed to be taking place – the Beast was growing more substantial, and Alex… waning. That was the only word which could adequately describe this, Mark thought. She was growing smaller, frailer – less *there*, with every passing second. A gout of flame bellowed from the hearth and she was lost in its midst; Mark's wail went unheard by all but the Beast, who simply smiled – an expression so far from humorous Mark cried at the sight. When the flames died down he was relieved to see Alex was still standing. But her clothes were gone now, the last scraps of cloth glowing gently as the flames died down and they melted away to nothing. Her bare skin was livid, traced head to toe in a network of fine white scars, more than he'd ever seen before – the fire seemed to have brought them out, somehow, undone all the operations and skin grafts she'd told him had been necessary after her… accident.

Except it hadn't been an accident at all, had it?

The Beast laughed, then, and stared down at him. *"Finally you see the truth."*

Alex had reached it (her) now; and stood beside it unconcerned. The creature draped an arm around her shoulders, and Alex smiled in approbation, basking in her mother's attention.

"The monk told the truth when he said evil still exists," it said. *"And it's true they burned me for my 'crimes', which were no more than a few love spells, some healing – until they burned me."*

"I don't believe you," Mark replied. "Why would you have been burned just for that?"

The creature laughed. *"Let's just say they disapproved of one of my 'cures'. I brought a man back from the dead, reunited him with his love – his murderer wasn't happy since he'd wanted the girl for himself."*

"You raised a corpse?" Mark blurted.

"Technically." The Beast stared down at him, lost in thought. Mark said nothing, knowing he was safer that way. He couldn't help gazing over his shoulder at the painting. Where *she* had been.

The creature shrugged, a gesture that struck him as disturbing in its ordinariness. *"I wasn't to know how he'd return."*

That simple phrase told Mark all he needed to know; she'd raised a man from the dead with complete disregard for the consequences, and he'd come back wrong. "What did he do?" he asked.

"He attacked his love, destroyed his murderer... several neighbours before he was stopped."

There was more to this, Mark knew. "He didn't kill his lover?"

"No. He spared her for the sake of her unborn child." The creature glanced at Alex then, and the tale was finally told.

So that's it, Mark thought. Aloud, he merely said, "You?"

Now she turned the full force of her gaze upon him, and he fell back, terrified. There was no pity to be found here, he knew, he had no recourse but for Alex... if she even remembered him. As if she'd heard him, she focussed on him properly and looked sad, lost even. As if in response, her mother's grip tightened around her shoulders. Alex flinched, aware now of the truth of her situation.

"Alex?" he whispered.

She made as if to move towards him, but the creature

grabbed her arm. Alex mewed in disgust and tried to get away.

The Beast clung tighter, and Mark saw smoke escaping from between its fingers as it fought to keep hold of its offspring. Whatever glamour had held Alex fast in its grip was gone now, and she fought to break free, to reach him.

"Let her go!" he shouted, launching himself up and forward, ready to do battle.

He grabbed Alex's other arm and pulled, causing her to scream in pain as the two opposing forces fought for her possession. Mark was helpless against that strength, and had to let go. Crying, he sank to his knees before Alex, and rested his head against her legs. "I'm sorry," he cried, "I'm so sorry."

The creature pulled Alex away, forcing another cry from her. *"Come, Alex,"* it grated. *"Come to Mother."*

Alex screamed, then rained blows on its head, forcing it to free her. She fell backwards, and landed in a heap on top of Mark, who still cowered on the floor before them. "Never!"

The creature roared, the ground starting to rumble; flagstones falling around them under the force of her displeasure.

Alex groaned, and spread her body over Mark's, taking the brunt of the falling masonry in an attempt to protect him. "Mark," she whispered. "Mark!"

Mark struggled to focus – a stray stone had clipped his temple, opening a gash there. His head throbbed as he fought to pay attention. "Alex? Wha…"

"There's no time, Mark, listen to me."

He nodded, groaning at the pulse of pain unleashed in his skull. "I'm listening."

"This is my fault," she said. "She came back because of me. *For* me."

He said nothing; there was no arguing with the truth, and both of them knew that now – knew she was, somehow, this thing's daughter.

She pushed him, gently; made him sit up. "You have to go. You have to get out of here."

"Alex, I can't! I won't leave you…"

The thing roared once more, and the heavens answered in kind. The storm was directly over them now, the sky itself trying to abate the force of this monster with the sheer weight of water it was throwing down on them. Lightning lit them all in stark relief, and Mark knew the strangeness of that vision would remain etched on his mind forever. Alex, naked and bloody but defiant still, knelt before the crazed creature that once had been her mother – and loved her still in its own demented fashion.

Alex raised her eyes, and the sorrow they held broke Mark's heart. "Blood calls to blood, Mark. My flesh knows the truth even if I don't want to." She gazed back at it, and groaned. "That's my mother – and I was ripped from her womb even as the flames took her flesh."

The ground shuddered, cracks appearing in the floor – snaking their way towards them. "See?" She tried to smile. "Even the earth knows she doesn't belong here. But she won't go without me."

"A-Alex, no," Mark stammered, "you can't go with her. You can't!" He touched her face, traced its contours with his fingers. "What will I do without you?"

"We can't think of that," she said, her voice breaking. "*I* can't. Mark, she'll destroy everything she comes across if I don't go to her."

Mark was crying now, knowing she was right. He

watched, helpless, as Alex rose and faced the thing that had birthed her with its dying breath. She paused for just a moment, smiled at him, and stepped forward.

The thing stopped screaming. It leaned forward until its face was nearly touching Alex's, and sniffed. Its face grew quizzical, and drew closer still, touched Alex's cheek with its own, whimpering as it recognised its child – and enfolded Alex in its embrace.

Alex moaned as it encircled her, fetid breath making her gag. Slowly, she brought up the arm she'd kept concealed behind her, not wanting to make the thing curious.

There was a scream that shook the building to its core as Alex brought her arm forward, plunging the shard of bone she'd hidden into the creature's chest.

Mark cringed, holding his arms over his head even as he tried to see what had happened. Blue light poured from the creature, light that sobbed and moaned and had a voice. *Voices*, Mark corrected – the souls it had devoured even as it stole flesh and bone to make itself whole were free now, seeking a peace that wouldn't be found here.

The creature itself was fading, the light that had signified its presence fading, gaps appearing in its frame. It clung to Alex, unwilling to let her go, even as the grave reclaimed it.

Alex was in its grip still, crying in pain as the creature dug its fingers into her shoulders, opening gashes as it did so. Blood poured down her chest, and the scars burned brighter still.

Mark watched as her flesh burned, even as her mother's had so long ago – and tried to picture her as she *had been*, before they'd arrived at this Godforsaken place. He watched his lover cry and struggle, knew that she'd never escape. She was too broken. Crying, he picked up a piece of glass – the base and stem of a wine glass, he thought, broken earlier – and walked towards Alex.

The creature hissed as he approached, but Mark sensed it lacked the strength to do him much harm. Alex smiled, nodded, and he thought he saw her mouth one word. *"Please."* With a cry, he drew his arm back, then plunged the glass deep into the creature's chest, watching as Alex slumped in her mother's arms, unconscious now; saw the creature wail in disbelief before it imploded – blue light collapsing, leaving a heap of bones and ash on the ground... around Alex's body, ravaged by her mother's fire, every bit of strength spent.

Dawn broke late, the first rays of the sun lighting Mark's progress as he dug a grave in the monastery's forecourt. The building blazed behind him, greasy smoke roiling into the sky. He grunted with each stroke of the shovel, dirt streaking his bare torso as he sweated and strained.

Finally, the hole was deep enough. Turning, Mark picked up what looked like a bale of black wool, then dumped it into the grave. An arm escaped, and he leaned down, covering the limp and bloody mess gently before standing up once more. He stared up at the sky, mouthing a prayer. This time there was no answer; this time it was done.

WORLD WITHOUT END

It was the same dream every night without fail, had been for weeks now. She was sitting up in a bed grown huge, as she herself had – so big she felt as if she filled the world, as if she *was* the world.

Her body fell away beneath her like the slopes of some vast mountain. She could just make out her hands, far off in the distance – islands in the midnight pool of her room. The walls of her room were lost in the darkness.

And then it came. A familiar sensation filled her mouth, causing her to clap her hands over it as if for protection – a tingling, burning sensation that rapidly increased and spread until it felt as if her whole body were on fire.

It was happening again. She could feel her teeth start to wobble, ever so slightly; the motion becoming gradually more pronounced. Her teeth tottered, one by one, rocking in their fleshy beds – eager to be free. One by one they began to fall, crashing and rebounding off the outcrops of her body; her breasts, her drawn-up knees.

Her vast hands flew after them like flapping wings before returning to her bleeding mouth; fingers gently cupping it in a desperate effort to prevent further loss. The lost teeth shone far below, huge monoliths on the coastline that had been her top sheet, once upon a time. She began to cry.

Tears poured down her massive face, dividing into streams and rivulets, creating tributary after tributary –

running freely down the channels of her nightgown – down to the vast ocean of her coverlet far below, lapping at her legs like the rising tide.

She stayed like that for what seemed like ages; keening and rocking. Her cries became the wind, howling across the moonlit landscape; until she was caught up in a tornado that span her back down into insignificance, her room her own once more. She fell back, exhausted, onto her sweaty sheets, and let the darkness cradle her fall into oblivion. Her last waking thought was a prayer, *Let there be no more dreams tonight*. She wasn't even sure who she was praying to, but prayed that no more dreams would disturb her that night. She wasn't sure she could stand it.

At the breakfast table next morning she sat quietly, subdued, worrying at her teeth with her tongue. All still there, just a dream after all. She played with her scrambled eggs, trying to delay the act of chewing as long as possible. Her mother noticed, and asked if she had a tooth-ache. Would she like her to make an appointment to see the dentist? She was quick to reassure her. The last thing she wanted was someone poking around in her mouth.

On the way to school, she hardly noticed her own surroundings. They seemed less real to her than the previous night's dream. She knew there were probably all sorts of fears exposed by her dream – fear of failure, of not being the best – of being exposed. Exposed as the seething mass of teenage insecurities she really was, rather than the confident, popular girl her family assumed her to be. She had friends, of course, but she wasn't on any mythical 'A' list, no matter how much she wished she was. There were plenty of parties she wasn't invited to. The day passed quietly, without incident – the more so as a result of her own reticence, even greater than usual. Her parents, noticing how introspective she was becoming, tried to coax her out of it – to draw her into their own seemingly banal round of concerns and anecdotes: the weather, where they should go on holiday this year, who was having an affair with their secretary, and did their wife know?

She played the game, and they were satisfied. Normality resumed, at least for them.

Life went on. Her days were a steady round of school, homework, and the usual teenage concerns – such as whether Gary from up the road was interested in her or her friend Louise. Louise maintained it was her, but then she would, wouldn't she? She knew that was wrong – had seen the way Gary looked at Louise.

Life went its usual humdrum way, at least on the surface; and yet underneath it all there lay the quality of a dream sequence from some old movie – just a series of images careering from one to the next, getting nowhere. Her dream was still waiting, lurking beneath the thin veil that separated sleep from waking, teasing her, making her more nervous by the day.

Monday. Almost a whole week since the last time she'd had the dream. Her mood had begun to lift as her night terrors receded further into the distance; reality crowding in to take its place. When she had climbed the stairs to bed tonight, she had been almost cheerful. She could see an end to the nightmare, it was almost behind her.

She should have known better.

In order to put it behind her, she had to confront it first.

Almost midnight, and she was woken by a wind – no gentle zephyr, this – whipping through her bedroom. Funny. She couldn't remember having left her bedroom window open. It wasn't something she usually did. Too easy for bugs of all descriptions to get in if the window was open. Bugs, however, were the least of her worries tonight. She sat up, shuddering, a sigh of negation dying stillborn in her throat.

It had happened again, as she had known, deep down, it must.

Her bedroom walls were disappearing, melting into the nothingness beyond; the wind rushing uninterrupted now to surround her. Stars loomed, pinpricks in the wall of darkness that fell like a curtain, heavy and velvet soft.

The wind almost seemed to carry the sound of sorrow; a high-pitched keening seemed to hover just behind each gust; barely audible. She felt it echo deep within, and was afraid. It was setting up some sort of resonance deep inside, she could feel it; layer upon layer creating a ripple effect. It felt as if it was jarring every atom loose, till she thought she could stand it no more and would just fly apart.

The familiar buzzing sensation was beginning in her mouth. Her gums started to leak crimson tears, and she prepared to watch her teeth fall once more, forming new land masses in the vastness of her room. She moaned, both in pain and resignation, even pleasure. Her body found it strangely enticing in spite of the pain. The paradox caused a perverse delight to caper, barely acknowledged, behind her fear.

The dream unfolded as before, with one difference. It seemed to her, this time, that she could hear echo upon echo – her cries repeated a dozen times or more. Layer upon layer of sound, reverberating both deep within her and all around, so that it seemed as if she were filled with it, resonating as with the pealing of church bells. A strange church, this.

She woke then, shaking, though for a few seconds her room didn't quite seem as it should. It, too, held echoes, as if others were imposed upon it; echoes of other selves.

Footsteps were pounding down the hall, then her bedroom door was flung wide. Light flooded in, and her room was hers once more, familiar in its singularity. She felt safe, at last.

Then she was in her mother's arms, soothed once more, falling back into sleep with almost ruthless speed. She could hear a storm raging outside her window as she drifted off, but it was too remote to bother her. She barely registered the fact that one of her teeth was missing.

She was brushing her teeth in the bathroom the next morning when that fact finally registered. Her eyes widened comically in the bathroom mirror as her tongue probed the sponginess of the empty socket. She looked like a fish. Fleeting images from her dream raced through her mind, but were quickly discounted. It must have been bad, that's all – some infection, maybe. Her mother agreed, and quickly made an appointment to see the dentist, to check and see if further action were needed. No mention was made of her dreams, but she'd heard her parents talking about her, whether she should "see someone." She resolved to keep her dreams to herself from now on.

The dentist concurred; there must have been some infection present. He gave her a course of antibiotics, "purely precautionary," he called it, and scheduled a check up in a couple of weeks. She was relieved, but couldn't bring herself to entirely believe him.

The daily round continued unabated and yet, she thought, there were rumblings. She was aware of a growing sense of unease – as if she were caught in the eye of a storm. She could see signs that things were in turmoil, and that they were all related. Her mother drew her attention to an article in the newspaper that evening. "ISLAND RISES FROM SEA IN VOLCANIC ERUPTION." Apparently some uninhabited island in the South Seas had been devastated when a seemingly dormant volcano had erupted savagely. In the aftermath of the eruption, massive tidal waves presaged the rising of another island, a little less than a mile away.

All this had happened the previous night. Hurricanes, tidal waves, everywhere. Devastation to echo the turmoil she had felt inside.

On the news, that night and every night, experts discussed it until they were blue in the face, blaming it all on the ozone layer, global warming, pollution – anything else they could think of.

But they didn't really know, did they. No one did. In her heart, she knew it was nothing to do with any of those things. She could feel the real cause; the maelstrom that presaged a new beginning – or maybe it was the end.

And it was getting stronger, coming closer.

Her family and friends, once so close to her, were gradually becoming strangers; her growing sense of isolation shunting them further and further away, to the periphery of her consciousness. Her mind was fully occupied with the strangeness she felt growing inside her. They didn't know her any more, and on some deep level, they didn't really want to. They were too afraid. She'd caused storms, somehow she knew that – although no one would believe her, were she to tell. If the dreams kept escalating, what else could she cause? She had to believe the dreams would pass, tell herself it was her imagination.

So she carried on – a solitary island marooned in a sea of uncertainty, sinking further by the hour.

Thursday – almost a full month since the last dream. Her terror had levelled off to an almost manageable level, the culmination she had sensed coming seemed far away, at least for now. Thinking the worst over, she relaxed her guard, not realising what lay within had been waiting for just that; eager for release.

The dance began.

Shaking. The walls were shaking. She awoke with a cry, certain the world was coming apart all around her. It had happened again. The walls of her room were fading, becoming inconsequential, the stuff of dreams – once more she dwarfed the surrounding landscape that logic told her should be there, even though she couldn't see it. She reached up and touched the moon. Grown vast beyond imagination, she cried out in fear – and the earth shook. Groaning beneath her weight, it began to crack and sunder.

She wasn't alone in her agony. Her cries were echoed again and again, it seemed the universe itself reverberated to their sound.

The burning sensation in her mouth grew, and as she opened her mouth to scream the first tooth fell. No dream this time. She watched in silent horror as it dropped, down and down, crashing into the depths so far beneath; the exact distance unfathomable. A faint splash, just a suggestion of sound, as it finally fell into the ocean her coverlet had been.

Another, then another, she could feel still more wobbling, becoming loose in their sockets – could tasted the blood welling up in their place, salty as the tears falling in torrents down her cheeks into the unseen valleys below.

Once more that juddering sensation ripped through her; making her feel as if she were coming apart at the seams. Every cell in her body seemed to be vibrating – a commotion that was growing by the second. She realised with a start that the feeling was no longer just inside her, if it ever had been. It was everywhere. Without even feeling it, she had shrunk back to normal size – at least she thought so; or maybe it was just that the others, containing and/or contained by her, had become more visible to her battered senses – and now it felt as if the house were slap bang in the middle of an earthquake. She held onto the bed, feeling it rocking manically from side to side; harder and harder, trying to pitch her off, in a last ditch attempt to return to normality. What had once been inanimate now animated beyond measure, and desperate to return that gift.

She clung to the mattress, wailing loudly for help.

No one came.

Her crying spiralled up and up, a formless wail that was almost beyond sound.

The wind keened around her, in her – a thousand voices in a discordant harmony, all crying of loss, and death, or both.

The world splintered around her.

To an outsider, if there had been any left, it would have looked something like a television picture breaking up, becoming grainy – as if the aerial had developed a fault. She appeared to shimmer for a moment, then distort.

Then she exploded.

She seemed to fly apart into an infinite number of pieces, worlds without end, as if she herself was the nucleus of one cell – life from death repeated to the nth degree; world without end, amen.

SOMEONE TO WATCH OVER YOU

Emily glanced over her shoulder again, hoping to find nothing – but her shadow was still there, keeping pace. She sped up, annoyed to find that the increased tempo of the tap-tap of her heels was making her feel worse, not better – the fact that they'd picked up a gruffer echo was something she tried to ignore. She was only a few feet from the stairs leading down to the exit now; and she cursed her penchant for sitting at the front of the train – all it had done was leave her with further to go to get to safety.

The lights in the waiting room went out, and she moaned – thank God she was at the stairs now. What on earth had possessed her to wait till the last train home when she knew damn well how dark it got on the platform at this time of night? East Finchley was a beautiful station, but it was also the first station going northwards that wasn't underground – and when the staff switched the waiting room lights off, it got dark quickly.

She heard her pursuer's breathing quicken and grow ragged as he started to run, and she launched herself at the stairs with little thought of how hard it would be to keep her balance at that speed. She clattered downwards, praying someone would hear her and come to investigate – but no one did. Towards the bottom she tripped, and felt herself grasped by strong arms – her rescuer stood her up and moved on before she had a chance to register who it was; her only impression was of strength and the cloying smell of tobacco smoke.

Then he was gone. She stood in the corridor and stared upward, scared her pursuer would still follow – there was a scuffle up there, then a cry, and finally the sound of squealing brakes as the last southbound train was brought to a sudden halt. An alarm sounded and she blanched, knowing what had happened. She just didn't know to whom. A shadow moved at the top of the stairs, and she saw a man's silhouette against the lights of the incoming train – a tall figure in a long, dark coat; a hat obscuring his features. He seemed to look down at her, just for a moment, and then he was gone.

Now staff arrived. She found herself shouldered to one side as guards ran up the stairs, and a very nervous young man tapped her arm, tried to shepherd her back towards the ticket offices, and the way out. "If you'd come this way, Miss …"

She nodded, and allowed herself to be led. From behind her came the unmistakable sound of someone throwing up.

As she walked into the office next morning, chatter stilled – she saw heads turn as she passed by, eyes drop as she sought to engage them and find out what was so interesting. Then she saw her boss, George Burrows, appear at his door and beckon her into his office, and her heart sank.

"If I could have a word, Miss Lane," he said, and stood back to allow her entrance.

She nodded and swept past him, trying to ignore the nervous muttering that swelled behind her.

He followed her in and indicated the chair opposite his, and waited until they were both seated before he continued. "I'm surprised to see you in this morning," he said, his tone kind.

"You are?"

"You've been up most of the night, after all," he went on. He registered the incomprehension on her face and smiled. "This is a newspaper, Emily, surely you realised we'd hear of a death on the line?"

Realisation dawned, and Emily was embarrassed. "I didn't think. I mean, I knew you'd hear about the body on the line, I just didn't connect the fact you'd find out I was on scene, as it were."

"You're tired, of course," George said. "There's no reason for you to be up to speed with the office at this hour." He pressed a button on his intercom and spoke to his secretary. "Can you bring those files in, please, Carole?"

The door opened almost immediately, and Carole swept in with a manila folder clutched to her frail chest, tattered pieces of paper creeping from its edges. She smiled at Emily, before a "humph" from George dissolved her grin and sent her scuttling back to her desk.

George opened the file, and took out various clippings – placing them side by side on the desk before her. "You're not the first one, you see."

"I'm not the first one…? I'm not following you."

He tapped the clippings, impatient now. "Look! It's right there, see?" He sighed at her confused expression, and sat back. "I wouldn't be a million miles from the truth if I said you were about to be attacked before this happened, am I right?"

Emily stared. "How…?"

"Look at the clippings," he said. "There have been a number of instances of 'phantom rescues' over the years; yours is just the latest."

"Phantom what?" Emily laughed. "I'm sorry, but just because I got the willies late at night on a train platform doesn't mean I was attacked."

"What were you scared of? Last night, on the platform?"

Emily laughed. "It sounds stupid now, but I thought someone was following me."

"And you felt threatened, yes?" George was bending forward now, his hands clasped in front of him, a finger on his lips.

Emily nodded. "Of course. A woman on her own, late at night, no one around … and someone's walking behind you, at the same pace as you, speeding up when you do…" She stopped, spooked all over again, her mind back with the events of the previous night, the man's heavy footsteps catching up with her own, each heel tap accompanied by a deeper echo …

"Of course." George sat back, satisfied he was right. "And then someone appeared, out of the night, and saved you."

"He saved me from falling, I suppose," she conceded, "but I hadn't actually been attacked, had I. I just got scared."

George shook his head. "I believe you were about to be attacked, and if you're honest," here he stared at her over his half-rim glasses, his expression serious, "so do you."

Emily attempted a smile, but failed miserably. "Because it's happened before, right?"

"That's right," he said, and nodded. "Read the clippings."

The clippings were of varying age, she saw, from issues of the paper as far back as the 1970s. All told similar tales – a young girl leaving the station late at night, complaining of a sense of being followed – a man attempting to catch up with them. All the girls had been grabbed at the head of the stairs (she'd been lucky, she realised, to get down them without being caught) and pulled towards the darkened waiting room. So far, so unsurprising. The odd fact was that, in each case, the girl concerned spoke of the smell of pipe smoke, and strong arms wrestling them away from their attackers ... and a brief glimpse of a manly shape in a long dark overcoat with square shoulders and a hat, brim down over the eyes, as it descended upon their assailant; a style that had been old-fashioned enough to stand out, even then.

Stapled behind each of these clippings was a shorter article from the following day – a tale of a body on the tracks, no sign of a struggle. One girl had seen her rescuer fall onto the line alongside her attacker, and screamed until help came – but the railway workers thus summoned only found the body of her attacker; there was no trace of anyone else having been at the scene.

She placed the clippings back in the folder, congratulating herself on the fact that the shaking in her fingers was almost imperceptible, and let out a breath. "They can't all be the same."

"And yet the similarities just keep stacking up."

"Someone's exaggerating, making things up."

George sat forward, frowning. "That doesn't track though, Emily, does it. Different people, different times ... yet all tell of a man in a coat and hat."

"Doesn't have to be the same man," Emily pointed out.

"I'll grant you that in the forties a lot of men wore dark coats and hats," he said. "But what about since then?

And all of them smelled of pipe tobacco?"

"Lots of people smoke," she tried … but she could see George already shaking his head.

"Not pipes," he said, sighing. "It's a very different smell, as you know. And besides, not that many people smoke anymore, compared to then. I mean, look at films – in the seventies everyone was doing it. Not these days, though; these days if a character in a movie smokes, he's usually a baddie."

Emily had no answers. "I didn't really see anyone," she said. "Just felt his arms, and smelled the tobacco."

"So you do admit it was tobacco and not a fag you smelled?"

"I have to, don't I," she said. "It was Dad's brand, Old Holborn."

"And the man was wearing a long coat, and a hat, just like the other times?"

Emily nodded. "I don't know what kind of hat, though … the name, I mean. It was like those old films – with that actor Dad loved. James Mason."

George laughed. "God, that's right – he did, didn't he?"

Emily stared out at her colleagues; all staring in, amazed he was laughing. "George, they're looking."

He frowned again, but the corners of his mouth were twitching, and Emily knew he'd be laughing again before long. He and Dad had been two of a kind that way, and she felt his loss all the more keenly when she was with her uncle.

"All right, lass," he said. "Best get out there and investigate this, eh? We wouldn't want everyone knowing the cub reporter's my favourite niece."

She smiled, then scraped her chair back and stood up.

Leaning forward to pick up the files she whispered, "Can I come and see you and Auntie Ann on Sunday?"

"Course you can," he said. "Can't see you doing a roast, somehow."

She grinned and held the files tight as she turned, forcing herself to look serious. "See you then, then."

Two hours later, poring over the files she'd found in the paper's archives, Emily was forced to admit George had been right. East Finchley station had, over the years, been prey to a number of these incidents – the earliest one she'd found had happened in October of 1972 when a seventeen year old girl had been coming home from a day visiting family in Camden Town. She'd been followed as she got off the train, and grabbed before she reached the stairs leading down to the exit. The only witness had been a middle-aged man in a black overcoat and a grey hat, who'd shouted for help and run to her aid. The two men had scuffled, and in the melée the girl had been thrown to the floor. She'd struggled to her knees just in time to see the older man grab her attacker as he made for her once more, knife in hand. In the struggle, both men had apparently overbalanced and fallen on to the tracks, into the path of an oncoming train. Both had died almost instantly.

No one had listened to the victim's protestations that her saviour hadn't fallen; he'd *pulled* her attacker down onto the tracks, and held him there as the train bore down on both of them. Emily didn't believe it either; who would willingly go to their own death, when all they'd had to do, really, was knock the attacker down and pin him there until help arrived – which in a staffed underground station shouldn't have taken more than a minute or two?

She spent another hour going through various other reports from over the years, but none seemed to quite fit the facts of what she'd been told by her uncle. There was a long and dispiriting list of the usual muggings, fights and accidents – some resulting in death, others in injury – none of these mentioned the man in the hat and overcoat.

Looking at the clock, Emily was surprised to see it was almost four o'clock; she hadn't even taken a lunch break, or had a coffee. No wonder she felt sick.

A shadow appeared at her left side and, looking up, she saw her uncle there, frowning again. "Any progress?"

She shook her head. "Not much; the usual list of violence – brawls, attacks, not much else." She reached into the hanging drawer on her right and drew out her handbag. "Do you mind if I go home a bit early? I've got a thumping headache."

"I'm not surprised," he answered. "You haven't left your desk all day, and you can't have got much sleep last night." He started to walk back to his office. "Go home, get some rest, but clear your desk first."

She nodded. "I will. Thank you."

"Bright and early tomorrow, mind," he called. "And I'll expect some progress tomorrow, alright?"

She groaned. She knew she'd better have something he could run by the end of the next day, but had no idea what to write. She trudged towards the exit, shoulders bowed. She'd worry about that later.

Twenty minutes later she was sitting on a train, heading back towards East Finchley. She glanced at her watch, and was comforted to find it was only four thirty. There should be plenty of people about when she reached her destination.

Sure enough, she hit the beginning of the rush hour, and East Finchley was teeming with people as she got off the tube and headed for the stairs. She couldn't help being over-cautious, jumping when anyone got too close – which earned her more than a few dodgy looks from people who couldn't decide if she was on drugs, drunk or just plain crazy. She was starting to think they might have a point – perhaps she was mad, after all. As she turned left at the bottom of the stairs, heading towards the ticket barrier and the High Road, she caught a glimpse of a hat. A very old-fashioned hat that looked uncomfortably familiar. The crowds parted and she saw that the hat belonged to an elderly gentleman, being buffeted towards her by the evening tide of commuters.

She stood back to let him pass, earning herself a few choice comments in the process, but she didn't care – he looked worried enough without being accosted by a loon of a woman demanding to know where he'd got his hat.

Keeping her head down so she didn't find herself getting into even more trouble, she made her way out to the High Road and hopped on a bus heading towards North Finchley. Twenty minutes later, she was letting herself into her flat above a shop just off Tally Ho Corner, trying not to fall over the cat winding its way between her feet and purring. "Come on, puss," she said, nudging the animal gently with her toe. The cat jumped and started off towards the kitchen. Emily laughed as she followed, shedding her jacket onto the bannisters as she followed. "You've got me right where you want me, don't you?"

Later, dinner cooked and eaten, cat fed and watered, Emily found herself channel-hopping as she thought over the events of the previous twenty-four hours. She felt such a fraud – it wasn't as if the man at the station the previous night had actually attacked her, after all. She'd been scared, yes, and he might well have tried to drag her off if the man in the hat hadn't …

Hadn't what, exactly?

She'd felt someone. She had. The feel of his body as he pulled her upright and the smell of pipe smoke that rose from his damp wool coat; she couldn't have imagined that. She examined her arms, and was a little surprised to find no trace of his clasp. He'd *hauled* her to her feet; surely there should be a mark? Something to show the strength of his grip? Whoever had been following her had definitely felt his strength – her rescuer had swept him off the platform to his death. Hadn't he?

She tried to focus on the TV screen before her, aware she'd just missed something important. Offering up a silent prayer of thanks to the great god Sky Plus, she picked up the remote and rewound. The local news was on, and a reporter was standing outside East Finchley station, microphone in hand, with a suitably solemn expression on his face. He was reporting the apparent suicide of a young man the previous night – a Warren Lytton, nineteen years old, a history of minor problems with the police; a couple of mugging convictions that seemed to consist more of aggravated shoving than outright violence, no one had been hurt, shoplifting … nothing too sinister.

Someone just off camera was shouting, and Emily strained to hear what was being said. No use; whoever it was had been pushed out of range of the microphone, and all she could make out was raised voices. A female voice, shouting, and more voices speaking in a conciliatory tone. The reporter stopped speaking, and in the silence that followed Emily heard quite clearly: "My boy wouldn't kill himself! He wouldn't do that!" The report cut back to the studio, and the newscaster shaking his head in disapproval.

Emily turned the TV off, her stomach churning. She ran for the bathroom and just made it in time before she doubled over and lost her supper. She sank to the floor, shaking, and wiped the sweat from her face. So it was being labelled a suicide. Perhaps it even had been, who was she to say? She couldn't help feeling a sense of relief that it was over – she'd been dreading more questions by the police. They'd been lovely to her, calming her down and taking her home – but no one had taken her story of the man in the hat seriously, that was obvious. She supposed in the absence of any sign of someone else at the scene they'd had no choice – no one else had even seen him.

She found herself crying, and rubbed her face clean of tears. She would not let this get to her. It was done, and she could move on now. She'd file a piece in the morning about the suicide, and that would be the end of it.

She smelled pipe smoke, and flashed back to the tunnel – she *had* seen him, she knew. So why had no one else?

The next morning found her at her desk bright and early, typing up the report of Warren Lytton's apparent suicide – she felt someone standing beside her and looked up to see George, reading the copy as she typed it.

"What about the attack?" he asked.

Emily shrugged. "What can I say? There's no record

of anyone else being seen at the station at that time, just this guy. Who knows? Maybe he slipped off the platform running away."

"You don't believe that."

"No," she answered. "I don't. But I don't want to look like an idiot, or crazy."

He said nothing.

"Would you?" she pushed.

George stared at her for a long moment before nodding. "Fair enough." Then he was gone.

Emily sat, nonplussed, not entirely sure from their exchange whether she should go ahead and file the piece or not. Gradually the office started to fill up, chatter replacing the peace of a few moments before; not making things any easier to focus on. Someone laughed and she whirled round, the voice familiar, but no one seemed to be responsible – most of her colleagues were by now seated at their desks, concentrating on the monitors in front of them.

She tried to work out why the laugh was familiar, but to no avail – it had been a man's voice, of that she was sure; probably an older man, but no one in her immediate area fitted that description.

Her nostrils filled with the scent of Old Holborn and tears welled up as she thought of her father; she'd loved to sit on his lap as a child, and this smell brought her back to those days in an instant. Yet no one around her was smoking.

She gave up, and sent her article to her editor, then closed the screen down. She needed some air.

As she left the building, someone jostled her, and as she automatically apologised she realised this was no accident. Her attacker's mother stood before her, her expression furious. Emily glanced back over her shoulder to see if anyone was on hand to help should it be necessary, but she was on her own.

"Excuse me," she said, and moved to side-step the woman.

Mrs Lytton, however, was having none of this. She stepped in front of Emily once more, her eyes narrowed.

Emily wondered if she thought this made her appear more intimidating, and bit down on the smile that threatened to bloom. Perhaps she'd have found it more frightening if she hadn't found herself looking down at the older woman.

Mrs Lytton took a step forward, not content 'til she was close enough to share Emily's breath, something Emily found vaguely distasteful, but not particularly scary.

"My boy didn't kill himself," she spat.

"Emily nodded. "You might be right," she said before adding with uncharacteristic cruelty: "But he's dead, so we can't ask him, can we?"

The woman gasped, and now she didn't look threatening – she looked heartbroken, and Emily felt heat blossom in her chest before spreading to her face. How could she have said that?

"I'm sorry," she said. "I didn't mean it to sound so …"

"Fucking cruel?" Mrs Lytton interrupted, and Emily had the grace to look sorry.

She nodded. "I'm sorry he's dead, I really am. But it's not my fault."

"Then whose is it?" the woman wailed. "Who killed my boy?"

Emma sighed, and steeled herself for the inevitable

response to what came next. "I didn't see anyone," she said. "I just heard a cry, and then the alarm. I was running away."

"From what?"

"From Warren." The woman hissed as if scalded, and Emma hurried to apologise. "I'm really sorry, but he was chasing me ... and then he was gone, and I heard him yell ... and then there were brakes, and ..."

"Stop it!" Mrs Lytton screamed, raising her arms as if to fend Emily off. "Bloody stop it, you lying bitch!" Her hand was up and planted firmly against Emily's cheek before either of them knew it was going to happen, and then she was gone, leaving Emily alone and sobbing, hand raised to the livid imprint on her shocked face.

Emily caught a whiff of that tobacco again, and shook her head. "No," she said. "Please don't." The smell faded, and she breathed out a juddering sigh of relief, "I'm going home," she said, to no one. "Alone."

No one followed.

Emily's piece came out the following day, and her phone started to ring as people realised she'd been involved.

The article made no mention of the attack she'd been sure was about to follow, but did mention her presence at the station; she found herself to be a celebrity, and decided – with her uncle's permission – to stay indoors for a few days, until something else of interest happened and she was no longer "interesting" to the gawkers and on-lookers that had crawled out of the woodwork.

A few days later Emily found herself making her way home alone once more, having spent the evening at a local theatre for a review of a play being put on by the local amateur dramatics society. *Blithe Spirit*. The joke wasn't lost, but Emily didn't think she'd ever find that funny again.

As she left East Finchley station, she saw a man leaning against the wall, hat pulled down low over his face, shoulders hunched against the cold. She slowed, then drew herself up and hurried forward – she'd be safe inside.

The man stood up as she approached, and as he lifted his head she saw she'd been scared of nothing.

"Uncle George," she said. "I wasn't expecting to see you here."

He smiled. "I thought you might want some company. Seeing as it's late."

"I'm glad you came. It's a bit quiet tonight, isn't it?"

George nodded, and took her arm. "Come on, we'll take the bus."

Emily found herself propelled down the hill, towards the bridge. "I normally get the bus at the next stop up," she said, trying to pull away. "It's a bit dark this way."

The bus stop they were heading to was closer, she knew, but she didn't like going under the bridge where it was dark. And there was a stretch of road just beyond the adjacent pub that was bordered by gardens with overhanging bushes – she preferred to be more visible, especially after …

George sighed, impatient. "It's all right, I'm with you." And kept pulling her on, past the bus stop they should have waited at.

As they reached the corner of Bishops Avenue, George pushed her to the side, and she found herself by a house with a low fence – and a lot of foliage.

"What are you doing?"

George laughed. "I thought we could take a bit of a walk."

"Why down here?"

George's grip on her arm grew painful, and she got ready to scream.

"Uncle George, what's going on? You're scaring me!"

"I'm sorry, love," he said. "I didn't want to do that. I just wanted you to see. I want you to make everyone see."

"You're not making any sense," she said. "See what?"

George nodded at the house, but had the grace to loosen his grip. "He lived here."

"Who did?"

"Your saviour. You were right; he's done this before – and it's time people knew."

Emily turned to stare at the house – unprepossessing in the gloom, she could see, nevertheless, that it was neglected. An air of loneliness pervaded its surrounds, making it stand out from the expensive, well-tended houses that adjoined it. "Who lived here?" she asked.

"A man called Arthur Fuller. I went to school with him, or rather your dad did. They were a couple of years below me."

"He knew Dad?"

"Very well. They were mates."

"What happened to him?"

George's eyes glittered as he started to talk. "He was killed. Walking home one night, late, he saw a girl being attacked by some thug at East Finchley station. Decided he had to have a go, save the girl." He laughed, the sound bitter in his throat. "Bloody idiot."

Emily didn't quite understand. "Why was he an idiot, if all he did was try to help someone?"

"The girl was your mother, and Arthur knew her, of course."

Emily stared.

"You look like her, you know," he said; and tried to touch her hair.

She flinched.

George grinned, his teeth bared white in the dark. "You see? You're just like her."

She took a step back, and he gripped her arm tighter.

"It's not like she was going out with your dad at the time," he said. "She was fair game."

"Oh, George," Emily moaned. "You were the thug?"

"So the papers called me. I just wanted a kiss, that's all. But she wouldn't be quiet."

"And Arthur heard her? Came to help?"

George nodded. "I always felt bad that he got hurt. I just pushed him off. I didn't see the car coming."

The smell of Old Holborn surrounded her now, and she felt herself relax. They weren't on their own any more.

George took a step towards her, and Emily stiffened. "I want you to tell his story," he said. "I want people to know he's still saving people."

"Why?" she asked. "Because you feel guilty?"

George nodded. "That, yes, and because people should know it wasn't just an accident. He was a good bloke, and he tried to help your mum. Just like he's still trying to help people."

Emily took George's hand, and peeled his fingers away from her arm, one by one. "I can't do that," she said. "It wouldn't be right."

151

"Why not?" he demanded. "Why shouldn't he get some recognition for what he did?"

"Because then they'd know what you did," she said, and saw the realisation dawn in his eyes. "And, even worse, what you nearly did to Mum."

George launched himself forward and pushed her towards the busy road.

She felt herself falling, but was overwhelmed by the scent of pipe tobacco, even as she felt herself being set back on her feet. She stood, gasping, as she saw the cloud darken around her uncle, a smoky figure reaching out for him and drawing him towards the main road. A bus was hurtling up the hill towards them, but she couldn't make a sound – and it was too dark for them to be seen, just yet.

George was trying hard to break free, but to no avail. As the bus drew close, the cloud solidified, and Emily saw her saviour, hat pulled low over his face, dark coat pulled tight around him. He pushed George down, and both men fell under the oncoming vehicle – brakes squealed, someone screamed, and Emily found herself witnessing everything this time, at close range, as Arthur held him there.

She saw George's hand, protruding from underneath the front of the bus – blood trickling towards the kerb. There was no sign of the rest of him. The hand twitched, just once, then was still. A woman who'd been walking up the main road was screaming: scream after scream pealing out, with barely time to breathe between. The bus driver was sitting in his cab, head buried in his hands – the few passengers were staring forward, shock etched on their faces. She could already hear the sirens.

Emily staggered to the kerb and threw up, and when she looked up, he was there. He smiled at her, and touched his fingers to his hat – an old-world gesture. The smell of Old Holborn caused her stomach to clench, and she vomited again. When she looked up again, he was gone.

She couldn't tell the story, she realised. And not because it would ruin her aunt's life, and her parents' memory. She couldn't tell the story because then everyone would know about Arthur – and much as she hated the idea of him continuing his vendetta, she hated even more the idea that he wouldn't be able to help any more girls daft enough to wander home on their own in dangerous places.

SUCH IS LIFE

Whoever said life is wasted on the young was full of it. It's wasted on the living. They wander around with their heads firmly up their own whatsits, bemoaning anything and everything whilst convinced they're invincible. It's raining. It's snowing. It's too hot. It's too cold. Make your fucking minds up.

What I wouldn't give to feel the rain slick against my skin one more time, or to feel a lover's lips brush against mine.

I watched a couple just this afternoon. Love's young dream. He was wandering down the road looking anywhere but at her, while she linked arms with him to keep him from walking ahead and prattled on incessantly in a vain attempt to get his attention. Her face shone with love, and the dumb fuck couldn't have cared less. All he could think about was what the score was, or how many pints he'd be behind his mates by the time he managed to ditch her and get to the pub. She would have done anything for him. And he couldn't even see how rare that was, how lucky it made him. He didn't deserve her.

I thought back to Helen. I'd been exactly the same with her. At first.

I wasn't such a bad guy. People seemed to like me, for the most part. I went through life trying to make things easy on myself, as people do. You know, don't get too close to anyone, don't let them hurt you. Don't hurt them, either. I thought that was the best way.

Except that wasn't really thinking, was it? If it was,

and if I had, I wouldn't be here now.

If you'd met me when I was alive, you wouldn't have looked at me twice. Most people didn't. I was a little over average height, about five foot nine, with dark hair cut short (but not too short) and hazel eyes. Loads of people have hazel eyes. I was forty, but could pass for thirty-five on a good day. I was like most other people in that I didn't like my nose much, or the fact that I could stand to lose about a stone. Nobody's ever happy with how they look though, are they? If you have straight hair you want curly, and vice versa. The list is endless.

Her hair was so soft. I remember the feel of it against my neck when she buried her head against my chest.

I used to get grief from my mum a lot. "When are you going to get married, Mark? When do I get to be a grandmother?" I'm sure you've heard it all before.

I just used to grin at her, and say, "When I meet the right one, Mum. I'll know when I meet the right one."

What I meant was, "I'll meet the one that's here right now, and worry about the rest later." I met a lot of those. Nice enough girls, for the most part. They'd give me the eye and laugh at my jokes, and I'd charm the knickers off them. It wasn't difficult, and as I say, I never made any promises.

Shouldn't that count for something?

Then I met Helen. She was really nice, I thought, and she seemed to like me too. We got on, as they say. We found out we frequented a lot of the same places, and wondered how we'd never met before. It didn't matter. I didn't want to just screw this one. She was too nice. So we dated, taking it slow, and things were good. Good for me, anyway. If she was a bit quiet sometimes, she'd put it down to her time of the month, or a bad day at the office. I never went into too much detail about what she did, or where she did it. Perhaps I should have.

We must have been dating for about a month before we slept together. Probably the longest time I'd ever been with anyone, whether sex was involved or not. I took her out to dinner, splashed out on a decent restaurant, a nice wine – we had a really good time together. When we got back to my place, it was business as usual to start with. She went to freshen up while I stuck a video on and got a bottle of wine out of the fridge. Then we curled up together on the sofa for a chat, and a bit of a kiss and cuddle, as usual.

There was something in her eyes that night. They shone. I don't even remember what we talked about, just her eyes gazing into mine, and the way she kept fiddling with her hair, because that one strand just to the right of her fringe would never sit right. She smelled wonderful.

Anyway, one thing led to another, and we ended up making love right there on the couch. Then we went to bed and did it again. Life, as they say, was good.

Things changed after that. Or she did, I'm not sure exactly which way round it was now. All of a sudden she started wanting to plan things. Like where we could go on holiday together, what Sunday did I want to go to her mum's for tea? What did I want to go to her mum's for tea for? I was happy as I was. I tried to tell her that, but she just sulked.

I guess that was when I started to change. I pulled away a bit. I was scared, see. Life was fine as it was; we were both adults, happy in each other's company. What did we have to get all serious for?

So anyway, we'd been going out for about three

months, sleeping together for the last two, and trying to pretend that nothing had changed. Then one Friday night I called round at Helen's a bit early, and saw a bloke leaving the house. He was in a hurry, and kept looking all round him as he rushed off down the street. I saw the net curtains twitch, and realised Helen was watching him leave

I hung around for a few minutes, then walked slowly up the front path and rang the doorbell. Helen appeared looking flushed, and she'd misbuttoned her top. Her chest was all mottled pink, the way it got when things heated up, and her lips looked swollen.

"Who was that, Helen?"

"Who?"

All bright and false, her voice was, and I could hear the panic in it.

"The guy that just rushed off down the road. He came from here."

"Don't be ridiculous, Mark. What on earth would some man be doing here?" Her voice shook a bit, and she seemed scared, which was fine by me.

I shouldered my way into the house, and a part of me felt triumphant when she shrank back. I kept my voice low and quiet. "I don't know, love. I was hoping you'd tell me." I grinned.

I never saw that bloke again after that, and I watched out for him. Helen was back to normal within two or three days, and the bruises were almost gone by the end of the week. I noticed she'd given up trying to organise me, too, and congratulated myself on figuring out what I'd needed to do. I told myself it was her fault; she'd pushed me into it.

What did I know?

Time passed, we moved in together, and Helen faded into the woodwork. I told myself it meant she was contented. I went to work, I came home, I put the money on the table. On a Saturday I'd give her one, thinking all the time of the new barmaid at *The Duke's Head*. If I closed my eyes, I could even pretend it was her. Helen seemed happy with that. If she was acting, I didn't notice.

I'm beginning to realise I didn't notice much.

About six months after the first time I'd had to put Helen straight, I met a girl at the supermarket. There I was, minding my own business in the cigarette queue, when suddenly I knew, just knew, there was someone looking straight at me. I looked up, ready to have a...disagreement, shall we say. And it was her. It was Sarah, the barmaid I've already told you about. She was dressed the same as usual, short tight t-shirt and leggings. Great big hoop earrings and short, spiky hair finished the ensemble.

She grinned, easily shifting her gum to her cheek as she did so. "Morning."

I grinned back, exuding what I hoped was an easy charm, but was probably just a leer. "Morning." I nodded at the kiosk in front of us. "Fancy seeing you here."

She moved closer, leaned in before whispering: "I'd fancy seeing you anywhere." She moved back, raised an eyebrow – waiting for an answer.

Just for a moment, I didn't know what to say. Thoughts of Helen flitted through my mind, but quickly disappeared. This was new, this was *exciting* – unlike Helen. A hint of danger danced in Sarah's eyes, along with the promise of an evening I wouldn't forget in a hurry. I opened my mouth to speak, and shut it quickly when all that emerged was a croak. I grimaced, smiled, cleared my throat and tried again. "How about tonight?"

She nodded, smiling broadly now. "After work, okay?"

"Sure, I'll be in around nine, half past."

"'Kay." A quick kiss on the cheek and she was gone, leaving me watching her hips swing saucily away from me, out of the shop and into my imagination.

Several hours and a row with Helen later, I was sidling onto a barstool, watching as Sarah fended off over-eager punters. She saw me, and her smile flashed white in the darkness, even as she took care of business. I nodded, and waited. Sure enough, a moment or two later a glass was slammed onto the bar in front of me and Sarah proceeded to pour a very large measure of Jack Daniels into it. I took out my wallet, frowning, and was delighted when she whispered, "On the house." She glanced sideways down the bar, where the manager was arguing with a belligerent customer that looked as if he'd already had far more than one too many. "Just don't let Charlie see."

"Sounds fair." I took a belt of the whiskey and let the air hiss through my teeth as it seared my throat. "Thanks." I put the glass back down, and watched in amazement as she topped it back up before disappearing in response to a summons from further down the bar. This was showing all the signs of being a very hard night.

I had no idea.

Alone at the bar as Sarah worked, I barely noticed her refilling my glass as I went over the row I'd had with Helen earlier. I couldn't even remember what had started it – but I knew how it ended. I'd shoved her up against a wall with my hand around her throat as I hissed: "Don't ever tell me what to do!" and walked out. All because she'd been suspicious about my trip to the pub. And didn't she have every right to be? I leaned my head back and swallowed, feeling the golden heat sink into me – and watched, befuddled, as a hand with long, claw-like nails held a bottle over my glass, refilling it. Dimly, I heard Sarah's voice. "Careful, darlin'. Don't get *too* drunk."

Too late.

Twelve o' clock, and I was shuffling down the road, arm slung over Sarah's shoulders. She was surprisingly strong for a little thing, I didn't seem to be causing her any problem at all. We stopped in front of a newsagents', and I stared owl-like at the ads in the window, trying to make sense of them as Sarah fumbled for her keys.

I don't really remember the door opening, or the struggle upstairs – my next clear memory is of lying naked on Sarah's bed as she straddled me. I think that must have shocked me sober.

The air was cold on my body, and I could see my breath plume as I gasped. She was beautiful. Slim and muscular, her skin – all dark veins against a milky white background – glowed like marble in the moonlight.

"Sarah?"

She looked down at me, her eyes black slits in the darkness. She smiled, and leaned over me, whispered in my ear. "Want to know a secret?"

The question seemed loaded with menace, somehow. I tried desperately to fathom what was wrong here, why I was terrified. She sniggered, and I knew.

"You're not Sarah."

"Oh I am, honey. Trust me." She trailed her tongue down my torso, and I screamed as it burned. "It's just that Sarah isn't what you thought she was."

She dipped her head lower, and I roared in pain as she encircled me with her lips. She relented, and raised herself over me once more. She threw her head back and howled, and as the moonlight fell fully on to her, I saw.

I saw what she was, what she'd always been, except I'd been too blinded by the chance of a quick fuck to see it. She was beautiful, yes, but that beauty was terrible. She started to writhe on top of me, and I felt myself succumb – desire was building to fever pitch, and I could feel the heat rising in response to her movements. It would be over soon. Her skin started to redden as if she were on fire, and in a way I suppose she was. She laid her hands on my chest and I howled in pain – angry looking prints were left there when she took them away. The temperature in the room was rising, higher and higher, the windows now weeping with condensation, my torso slick with blood – drawn expertly by her nails every time she touched me.

I felt myself coming to a climax, even though I'd never known such agony; and as I came she screamed in pleasure, brightening the room until it was like day as she glowed with heat. Finally she relaxed, and climbed off me, patting her stomach – already starting to swell.

"Poor Sam," she crooned, careful now not to touch me – she'd done enough damage, and I was dying in front of her.

"Helen…" I croaked, and watched Sarah's face darken.

"You should have thought about her before," she

whispered. She stood, and the air cooled. I whimpered in gratitude, too scared to look down at the burns she'd inflicted. Breathing was becoming difficult, now; my lungs felt as if they were full of soup, and it was getting worse by the minute.

She moved to the door, and turned to face me, eager to impart one final piece of information. "I guess you know what I am by now, don't you?"

I groaned, and she took that as a plea.

"You do know what a succubus is? I kill my lovers, Sam, every single one."

"D-Death would be…pretty good right about now."

"It won't be long, lover, I promise." She stood in the doorway, smiling as she listened to my tortured breathing. Then she fired the final shot. "You should know one more thing about me, though."

"Huh?" I was beyond caring, just wanted to die – wanted the pain to stop.

"I can't just roam as I will." She saw the truth dawn in my eyes and nodded. "I have to be *sent*. Now who would want to send you a succubus, Sam, hmm?"

She was gone, and I was dying. I lay there for twenty more minutes, trying to cry but only choking on my own fluids as I burned up from the inside.

Helen. You bitch!

So now I wander around, staying firmly away from any sign of 'the light', eager to ruin what remains of Helen's life. I've managed to scare off four boyfriends so far.

She knows it's me. I can see it in her eyes, each time one of them calls to stammer out an apology. I stand right behind her as she answers the phone, and laugh in her ear. If I'm having a good day I can even make her flinch, as she smells the cooked meat stench I left behind.

I know she hopes I'll pass on, let go my hate, *forgive* her and leave her alone.

Fat chance.

Life might be a bitch, but dying is so much worse.

And it lasts much longer.

PLAY TIME

Tommy stood still, head cocked to one side, listening to the night-time noises of the playground. By day these places were full of the sounds of children squealing with delight, maybe crying at some mishap – a fall, or a bang to the head or knee, perhaps an argument with a friend or a tussle with a bully. But overall playgrounds were happy places, full of joy. Even their name showed that to be true.

Night-time was different. By night the only sound was the wind moaning through the creak of the swing's chains and the whispering of the leaves on the trees – the slow sigh of the night's chill as the playground waited for morning to come and banish the darkness. That was all the noises could be, he decided. He'd listened to, and catalogued, each of these sounds, one by one, until he was satisfied, huddled as small as he could make himself: a small dark shadow on the last swing on the row.

He sighed, wishing it was earlier. There was no-one left to play with – all had gone home for their dinner, full of the day's adventures and ready for sleep to claim them; only to release them in the morning, eager for more. Their mothers had come for them, reducing their number by degrees until he was the only one left. He eased his weight back and kicked off with his feet, letting the swing carry him gently backward – he wasn't sure where his mother was; and it was late. *Shouldn't she be here by now?* his mind whispered, and he told it to shush. *She'll be here. She'll come.*

He tilted his head at a new sound – one unexpected at this hour. There it was again, the high-pitched tinkling of a girl's laughter. He craned his neck to look behind him into the bushes, then scanned the rest of the playground, but could see no-one. Digging his heels into the earth below him, he brought the swing to a standstill, quieting the creak of the chain against the crossbar. A sudden gust of wind whispered through the trees, and errant leaves danced in the air before him.

Tommy...

Now he knew he was imagining things, because the wind couldn't know his name. Footsteps skittered off to his left, and he whirled around to see what was there. The sodium light guttered fitfully, barely illuminating a small circle around it, but it was enough. A shadow was cutting off part of the lit circle – a girl shaped shadow, from what he could see. Boys didn't have pigtails. *Maybe it's not pigtails,* his mind whispered again. *Maybe it's horns!* He whimpered, and this time the laughter wasn't just in his head. It rang throughout the playground, and Tommy saw a light come on in a house behind the park.

"Silly, girls don't have horns."

Tommy gasped – and felt icy fingers play his spine. The voice – and the pigtails, apparently – belonged to the girl standing at the edge of the light, staring at him as if he'd said something stupid. He hadn't, had he? He was only thinking.

The girl grinned at him, then, and he knew, he just knew, that she could hear what he was thinking – even if she said nothing about it.

He took a deep breath before asking, "Who are you?"

"Who do you think I am?"

Tommy frowned. "That's kind of a stupid question,"

he said. "How am I supposed to know that?"

The girl moved back a little, so that all he could see was her eyes. The rest of her stood in darkness, but her eyes glowed with yellow light, and oh, how they danced.

"I guess that's true." She moved a step closer to him, and the wind screamed. "My name's Mary."

"You're out kind of late, Mary."

"So are you," she retorted, and she inched a step closer, twisting the cloth of her dress in her fists. "Shouldn't your mother have come for you by now?" Her skin was pale, her mouth pinched – she looked so *cold*.

Tommy looked around at the gate on the far side of the playground, and sighed. No one was there. "Yeah, she should." He looked at Mary once more, his face hopeful. "Maybe she got delayed, met someone…you know, got talking." It wouldn't be the first time his mother had been a little late, delayed by another mother who wanted to chat; but it was never more than a few minutes, and she always ran so *fast* to get to him, so he wouldn't worry. He looked towards the gate once more, hoping he'd see her racing towards him, her red hair flying back in the wind, showing him her relieved smile when she saw him waiting. There was nothing.

"Kinda late, though," Mary offered. Her voice shook, and Tommy wondered just how long she'd been waiting here. "I mean, it's *dark*."

"Yeah, it is," he replied. He took a closer look at the girl; her eyes were huge with fear. "You're not scared…are you?"

"Who, me?" She laughed, but he wasn't convinced. "Nah, not scared." She looked around, seemingly bored, and when her gaze came to rest on Tommy again there was something there that hadn't been before. "You get used to it." Yep, it was there, all right – it was anger, bleeding into her voice more with every second.

"How long have you been here?"

"I don't know." She wouldn't look at him now. "Long time, I guess."

Tommy tried to think if she went to his school. She really didn't look familiar, and it wasn't that big a town. He should know her, if she lived nearby. "Where did you say you live?"

She grinned at him, then; her small teeth almost too white in the darkness. "I didn't." She moved a step closer. "What's the matter, Tommy? Scared?"

"No, I just wonder where she is, that's all." He inched back from her, wary of allowing her too close even while calling himself stupid for letting a girl rattle him like this. "It *is* late."

Mary stood back suddenly, turned and walked towards the roundabout at the edge of the playground. "You're going to freeze if you sit still like that." She started the roundabout turning, pushing at the ground with her foot as if she were on a scooter. "You might as well play while you wait, it'll keep you warm."

Tommy hesitated. His mother would see him clearly while he sat on the swing, he knew…but the roundabout wasn't that far away, was it? She should still see him…and he'd definitely see her. The roundabout squeaked as it turned, and Mary giggled. That decided it. At least if he played with Mary for a while he'd be warm, and – more importantly – he wouldn't be alone any more. He cast one more glance at the gate and then ran to Mary, yelling: "Wait up! I want to play!" The two children laughed as they played, and the darkness crept up and wrapped them up in its embrace.

Sarah Warner stood impatiently at the playground gate, trying to stop her hair from getting too messy in the wind. This wasn't the kind of day she'd have picked to go to the park but then her sister wasn't her – that much was painfully obvious. Sarah checked her watch yet again, as if catching the minute hand in the act of moving would magic Lauren into existence.

"What are you doing?"

The voice was unfamiliar, and it took Sarah a moment to realise the words were meant for her. Looking down, she saw a small girl, maybe eight or nine years old, wrapped in a shabby coat and with her socks rolled down around her ankles. One knee was scuffed, but she didn't seem to mind. The girl waited patiently, and Sarah forced herself to be polite. "I'm waiting for my sister."

"Is she coming here to play?"

Sarah suppressed a grin. "No, honey, she's not. We're going shopping."

The girl frowned, thinking hard. Her question, when it came, was so obvious Sarah could have kissed her. "Then why meet here? Is she leaving her kids here to play?"

"No." Sarah didn't want to talk about that. "No, she doesn't. She just likes to see kids having fun, I guess." No need to involve this child in the misery of her sister's life; the emptiness.

The child said nothing, just stared at her, and Sarah found herself getting nervous. Why, for God's sake? This was just a kid! Someone called Sarah's name, and both of them looked down the hill – Lauren was bustling towards them, her dark hair unruly and a big smile plastered across her thin face.

"Hi! Who do we have here?"

Sarah didn't know what to say. The little girl looked Lauren up and down, her face serious – Sarah stifled the urge to laugh. Then she grinned, and her face lit up.

"I'm Mary. I was just saying hi." She looked from Lauren to Sarah, and then back to Lauren. "You two don't look much like sisters."

Sarah took Lauren by the arm, not wanting to prolong the hurt for her sister. "No, we don't, but we are." She grinned at Lauren. "Sometimes we even act like it. Come on, hon, time to shop."

Lauren followed her, then turned and waved at the little girl, who grinned and waved back before disappearing into the crowd of children. "Cute kid, huh?"

Sarah searched the playground, but saw no sign of her – she'd melted from view completely. "Yeah, she was great. You hungry?" She urged her sister forward when she nodded, and tried to listen to the prattle – ignoring the feeling that the little girl was still watching them.

The clatter of cups on saucers and plates on trays in the heat of the café was almost painful after the quiet of the park in the cold. Sarah felt her face flush in the heat, and managed to get herself out of her coat without having to stand up, which was a relief in this small space. Lauren looked as pale as ever, and Sarah envied the way she never flushed. She took after their mother, pale and dark; while Sarah favoured their father, a man of far ruddier complexion and chestnut hair. She even had his freckles.

The waitress pushed mugs of hot chocolate in front of them, then trudged over to the next customer, already gesturing impatiently. Sarah took a sip of her drink, wiped the foam off her lip, and looked up to see her sister staring at her, deadly serious.

"What's the matter?"

Lauren had the good grace to look abashed. "Another kid went missing last week."

"Another one? Really?"

Lauren nodded, her enthusiasm escaping now she knew she had her sister's ear. "From that playground."

"From the one I met you at this morning?"

Another nod.

Sarah sighed. "Is that why you were so keen to meet there?" Lauren's face fell, and Sarah fought hard to stay kind. She didn't want to frighten her off. "Honey, this isn't healthy."

"What do you mean?"

Exasperated, Sarah blew her fringe out of her way, a habit Lauren knew only too well. Her chin set, as she grew stubborn in return. Sarah sighed. How long was this merry-go-round going to keep running? How many times were they going to end up right back here? "You can't keep obsessing about kids that go missing."

"I'm not obsessing!"

"You're scoping out the playgrounds where they disappear! How is that not obsessed?"

Lauren stared into her mug, her face solemn. A single tear spilled over onto her cheek and cut a track in her make up as it fell. "It's not fair."

Sarah reached for her hand. "No, it's not. And I'm sorry, honey, really I am." She squeezed her sister's hand and handed across a tissue. Lauren ignored her, wiping her eyes and focussing on her cup. "Lauren, kids go missing. All the time. Sad but true."

Lauren glared at her. "That doesn't make it right!"

"No, it doesn't. But it doesn't make them yours,

either."

Lauren flinched at that, but Sarah pressed on, hating herself – and hating Lauren for making her do it. "There are ways, Lauren, we've talked about this. Adoption, fostering…"

Lauren was shaking her head, vehement in her refusal to listen. Sarah grew exasperated. "Why on earth would you think hanging around playgrounds is a way to get a kid? It's creepy!"

"I don't know." Lauren's voice was low, choked with grief and self-loathing. "I just like being near them, okay? It makes me feel less…"

"Less what?"

"Redundant. Alone." She glared at her sister now, fierce in her contempt. "I know how that sounds, you don't need to tell me." She wiped her eyes, stared out of the window, at the people wandering by with no idea how hollow her life was. "It just helps."

There was nothing to say, thought Sarah. There were no words that could help here, it was just sad, and raw, and hurtful. And that wouldn't stop anytime soon. She joined her sister in gazing at the world as it passed, blurry in the steamed windows; and perhaps better for it.

Lauren sat staring out of her living room later that night, watching the first snow of the winter. The flakes danced out of the sky as if they were bestowing a gift upon the earth – and Lauren thought maybe they were. All the usual ugliness that surrounded them was buried under a pristine, white blanket. Everything was clean and new, just for a little while. She raised her fingers to the glass and traced the shape of a heart, touched her lips to it and smiled.

The smile died, nascent, as tiny, unseen fingers echoed her movements on the outside of the window; leaving icy trails around the outlined heart, setting it hard.

The playground looked different tonight. It was colder, thought Tommy, but that wasn't it. The place looked deserted, forlorn – as if kids had stopped coming here. The chains on the swings screamed, and Tommy realised that was because they were rusty. How long had they been here, anyway?

As if called into being, Mary ambled past him into the middle of the playground, her gaze disinterested. "Don't worry about it, they'll come back."

"They will?"

"Sure, they always come back."

Tommy didn't like this. "Why did they leave?"

Mary smiled at him, then, and Tommy cringed. He'd learned to be wary of that smile – the real Mary came out when she smiled, and she wasn't the same. Tommy wasn't even sure if she was a real little girl, when she smiled. He thought that she might be some *thing* that just wanted to play the part of a girl, or even lived inside her. But if there was a thing inside her, where was the real Mary?

The girl scowled, her voice rougher this time. Deeper. "I've told you. Best not to worry about that. It's not for you to know." She cuffed him, and he stumbled. "Let's play." He followed her, too scared to say no – wondering, not for the first time, where his mother had gone. And why hadn't she looked for him?

Lauren stumbled in the snow, her breath coming in harsh gasps, her lungs burning with the cold. As she trudged up the hill, she searched for the child that must surely be out here. Who else had drawn on her window? Such tiny fingers, they'd die out here if they didn't get warm. Such thoughts buzzed in her head as she homed in on the playground, sure that whoever was lost would find their way here – in the hope that their mother would find them. She hoped that Sarah would find her soon, would help her find whoever was lost. What would she think, when she heard her sister rambling about lost children and icy fingers on her answer phone? She almost laughed, then realised she'd probably given Sarah enough ammunition to make a doctor listen. And then what would she do?

She realised she didn't care. Throughout her life, all she'd wanted was a child – and the one time that had been imminent, her chance had been taken away in an instant: her unborn child crushed by the steering wheel of her car as she careened into a wall to avoid an accident. There would be no more chances, not for her. There'd been too much damage, they said. It hadn't taken Dan long to leave after that, although in all fairness a lot of the blame for that lay at her door. She couldn't look at him, knowing what she knew – and he grew tired of promising he didn't blame her and it didn't matter.

Too late now to worry about all that. A cry in the darkness energised her, and she moved forward more purposefully as the park's gate hove into view.

Mary turned her head as she pushed her heels into the ground and halted the swing. Tommy, still in mid-swing, followed her lead as soon as he was able. He'd learnt to listen to her, to do as she said. It was less painful that way.

"What is it?" His voice was shrill in the night, his

breath plumed out in front of him like morse code, staccato evidence of his fear.

"She's here." Mary smiled, and stepped off the swing, her mood suddenly light.

"Who's here?"

"You'll see." She was making for the gate, eager to find…what?

Tommy raced after her, not wanting to be left alone. Not here. "Mary, wait!"

She took no notice, just skipped down the path, humming tunelessly as she went. She threw a glance over her shoulder, just once, "Come on, Tommy," and then she was gone. The lights went out suddenly, and he was alone in the dark.

The temperature dropped.

Lauren reached the gate, almost sobbing with pain as the cold air burned its way into her lungs. The sound had gone. Just for a moment, she'd thought she heard a cry – but then maybe she'd just wanted to. There was more light, suddenly – just by the gate, but Lauren couldn't see where it came from. And there she was. A little girl had stepped into the light, and stood gazing solemnly at her. As Lauren ground to a halt, she smiled, and watched delighted as Lauren sank to her knees.

"You're real," she sobbed.

The little girl nodded, her face wise. "Of course I am. We both are."

"Both?"

Again she nodded, and Lauren became aware of someone standing just behind the girl. A boy, this time. Hadn't she seen his face somewhere before? Recently? He edged forward, his face shy, hopeful. "Do you know my mum?" he asked.

"I'm sorry, love, no. Are you lost?"

"No." The boy grew mournful, and stepped back. He seemed to fade a little. "She is, though. She never came."

The boy's face clicked into place for Lauren then. Tommy Ryan. He'd gone missing from the playground only a week ago, and his mother's body had been found just outside the gates, her throat torn open.

The little girl broke in, cross at no longer being the centre of attention. "She didn't want you, Tommy. Remember? She would have come if she did."

"No, honey, I'm sure that's not true."

"It is!" The girl stamped her foot, and the world darkened. Something grated underfoot and Lauren sat back, stunned. "I told you, Tommy. No one wanted you, just like no one wanted me!"

Tommy's face fell, and as he stared at Lauren she felt her heart break. "Tommy, it wasn't your fault. You have to know that."

The boy shook his head. "Mary's right. If she'd wanted me, she'd have come to find me."

Lauren had to at least try to help him. "Maybe something stopped her."

Mary growled at her, and she recoiled. "Careful, you'll frighten him."

"I just want…"

"To what? Make Tommy think he belongs? He doesn't, anymore than I do." Mary took a step closer, and a cruel smile twisted her child-like features. "Any more than you do. You're alone, too, aren't you."

Lauren nodded, bereft.

"They left you, didn't they."

Again, Lauren nodded, dumb with grief.

Mary sidled closer, and Lauren felt a small hand worm its way into her own. She clasped her fingers around it, feeling a warmth grow inside her. "We're alone too."

Lauren looked up at that. "You don't have anyone?"

"Just Tommy." She looked back at him, and he attempted a smile. The effect was repulsive – he looked like he was facing Hell itself. Mary beckoned him closer, and he reluctantly took a step closer, then another. "Tommy and me belong together." She ruffled his hair, and he cringed. His eyes remained locked on Lauren. "Don't we, Tommy?" Tommy said nothing for a moment, then nodded, all hope lost.

Lauren reached for his hand, took it into hers and squeezed. He moaned, and wrapped his arms around her in a hug. He whispered: "Please stay with us. Don't leave me alone with her anymore."

Lauren hugged him tight, tears blinding her. "I won't, I promise."

Lauren's mobile phone shrilled into life, breaking the spell. For a moment she saw Mary as she really was, wizened and old, and needing their warmth to survive. No child, this, rather a creature that might have been a child once, but had been corrupted into this parasitic monster, eager for warmth to keep her here, and for other lives to keep hers going for a little while longer. This creature was hungry, and was prepared to kill to keep her playmate, Lauren saw. The vision of Mary going to Tommy's mother for a hug floated into Lauren's mind, and she cringed as she saw the woman wiping her tears away, and holding her close. Close enough for little teeth to rip into her throat, and tear it wide open.

Mary laughed, softly. "Aren't you going to answer it?"

Lauren stared at the display. It was Sarah. As she clicked the button to take the call, Sarah's voice rose into the night, frantic. "Lauren! Thank God, where are you? Listen…" Lauren dropped the phone, and the tinny notes faded from her mind. She looked at Tommy, and she made up her mind. What did life hold for her, anyway? An empty house and an empty womb, for ever and ever, Amen.

The mobile phone dropped to the ground.

Lauren stood, and took both children's hands. She tried not to cringe from the touch of the little girl, but the child didn't seem to notice. Tommy hung on, pathetically grateful for her affection.

"Come on, kids. Time to go."

Darkness fell, and when the lights came back on they revealed an empty playground, save for a red scarf puddled in the snow, cradling a mobile phone, its volume fading as the battery died.

The sound of children laughing rang in Sarah's ear, as her sister sang a nursery rhyme.

Then they were gone.

INSPIRATION POINT

Her first thought was that she was blind. She'd opened her eyes, she *knew* she had – yet all was dark, not as much as a chink of light anywhere. She stilled her breath and listened, but heard nothing. When she could hold her breath no longer she inhaled fast – a great, whooping gasp – and was relieved to find that she could, at least, still hear.

Her hands were bound, and so were her feet. She could feel the ropes biting into her skin at wrist and ankle, blood welling around them – she must have been struggling, then. Try as she might, she couldn't remember how she'd got here, or who had done this to her. The floor was hard, damp, and things scrabbled about in the dark – perhaps she was in a cellar? She tried not to think about rats, but couldn't help it. The scrabbling came closer, and she flinched, relaxing only as it faded away again – but not completely. Checking herself for injuries she was relieved to realise that – apart from a throbbing at the back of her head – she seemed unharmed. She tried to sit up higher, and her head started to swim. Dimly, she was aware of everything fading out, then it was gone.

"What's your name?"

"What?" Reality flooded back, and she realised she'd passed out. She tried to sit up, unsure of what she'd heard, if anything.

"I asked, 'what's your name?'" the voice said again. It was a girl, perhaps around her own age – she certainly didn't sound old; maybe nineteen, twenty. The sound came from her left, and, she thought, a little behind her. She twisted as much as she was able, but saw nothing – pain in her protesting skull the only reward for her trouble. She groaned, and relaxed back against the wall as much as she could.

"Marnie," she replied. "My name's Marnie." The answer surprised her; for a moment there she'd had no idea.

"Marnie what?"

Now that did fox her. She couldn't remember. Marnie's head throbbed, making her stomach roll, and for a moment she was worried about exactly how hard she'd been hit. She tried to sit upright, and this time she almost succeeded. There was a coppery smell she realised must be blood, and the thought it was her own made her nauseous again. Defeated, she slumped back against the wall.

"Can't you remember?"

Marnie shook her head, regretting the action even as she did. Her stomach lurched; she took a deep breath to try and quell the nausea. What if she'd done something serious to it? What if no one rescued her and it just kept on getting worse? What if…

The voice came again. "Well, I can't see you, but I'm guessing the lack of response means no."

Marnie sighed, brought back to earth by the intrusion. "I'm sorry," she said. "I mean no, you're right. My head hurts."

"Did you bang it?"

"*I* didn't," she said, "but someone else certainly did."

The voice oozed sympathy. "Oh, poor you," it said. "Are you bleeding?"

"I don't think so," Marnie replied. "Not anymore, anyway."

There was silence for a while as Marnie tried to gather her thoughts. Her companion gave no sign of wanting to continue the conversation, which suited Marnie for now.

The darkness was slightly less pervasive now, she thought. It was still dim, but she could see a lighter patch off to one side, presumably a window. Perhaps it was dawn? Turning her head to the other side, she could see a line of light some distance above her. At a guess, she figured that to be where the cellar door was. She smiled to herself as she realised she'd worked out she was probably in a cellar. That was no practical help, she knew, but it seemed to help, a little.

Something scraped on the floor above, then thumped, and Marnie tensed. The noise passed, and she dared to breathe once more – then remembered she was no longer alone. "What's your name?" she asked.

"Annie. Annie Bourne." The girl's tone was matter of fact, a slight tremble in her voice the only sign she might be scared.

"How did you get here, Annie?"

"I'm not sure," she said. "I remember sitting down on a bench at the bus stop... and then I woke up here."

Marnie thought about that. Her own last memory prior to this was of walking home, and a blinding pain at the back of her head. "You don't seem scared," she said.

"Oh, I am," Annie answered. Her voice got small. "I just . . . try to make the best of things, I suppose."

Marnie laughed. "Not sure how to make the best of something like this, but I admire the sentiment."

"Do you think we'll get out of this?" Annie's voice

was less certain now; a quaver had crept in, revealing her lack of confidence.

Marnie cursed herself for undermining the girl; she was just trying to keep herself under control. "Of course we will," she answered; unwilling to deal with Annie if she was going to have a meltdown. They needed to stay calm, figure out what was going on.

The scraping over their heads sounded once more, and Marnie felt the other girl huddle in closer. She hadn't realised how close they were, or how tightly Annie must have been holding herself – so had she, come to that. The warmth of her companion's body was welcome, and Marnie felt the aches in her own body complaining at the unaccustomed increase in temperature, however slight. A floorboard creaked, sending a shower of dust down on to their heads, and Annie whimpered.

"Sshh," Marnie whispered, and the girl huddled even closer. For long moments they sat there, barely breathing, waiting for some sign they'd drawn the attention of their gaolers – nothing came.

Gradually, the two girls relaxed. Marnie could see more now – the lighter patch over to her left was indeed a window, covered with what looked like a piece of grubby sacking nailed roughly over the frame. With the increased visibility, Marnie realised she could now probably get at least an idea of what Annie looked like.

"Annie?"

The girl was silent, Marnie could sense no movement. Had she fallen asleep? She started to turn her head, moaning at the pain induced by this movement – both the wound at the back of her skull and the stiffness in her neck protesting at such treatment. She winced as something pricked her hand, and darkness fell.

"Marnie?"

The voice was shaky, struggling to maintain calm, and Marnie recognised it as Annie's. She flicked her tongue across her lips, attempting to soothe her cracked mouth, but it felt too large, somehow alien – dry and rough.

"*Marnie!*"

It was more insistent now, and Marnie realised some sort of response was required – but nothing came. Her wrists were agony, she'd slumped forward and the ropes were biting into the soft flesh there – so there wasn't just a wall behind her after all, was there. Or if it was just a wall, there was a ring or a hook or something that her ropes were fastened to. She forced herself upright, and gasped at how badly that hurt her. She tried to speak. "I'm here. . ."

"Oh, thank God."

Annie had given up looking on the bright side, it seemed, and Marnie had to feel a twinge of sadness at that. She tried again, and this time was more successful. "I'm okay. I think."

She became aware of various pains she hadn't noticed before – her hand stung where something had scratched her before . . . before what? Her back ached, and her ribs felt bruised – there was a sharp pain when she tried to take a deep breath, so she struggled to keep her breathing light. Why wasn't that as easy now?

Annie was almost hysterical. "I thought you'd died! You went all quiet and then you sort of . . . drooped, and wouldn't answer me! I thought you'd had a stroke, or something! "

"Annie!"

The girl stopped in mid-flow, her breath hitching as she tried to regain control. There was no trace now of the brightness she'd displayed at first.

Marnie tried to temper her tone, sorry she'd been sharp. "Calm down, okay? We need to figure out where we are, what's going on."

Annie muttered something incomprehensible that Marnie chose to take for assent, and she turned her attention to what little they knew of their predicament.

"Neither of us know how we got here, right?" she asked.

"No," Annie said.

"Are you hurt at all?"

"No," Annie answered.

Marnie pondered that one for a while. She'd been hit on the head, knocked out with what she suspected was an injection this time around, then apparently beaten whilst unconscious. At best. How had Annie not been touched?

She tried again. "Are you sure?"

There was a pause before Annie answered. "My wrists are a bit sore, but that's the rope, isn't it."

"Nothing else?"

"No," Annie said. "But you've been here longer than me, I think. And what if . . ." Her voice trailed off.

"If?" Marnie prompted.

"What if they're saving me for when they're finished with you?"

Marnie hadn't thought of that. She sat and listened to Annie as she started to cry softly, and couldn't think of a thing to say.

Time passed, and the silence held. Marnie was frozen, horrified at the thought that Annie might be right, and she was meant to be Marnie's replacement, ready for when she was all used up – and presumably dead.

Annie herself didn't seem to want to intrude, leaving Marnie to her thoughts – for now, at least. Marnie was grateful for that. She tried hard to remember the events that had led up to this incarceration – and could only remember walking home from a night out with Cal, then a sudden blow to the back of her head. Then the cellar. She thought about her injuries, tried to catalogue them. There was a bump that felt the size of a mountain on her head; her ribs ached in several places and she still couldn't breathe deeply without a sharp, stabbing pain in her side – probably a broken rib, and she could only hope it wasn't digging into her lung. No coughing yet, so she guessed she was okay so far. Her back was sore, too – part of this was probably the prolonged period spent sitting on the hard floor (her tailbone was sending bolts of pain up her spine every time she tried to shift her weight a little), part of it was probably down to landing like a sack of coal when she'd been hit on the head.

She couldn't feel anything else, other than the ubiquitous pain in her wrists. She leaned back, and hissed as they complained at this renewed pressure on them.

"What's the matter?"

Annie sounded much more guarded now, and Marnie wondered how much to tell her. "My wrists are sore, that's all," she said. "I daresay yours are, too."

Annie's reply was a non-committal "Mm," and Marnie wondered what was wrong. She tried to crane her neck to see her companion, but Annie had shifted to one side and Marnie got no more than a glimpse of dark hair at the level of her own shoulder before she lost sight of her companion.

Silence fell again. Annie didn't seem interested in talking, and Marnie was running recent days through her mind, looking for a reason for someone to do this. She let her thoughts roam to her boyfriend, Cal, and a smile teased the corners of her mouth. Three days ago they'd been at a party, dancing close, laughing and – as always, with them – talking. She couldn't even remember whose party it was, other than some friend of Cal's. She closed her eyes and pictured Cal as he'd been that night; happy – green eyes crinkling at the corners in the way she loved when he laughed. Dancing had never been a strong point for either of them, and she smiled as she remembered his emphatic apologies when he'd trodden on some girl's foot. Cute thing, small and dark, and dancing way too close to Cal for that not to happen.

She opened her eyes. Cute, small, dark. Something shifted at the back of her mind, something she couldn't quite fix. Annie moved, and Marnie tried not to flinch. Then wondered why.

She'd had no warning, this time, of darkness falling. One moment she'd been thinking about. . . what, exactly? It had started as a nice memory, she was sure of that, but then. . .

It was gone, no use trying to get it back now. Her head felt bruised, *her whole head*, as if someone had bounced it around, banging it off walls and floor whilst holding on by her ears, which now felt huge and very hot. Not possible, she knew, but the pain was impossible to ignore – or to explain.

"Annie?"

No answer.

"Annie? Are you there?"

Something shifted overhead, and Marnie froze. She listened, breath held for what seemed an eternity, as footsteps roamed over her head. Her chest was burning now with the effort of holding it all in, but still she couldn't bring herself to let out any air – what if she was heard? Then she couldn't wait any more, and let out a sob as everything escaped. She stiffened in terror, sure she'd bring someone down to investigate the noise.

Nothing. No one heard, or if they did they weren't about to come downstairs, and she was grateful for that. Still, she breathed now – short, shallow sips of air that she could let out with little or no discernible noise, even by her.

There was a sharp bang from overhead, making her jump, and then a scraping noise – and Marnie was ashamed to realise she'd wet herself. She sat there, the warm fluid spreading beneath her, and started to cry. Had she really sunk this low, after what couldn't really have been very long locked in a cellar?

Apparently she had. The scraping noise stopped, and Marnie heard a groan – a man's voice, she was sure, and strangely familiar. Muffled voices rose in what sounded like an argument, then there was another thud, and silence fell.

Marnie was starting to doubt her own sanity now. Still no Annie, and the light – what little there was of it – had waxed and waned at least twice. Now she was in darkness again, and no one had been near her for ages. There hadn't been any further sounds from upstairs since she'd wet herself, and part of her was thankful.

Groaning, she shifted her weight and wondered how long it took for pressure sores to start. Her backside and tailbone ached like a bitch, and her head now felt too big – at least it didn't hurt anymore. The smell of stale urine wafted up as she moved, and she felt the shame of it all over again. This time intermixed with anger that she hadn't been allowed to relieve herself, had instead been kept chained like a rabid animal and neglected for God knows how long. Her stomach growled, and Marnie tried to think how long it had been since her last meal – she'd gone from raging hunger pangs to an empty, pinched feeling in her stomach, so she'd guess quite a while. Annie was gone, and had been for some time – Marnie was beginning to think she'd imagined her in the first place, made up a companion to alleviate the loneliness a little.

Something creaked, off to her left, and Marnie whimpered.

"Annie?"

No answer, save for a badly stifled giggle, and Marnie's fear ramped up several notches.

Something thudded against the wall by her head, and she started to cry. Up to now, most of the indignities she suspected had been inflicted had occurred when she was asleep, or unconscious. Now she prayed that her attacker would knock her out again, showing at least a little mercy.

Something scraped along the floor, metal on concrete, close by – mercy seemed to have run out. Marnie yelped as something prodded her in the thigh, and again there was a giggle – whoever it was didn't bother to stifle it this time. High pitched and cruel, Marnie recognised the tone. "Annie. I should have known."

So she had been real, that much was true. But she hadn't been a prisoner at all. She'd been Marnie's tormentor all along, pretending to offer a sympathetic ear.

Someone cleared their throat, off to Marnie's right, then there was a click – and the cellar flooded with light. Marnie clamped her eyes shut, too late; her head throbbed with the impact on her sight after so long. She felt someone fumbling with her chains and heard a click; then footsteps, running upstairs, and a door opening.

Silence.

For long moments Marnie didn't dare to move. Finally, she unscrewed her face and allowed her eyes to open a crack, then a little more, trying to lessen the pain this new and vivid light incurred.

She was in a cellar; she'd been right about that. The concrete floor was clean, more or less, bloodstains dotting the floor here and there. Looking up, she could see shelves lining one wall, facing her – boxes and paint tins, presumably the usual cellar detritus ranged along their length. Over to her right there was a flight of wooden stairs, a single light bulb swinging over them, making them appear and disappear as it moved. There was another click, and now she could see that the door at the top of the stairs was ajar; someone had turned on the light in the room behind it. She heard laughter, high and shrill, then silence fell once more.

Marnie waited, aware that she had to gauge her situation correctly here; any mistake could be her last one. For a while she could sense (or maybe imagine) someone waiting just the other side of the door, ready to fall on her when she walked through it.

Still she waited. After a while she remembered the fumbling at her wrists, and tried once more to raise her hands. She was so stiff she nearly didn't manage it, but slowly her arms rose and she could rub her wrists, crying at the pain as blood flow was properly restored. She groaned again as she put her weight on her hands and attempted to push herself upright. Her first attempt failed, and she slumped back to the floor, demoralised and wary of trying again. Then her new position started to get painful, and she realised she had to.

"Nothing ventured, nothing gained, right?" she muttered to herself, and laughed at how alien her voice sounded. Cracked and thin, the result of dehydration and lack of use for what must surely be several days. Something small skittered away at the unaccustomed noise, but Marnie wasn't scared of that now. After the events of the last few days, a mouse – or even rat – was the least of her worries. She knelt, feeling her knees pop and her back protest, and put her hands to the floor. She paused, then, just for a moment – taking a last look around at her prison, making sure it was safe to stand. Then she pushed up with her hands and hauled herself to her feet. She swayed a little, and almost reached out to support herself on the shelves, but then the floor stopped moving and she started to feel steadier. Her heart was racing as if she'd run the 100 metres, just from the effort of standing up, and she wondered again how long it had been. Would she deteriorate so much, physically, in a matter of days? When her heartbeat started to settle down, she moved forward towards her next target: the stairs.

They were creaky, and she moved up them as quietly as she could – flinching at each creak and crack of the ageing wood. Finally, the door was within reach – and she found she was too scared to push it open. In her head, her attacker was standing on the other side, waiting for her to walk through the opening so he or she could attack, and push her all the way back down – happy to watch her crack her head on the concrete floor, maybe even bleed to death or fracture her skull.

"Don't be stupid," she told herself. "You've got this far." Thus cajoled, she reached forward and took hold of the doorknob, her hands quivering as she forced them to do what she wanted.

Marnie's brain refused to process the image in front of her. She was in a kitchen, that much she could understand, but the sight of Cal tied to a wooden chair in the centre of the room, bloodied and bruised, would not compute. She whimpered, and saw him twitch; some semblance of consciousness remained, then.

"Cal?"

His head lifted slightly, then slumped again. He had no strength to lift it.

Marnie looked at the floor around him, noting the blood that had pooled and dried, and dripped again. How long had he been here, no more than what – fifteen, twenty feet away? She could hear him huffing as he tried to breathe through his nose and failed, having to almost cough his breath out through his mouth before hissing more in.

No one else seemed to be here, but Marnie knew she couldn't trust that. She inched forward, hoping that Cal would look up, and that he'd know her. That he'd be able to stand, and that they could get out of here.

She tried again. "Cal?"

This time he managed to raise his head a little higher, and Marnie gasped as she saw the extent of the damage to his face. He tried to speak, but managed only to moan, and drool more blood on the floor.

His eyes were puffed shut, and navy blue. His nose was smeared across his face, and thick blood massed around his nostrils, bubbling when he tried to breathe. His mouth was worst, though. His lower jaw was hanging, but at entirely the wrong angle – hanging off to the left, tongue lolling down. That was swollen and bruised, almost purple, and blood was welling from a jagged cut down its side – the cut seemed to have come from the ragged remnant of one of his canine teeth. His teeth were broken, shards of enamel littering his shirt, gleaming white against the crimson stained cloth.

"Oh God, Cal," she said, and went to him – all thought of danger forgotten now. She went to the back of the chair and saw that plastic ties were sinking into the swollen, puffy flesh of his wrists – the flesh below them already blackening and distended. Looking around, she saw a knife on the worktop a few feet away and grabbed it, trying not to cut him as she worked the blade under the ties and cut through them.

He groaned, but left his arms hanging – she lifted them into his lap, started rubbing them to try and get the blood flowing again.

"Not so pretty now, is he?"

Marnie flinched, and whirled to face the sound. "Annie."

Annie giggled, delighted. "*Ta dah!* Bet you thought you were going mad, didn't you." It wasn't a question.

Marnie turned once more, positioning herself between Annie and Cal. Annie stood in the doorway to the kitchen, head cocked to one side as she watched Marnie; eager to see some sign that she'd broken her.

Marnie straightened, stood with her feet firmly planted hip-width apart, and stared right back. "I gave up on that a long time ago," she said.

Annie's smile faltered. "I'm sorry?"

"You will be." Marnie took a step forward, and was gratified to see Annie take a corresponding step back. "I've played the nice girl long enough, I think." She turned and looked at her boyfriend over her shoulder. "Don't you, Cal?"

She was rewarded by a grin from that broken mouth, which quickly dropped when Cal's gaze turned to Annie.

Marnie's mind was clear now. The fog of the last few days had lifted – Annie had drugged her, she could see that now. How dare the little bitch? The flash of memory she'd had earlier returned, of dancing with Cal while a small, dark-haired girl glowered at them – and this time she recognised the girl as Annie. She was a little disappointed that all this was just a jealous 'screw you' from some lovelorn kid but she had to admit Annie had potential.

As Marnie watched, Annie seemed to gather herself. After a nervous glance at Cal, presumably making sure he wasn't able to come to Marnie's aid, she said – in a voice far braver sounding than she looked – "You had no idea it was me."

"No," Marnie said. "I didn't." And now her smile was brilliant, making Annie flinch. "I have to admit you were a surprise."

"I don't know what you mean," the girl answered, and now her voice was quavering. "You always seem to get what you want, and you're so bubbly and pretty. You're always so nice to everyone . . ." Now her gaze swept across Cal's ruined face again. "You're like a flame."

Marnie followed Annie's gaze. "And he's what, a

192

moth?" She started to laugh. "You thought you'd teach me a lesson? Show me I can't always have what I want? That it doesn't pay to be *nice*?" She remembered the knife in her hand, and launched it at Annie, laughing all the more when the girl screeched in fright as it slammed into the doorframe not far from her head.

She ran towards Annie, who shrieked once more and fled down the hall. Gripping the knife by its handle and hauling it back out of the frame, she yelled after her: "Newsflash. I'm not that nice."

Marnie heard the scrape of chair legs on the tile floor behind her and turned, happy to see Cal staggering to his feet. His face was a mess, but other than that he seemed essentially unharmed, if a little groggy. She moved back to him and stood on tiptoe, kissed his forehead. "Welcome back, lover. Want to play?"

He nodded, sending a spray of blood onto the floor, and grimaced. "Think I'll take the dentist's fees out of her flesh."

Marcie saw the pain speaking caused him, and could barely understand his words. She frowned. "Sounds fair to mc," she said, and moved forward again. "Come on."

The upstairs appeared deserted. Marnie stood motionless in the hall alongside Cal, listening. She could hear the wind, and from the sound of it rain was coming down hard, which suited her mood. It felt like the right time for end of the world weather. A floorboard creaked and she cocked her head – there it was again; no random giving of wood, this. Annie. The sound came again, and Marnie realised it was coming from the second room on her left. Floorboards creaked again, followed by the sound of a door snicking shut, and Marnie smiled.   She nodded towards the room, and motioned for Cal to follow her as she moved forward.

She eased the door open as slowly as she could, not wanting to alert Annie to her presence too soon. The room appeared empty; bare floorboards were covered by a thin film of dust which showed Annie's footprints clearly as they led towards a door on the other side of the room – either an en suite bathroom, Marnie thought, or a fitted cupboard of some kind. Either way, she was trapped.

Cal moved past her and positioned himself to one side of the door so that, if she opened it, he'd be behind her and well placed to grab her and hold her, so that Marnie could go to work on her.

Marnie let out a slow breath that shook with desire. This was what she loved; not the pretence of normality that she had to maintain day by day so that no one would suspect; not the playing nice that ensured people liked and trusted her, and by extension Cal. No, what she loved was cornering the mouse and starting to play, seeing the fear on a victim's face as they realised both their miscalculation and the fact that their error was about to prove fatal.

A sob, quickly stifled, came from behind the door, and Marnie relaxed into her role. She strode forward and opened the door, revealing Annie cowering in a cupboard, tears etching a path in the dirt on her cheeks.

"I'm sorry!" she wailed. "I didn't know!"

"That's an excuse?" Marnie said. "Pretty poor one, if you ask me." She looked over her shoulder. "What do you think, love? Should we accept her apology?"

"Not much of an apology," Cal growled. "I don't think she means it."

Marnie reached in and hauled Annie out of the cupboard, dumping her on the floor in the centre of the room. Now that the drugs were out of her system she was more than a match for the smaller girl, and ready to take her revenge.

She knelt down in front of Annie, pulled her hair to force her to look up and into her eyes. "You ruined our game, Annie. We were playing nice, lining up the next one."

"The. . . next one?"

Marnie nodded. "That's right. It's been months since the last one, and we were starting to get bored."

"The last one?"

"What are you, a parrot?" This from Cal, who aimed a kick at Annie's behind, and laughed at the cry of pain that ensued.

"Not yet, Cal," Marnie said. She turned to Annie. "I'm sorry about him, he's a little. . . testy about the way you treated him." She thought back to the party. "I thought you liked him; you certainly seemed keen at the party."

"He didn't want me, though, did he," Annie said. "He only wanted you." She looked down at the floor and went on, "It's always the same. They never want me." She looked back up at Marnie, and her gaze was defiant. "Why should girls like you always get lucky? Just because you're confident, and nice, and. . . ." She realised the error in her assumption and faltered.

"So you thought you'd ruin him for me, is that it?" Marnie asked. "Spoiler tactics?"

Annie nodded, her gaze once more firmly on the floor.

Marnie tapped the knife blade against her thigh,

thoughtful. She and Cal had travelled a long way together, finding a mark wherever they went; playing nice, earning trust. . . then obliterating their victim before covering their tracks and disappearing again. This time felt different. Their intended victim had been an insipid little thing with a crush on Cal, and both Marnie and Cal had taken great pleasure in encouraging her affections. Annie, though. . . Annie had shown guts. Sick to death of being passed over in favour of the prettier, more vivacious girls, she'd shown some spunk and decided to take her revenge. You had to respect her work ethic, Marnie thought. Then again, she needed to be punished, and she was going to be so much more fun than their intended prey.

Leaning forward, she whispered into Annie's ear. "You know we have to make you pay, don't you?"

Annie nodded, her sobs coming more strongly now.

"I'll tell you what, though," Marnie continued. "You showed promise, down in the cellar. I'll make you a deal. We can leave you alive; you can take this as a lesson, a starting point." She pulled the girl's head upright and stared into her saucered eyes. "Do you understand?"

The girl tried to nod, winced. "I . . . I think so, yes."

"And when we're finished," Marnie said, "we'll give you her name. She can be your first. You always remember your first time, after all."

Silence. The wind sighed in the eaves, and the three of them sat motionless as Annie thought about that.

She nodded, and Marnie grinned as she raised the knife, watched the light glint off the blade before she went to work on her almost willing victim with its point. It wasn't every day you got to inspire someone.

A GARDEN FOR LILY

Lily screamed in pain as a sudden nip to her ankle drew blood. She was standing in the middle of a jungle overgrown with plants; roses, hydrangea – the strange but suddenly aptly named snapdragons: all were attacking her. The roses bore down from a height no normal flower would reach as they tried to impale her flesh on their thorns, their scent – usually so beautiful – now so thick it did little but inspire nausea; the hydrangea bushes sought to ensnare her even as they capered and shuddered in the wind, branches slapping into her with ever-increasing force; snapdragons nipped at her heels, drawing blood as she passed. But she couldn't stop.

"Darren!"

No answer. She pushed deeper into the undergrowth, searching for her husband, sure that some terrible fate must have befallen him – he'd have answered her otherwisc…wouldn't he? "*Darren!* Answer me!"

Silence. The wind sobbed and moaned through the trees that loomed ahead in this morass of a garden, and there was still no sign of her husband. She was alone, and she was utterly lost.

She heard a splash, somewhere nearby, and something laughed; a soft, lunatic sound from the depths of the surrounding vegetation that froze Lily where she stood. She remained motionless, shuddering in the cold as she searched for a glimpse of Darren in the bushes, but nothing seemed familiar. This was their dream home, sold to them as a 'fixer-upper' opportunity, and they had fallen in love with it at first sight. Now it was trying to kill her; had probably already killed Darren.

Two ice blue orbs blinked into existence a few feet in front of her, accompanied by that gibbering laugh once more – and she understood somehow that they were eyes. She was surrounded by the smell of stagnant water, and worse than that – something *rotting*.

Lily opened her mouth wide and screamed until her throat was raw…

"Lily!" Someone was shaking her, their fingers digging deep into the meat of her arm in an effort to keep hold as she struggled to escape. She heard her name again, and the panic in the speaker's voice… Darren's voice. Her eyelids flickered, the pressure on her arms increasing as she was shaken once more.

"Ow!"

The hold on her arms eased immediately, and she felt the rush of blood to the sore spots, points that she knew would bruise within hours. As she opened her eyes she rubbed her arms, tears threatening. "Jesus, Darren, what was that for?"

Her husband sighed, and she saw embarrassment start to overtake the fear that had been etched on his face just a moment before.

"You were screaming again, Lily." He sat back, rubbed a hand across his face, still shaky. "I'm sorry about…" Darren gestured at her arms, where the marks of his fingers were rising quickly; a dark, purplish red that would be almost navy blue by morning. "I didn't mean to hurt you, but you wouldn't wake up."

"I know you didn't, love." She lay back down, relieved to be back in the here and now, safe. The pain in her arms began to subside as she rubbed them.

Darren lay down beside her, hooked an arm under his head and pulled her close, the tension apparent in his voice as he asked, "So what were you dreaming?"

Frowning, Lily replied, "I don't know, not properly. It was dark, and I was in a garden. It felt like it was *our* garden, but I couldn't get my bearings; I was completely lost. The plants were huge; I couldn't fight my way through them, and there was something..." Her mind shied away from that detail and she curled up to Darren, relishing his warmth. "I couldn't find you."

Darren's voice was calm, and somehow she knew he was smiling; she could hear it. "Doesn't sound too scary now, does it? Big plants and I wasn't around? I mean, we haven't even got a garden!"

"Well, no," she said. "But it wasn't just that. There were these eyes, all cold and blue and scary. And a smell..."

"So far, sounds like me after a bad night."

Lily snorted laughter against his chest, and relaxed against him as he pulled her close. His voice was growing lazy as he said, "Sleep now, babe. I've got you."

She was already halfway there, and fell asleep quickly in his arms. There were no more dreams.

The day dawned bright and warm, as far opposed to Lily's mood as it was possible to get. She kept quiet while Darren got ready for work, and pulled the curtains closed the minute he was gone – it felt better to be in the gloom, away from the light that hurt her eyes and made them itch. Maybe she was coming down with something, she thought – or then again, given her dreams, maybe she was just plain tired. She went through the motions of cleaning the flat, shopping for groceries (her poor eyes protected from the sun by a hat and sunglasses, even though the day wasn't anywhere near as bright as it felt to her) and starting dinner, ready for when Darren came home. In the three months since the doctor had signed her off work following the... as usual, her mind tried and failed to refuse the word *miscarriage*... first to allow her to recover from that, then from the near-breakdown that had followed, she'd grown quite used to her own company, her own schedule, and was no longer sure she wanted to go back. She had no wish to face her colleagues' sympathetic glances and comments. She was happier at home, by herself.

Lily was just setting the table, clattering the cutlery down in a huff because Darren was late (it was half past six; he was never this late), when she heard the scratches at the door.

"Very funny, Darren; just come in for dinner, will you?"

No answer. The scratches came again, somehow *craftier* this time, and it crossed Lily's mind that perhaps someone – or something – other than Darren was outside the door. She smoothed her skirt flat with her hands, picked up a knife from the table, and moved closer to the door. The scratches grew louder, more insistent, and she realised she was gripping the knife so tightly that her fingernails were embedded in her palm. Forcing herself to loosen her grip, she took a deep breath and let it out slowly, surprised at how shaky that breath was. "Darren?"

There was a *snuffling* sound, and the scratches stopped for a moment. To Lily, it seemed as if those few seconds stretched out for ever, and she nearly cried with relief when the scratches returned – this time followed by the unmistakeable sound of a key rattling in the lock.

The door swung open to reveal a rather sheepish Darren swaying in the hall, keys dangling from his hand. "Sorry, pet, had a pint with the lads on the way home." His gaze took in the knife still clutched in his wife's hand, and the fear on her face. "Whoa, love. It's just me, okay? I didn't mean to frighten you."

Lily quickly hid the knife, forced a smile. "I wondered what the noise was, that's all."

She turned and headed back towards the kitchen, her hands shaking. What was wrong with her?

Darren followed a little more slowly, banging into the wall now and again. He pulled out a chair and sat at the little table, but said nothing. He watched Lily as she went through the motions of dishing up their meal, clearly nervous at the change he saw in her.

She clattered the plates down on the table, fetched glasses of water, sat down opposite him and started eating, reluctant to say anything that might make things worse. It made for an uncomfortable meal, as Darren, in turn, said nothing – and she knew that was his way of avoiding anything that might provoke her.

Finally, Lily relented. She put her fork down, smoothed an errant curl behind her ear, and stared up at him. "What was the occasion?"

"Sorry?"

"The pint you went for, remember? What was the occasion, something special?

Darren opened his mouth to speak, cleared his throat, then closed his mouth again – he seemed unsure of what to say.

Lily said nothing, just waited, a little frown creasing

her forehead.

He tried again. "I've got good news."

She smiled now, and finally her face relaxed – the warmth that expression brought with it enough to erase all the worry of recent months, if only for a moment. "That's great. What is it?"

Now he smiled. "I've found a house."

Lily stared at him, the frown back. "Don't joke about it, Darren. You know we can't afford a house."

"We can afford this one, love."

Lily snorted. "Why? Is it falling down?"

Darren's smile slipped a little, but he didn't say anything. Lily waited – sure there was something here that wasn't being said. Something important.

"Besides," she said, and now she was struggling to keep her voice even, "we don't really need one now, do we? Not yet, maybe not…"

"Don't talk like that."

"I'm sorry, but we don't know that we'll…"

"We'll have a family, Lily. I know we will." Darren's voice was firm; he wouldn't brook any dissent on this point. "We just need to give it some time."

Lily said nothing, not willing to open the door to hope; not yet. Not on that. It hurt too much.

In the end, Darren sighed and took her hands in his, pulling gently when she resisted. "It needs some work, that's all; but it's beautiful, Lily. You'll love it, you'll see. And we can take our time doing it up." There was a wheedling tone in his voice that she didn't like, and found herself questioning.

"What's the catch?"

Now Darren let her hands go, and returned to his dinner. He wouldn't look at her, visibly annoyed that his surprise hadn't been welcomed with open arms. "There is no catch, for God's sake. It just needs a bit of TLC, that's all." He sawed angrily at his steak and blood flowed onto his plate, making Lily feel sick. "We're viewing it on Saturday, okay? Just try and keep an open mind till then."

Silence fell, punctuated only by the sound of cutlery on china – Lily nodded, wary of aggravating him further. Maybe she'd been unfair. He'd only been trying to do something nice for her – just like always, and especially so since… "Okay, love. I'm sorry."

He grunted, but didn't reply; just concentrated on his food. Conversation, and along with it all hopes of a pleasant evening, were over.

Wind howled outside their window, and Lily tried to ignore the keening sound the trees made as leaves were ripped away by its gusts – Lily lay and stared at their skeletal fingers scratching across the moonlit ceiling and tried not to cry. She was badly frightened, though if asked she wouldn't be able to say why – she just had a feeling something was wrong.

And was going to get worse.

Saturday dawned clear and bright, and Darren was annoyingly upbeat no matter how much his wife dragged her feet. "Come on, Lily; we're nearly there!"

They turned another corner, and Darren stopped before a rambling Victorian cottage. "We're here!"

Lily said nothing, just took in the building he was clearly so excited about. Made of Derbyshire stone, it was a pleasant, buttery yellow cottage – with crimson roses climbing a ramshackle trellis that was bowing under the weight of its burden. The windows were old-fashioned, small panes of glass with what looked like a bubble in the centre – Lily felt herself start to smile, and as she did, became aware of Darren relaxing beside her.

"You like it?"

She nodded, then looked sideways at Darren, squinting against the sunlight. The effect was oddly disconcerting. "I'll reserve judgement until we've seen inside, though."

"Of course." Darren rushed to open the front door, fishing a key out of his pocket as he went. The door swung open with a creak, and they stepped over the threshold to find themselves in a pleasantly cool, dim hallway. Yellowing wallpaper peeled slightly at the edges, a pattern of roses – now so faded they were barely visible – splashed across the walls. *They certainly loved roses*, Lily thought, and smiled. She peeked into the rooms that led off the hallway as they made their way to the back of the house, and saw nothing that perturbed her. It needed some care, that was true, but she knew they could give it that. She felt no draught, despite the fact it was a windy – if sunny – day, no doors or windows creaked or banged in the breeze.

Darren pushed open a door at the back of the house, and sunlight streamed towards them, bathing them in warmth. Lily exclaimed in delight as she rushed forward, finding herself in the kitchen.

"Oh, it's beautiful!"

Darren stared at her, a little bemused. "It is?"

Lily looked around her, seeing the things he saw – cracked and peeling pale yellow paint, tatty cupboard doors in a hideous avocado green formica (*Thank you to the sixties*, she thought), and a big, cracked old butler sink in front of the huge windows. It needed a complete overhaul. Nevertheless, she loved it – the whole room was filled with light, and there was plenty of space. In her mind, she'd already started planning how she could bring this room up to date, make it hers. She moved to the window and peered out – her face falling as she took in the view. The windows looked out onto a huge, overgrown garden; roses, hydrangeas and clematis grew in abundance everywhere she looked, their heady aroma filling her senses – and to say it was overgrown was an understatement.

"Darren, I…"

He moved to her side, slipped an arm around her shoulders. "Beautiful, isn't it?" He looked down at her, and she saw his face stiffen when he saw the fear in her eyes. His face fell. "Not this again."

"But it's…"

"It's not the garden you dreamed about, Lily. How can it be?" His expression hardened, became stubborn.

Lily chanced another look out at the wilderness outside the kitchen window, and took a deep breath. She forced herself to take in the whole of the garden – the plants, the grass that needcd cutting back… she couldn't be sure it was the same garden, no. She just knew that looking at it filled her with foreboding.

Lily turned to Darren, trying to keep calm. He'd leap on any sign of what he viewed as hysteria. "I know it can't be," she said, "but it looks so much like it."

She waited, fearful of Darren's reaction. She knew how much he loved the house, and worse, how much he wanted her to love it.

His reaction, when it came, surprised her. "How about we get it cleared first?" he said. "Once it's all cleared and tidied you might feel differently."

She thought about it. Much as she wanted to say no, it was the same garden, she knew that was neither fair nor even realistic. It wasn't fair to project a dream onto a place like this. She stared out at the jungle that seemed to be slowly encroaching upon the house, and took a deep breath. Gardening had never been her strongpoint, nor had it been Darren's – but they could find someone, easily enough. It wouldn't take somebody who knew what they were doing long to put things to rights.

"Okay," she said. "And if it still scares me? If I hate it?"

"Then we can concrete it over, okay? Decorate it with pots or something." His tone was tightly controlled, and she knew he was trying hard not to get annoyed.

She snaked an arm around Darren's waist, hugged him. "Then I love it. But can we really afford it?"

Darren sighed, a huge release of pent-up tension, and she realised then just how worried he'd been. His voice shook as he answered, "Just about, love." He gestured vaguely around him, frowning. "It needs quite a bit of work, which puts the price in our favour – but it's going to take a lot of time to get right. Are you sure you're up to it?"

She frowned. "I'm not as fragile as all that, you know; I can help."

"I know you can, love," he said, and squeezed her waist. "I just don't want you overdoing it, that's all. You know how you get."

Lily had the grace to smile. She did have a tendency to get a little obsessed with whatever project she took up; she was sure this would be no different. "I do, but it'll be worth it, won't it?" She gazed once more into the garden, seeing not what was really out there but her ideal – a deck they could sit out on, flowerbeds, maybe a rockery… Her dreams flashed into her mind, and she shivered, then told herself they didn't mean anything; this wasn't the same garden. They didn't even need to *have* a lawn if they didn't want to, and the flowerbeds could be easily tended so they didn't get overgrown. They could even use pots, if it came to that. She turned to Darren, hiding the fear she'd felt for a moment. "I mean, this could be our forever home."

Darren nodded. "I think it could, yes." He rested his hand gently on her stomach as he went on. "There's certainly room to grow." He smiled at her, then loosed himself from her grip and headed into the hall, mobile phone in his hand as he punched the estate agent's number. Lily heard him start to talk, putting things in motion, and took a deep breath. *Please God*, she thought, *let this work out.*

It did work out, finally; after what seemed like endless wrangling and battles to beat the price down because of work needed (taming the jungle in the back yard, for a start) it was really little more than two months before it was theirs. Ten weeks after first viewing the house, Lily stood outside the front door of their new home with the keys in her hand, grinning as she realised this was it. This was theirs now, and if they could sort out the garden stuff it could be their *forever* house, where they would raise their family – should they get lucky enough to have one.

"Penny for them?" Darren stood just behind her, all proud of himself.

"Just thinking you did great, love." She squinted up at the top floor, sunlight blinding her momentarily. "You did really great."

"Thank God for that," he said, laughing. "Come on, time to get on with it." He took a measuring tape out of his pocket. "You got the notebook?"

She waved it in the air. "Yep, and the pen – let's go measure up."

A pleasant few hours passed as they measured the rooms for carpet where needed, and the windows for curtains – wary of anything going wrong with the purchase, they'd been too superstitious to do this until now. Lily could already see how it might look, given a little time and a lot of love. The splash of sun that had marked the hours' passage was low on the wall when Darren walked back in, dusty and dishevelled.

"You ready, love?"

She looked up from her notepad and nodded. "All done, we can go home now."

Darren smiled. "Not home. This is home now, or soon will be." He headed out into the hall, out of her sight. "The flat doesn't really feel like home anymore."

He was right, it didn't. Lily lay in bed there that night, listening to the murmur of next door's TV and the sounds of the family upstairs getting ready for bed – and sighed. Living in a house of their own was going to take a bit of getting used to, she knew – and there was still the garden to worry about. She consoled herself with Darren's promise that they could concrete it if she hated the tidied-up version. But she couldn't wait to start this new chapter in their lives, and to move on from the sadness they'd endured here these last few months.

The house – this was *their* house, she knew; she could feel it even if she couldn't see much – was bitterly cold, the air she breathed wet with condensation. Someone was sobbing in the dark, and she had an awful feeling that she should recognise this phantom; it was someone known to her of old. She reached for the bedside lamp (if she could only see…) but it wouldn't work. She padded over to the wall and toggled the main switch, frustrated, but it was useless. Neither light worked, so a fuse had probably blown somewhere. She had very little choice now; get back into bed and wait in the dark for Darren to come home (where was he, at this time of night?) and tell her everything was alright; or head down to the kitchen, find the fuse box. She chose the latter and began to inch sideways, searching for the door handle. She regretted it almost immediately, as her foot crunched down on something unexpected on the bare wooden floor. She cried out in disgust as it scuttled away, chittering. *What in God's name was that?* She shuddered, and – instead of stepping – started to slide her foot sideways on the floor even as her hand swept the wall in search of the door handle. Her hand scraped against the door jamb and she almost cried with relief when her fingertips brushed a handle almost immediately afterward. She grasped it firmly and turned, stepping forward before she could change her mind and crawl back into bed.

She walked out into the hall and things whispered in the darkness. She took a deep, sobbing breath and groaned at the feeling of its warm vapour pluming out in front of her; her heat being sucked out by the chill of the night air.

Now she was downstairs in the kitchen, just like that – no transition, just there. And the quality of the light now filtering through suggested it was dawn. *Ah, I'm dreaming, then.* That realisation should have brought relief, but menace hung heavy in the air and she was frightened to look out of the kitchen window, even though she knew she must. Slowly, she turned her head, every tendon in her neck screaming in protest.

The bushes outside were heaving themselves to and fro in the wind that shrieked through their leaves; rain slashed against the glass, running down the panes in torrents and she could hear scrabbling at the base of the back door as something tried to scratch its way through, or even get underneath. This was the source of her fear. This was where the danger lay, and it was doing its damnedest to get in. Lily tried hard not to breathe. Something was out there, in the middle of the maelstrom, something that stood quite still and dark in the middle of the madness and beckoned to her, its glacial eyes shining.

Lily woke up screaming, Darren holding her and rocking back and forth, his voice panicked as he shushed her. "Lily, it's okay! Lily! Come on, it's just a dream!" She collapsed into his arms and shut her eyes, held him tight as the sobs forced their way out of her.

"The garden again?"

She nodded, face buried in his chest. "It was trying to get in."

"You're safe, love; I'm here."

She shook her head, a small storm of fear in his arms. "No?"

She shook her head again, but wasn't ready yet to verbalise her reasons. She hung on for a few more moments, allowing his touch to calm her and ground her back in the here and now, then she sat up and leaned into him. "What if it *is* our garden?" she asked.

"Eh?" The confusion in his voice was plain to hear. "You've lost me now."

She sighed. "I keep dreaming about an overgrown

garden, yes? With something in it; something not right. And this time someone was crying… What if it really is our new garden?"

Darren was silent for a moment, as he tried to digest what she was saying. "I know you're scared, okay? I know you keep having this dream, and now we're buying a house that just happens to have an overgrown garden and it's freaked you out somehow – and I can see how you'd make that leap, I really can. But…" He hesitated as he looked for the right words.

"But?" Lily had sat up straight now, her back stiff and straight.

"But we've been through all this. It's just a dream, love. There's nothing to be afraid of. You'll see, once we've moved."

Lily said nothing, but she was still frightened. She shivered, suddenly frozen again, and jumped when Darren laid a hand on her back.

"Besides," he said, "I promised we could concrete the thing if you still hated the finished version, remember?"

She did. Lily allowed herself to be calmed, now, enjoying the feeling of Darren rubbing her back. "Okay," she said, "okay." She laid back down, feeling calmer about the move now. You couldn't get lost in a garden that was cut right back, or covered over.

Darren turned towards her and snaked a hand across her stomach, a leg over hers. He kissed her cheek, but said nothing more, and Lily lay listening to his breathing as it gradually softened and became deeper. He was asleep. She wished it was that easy for her.

Moving day dawned bright and sunny. Lily took a last tour around their flat – a job of no more than a few minutes – and surveyed the pile of packing boxes stacked in the living room, the kitchen… hell, everywhere. The walls of the flat looked even dingier with all their pictures and bits and pieces taken down; brown marks stained the walls where they'd been, the wallpaper brighter where it had been protected. She was surprised to feel a twinge of sadness at the idea of leaving this place. It might not be much, with only one bedroom and a tiny kitchen, and it held some bad memories, but it had been home for quite a while now.

Darren walked into the living room and saw Lily standing framed in the light blazing through the window. She looked… not there, almost, and he shuddered at the prickle that ran up and down his spine. *Silly sod*, he thought. *She's right here, with you – you haven't lost her, and you're not going to.* He forced a smile onto his face and crept up behind her, wrapped his arms around her waist – and was shocked by how fragile she felt. Bones lurked just below the skin, no padding on them now; she felt brittle, easy to break.

As if in answer, Lily struggled round to face him, her expression half-happy, half-pained. "Not so tight, love; you're hurting me."

"You're losing weight? How come?"

She dropped her gaze, then, and snuggled into his neck, her face hidden. "Not much," she muttered. "I haven't been that hungry lately."

He loosened his grip and forced himself not to rise to this, not to try and force the issue. They'd be in the new house soon, and she'd start to put the dreams behind her once the garden was sorted to her satisfaction – it was just worry over the move, he reasoned. She'd be fine.

"Come on, time to go."

Lily eased herself out of his grip, and nodded. Picking up her handbag and a small holdall, she sighed – swaying slightly for just a moment before heading towards the front door. "I'll miss this place, won't you?" she said.

"In some ways," he said. "Not in others. It's too small; time for us to have a place we can spread out in, settle down and start a family, maybe." He gazed towards the bedroom, his expression pensive. "Too many reminders here," he said.

She nodded. "Yeah. Fresh start. I'm looking forward to that." Then she was gone, and he heard her feet clatter on the wooden stairs as she headed for the waiting cab.

Darren took one last look at his old home, their first home together, and smiled as he slammed the door shut and locked it. "That's the last I have to see of you," he said, and turned to follow his wife.

The next few weeks passed quickly in a blur of painting, wallpapering, and generally putting their new home to rights. The repairs had been completed before they moved in; all that remained was to make it truly theirs. Darren watched his wife as she went about her work; she hadn't said anything but she was still whimpering in her sleep, tossing to and fro as she fought to escape whatever demons were chasing her. He knew she was eating, he'd made a point of ensuring that – treating them to takeaways he knew she loved, cooking when she was tired, which was most of the time now – although he had to wonder whether part of that was an attempt to avoid having to go into the kitchen wherever possible, so she wouldn't have to see the garden outside the window. Yet still the pounds kept falling off. Now, a month after they'd moved in, the interior work was almost done and the new house was finally starting to look more like home. He watched as Lily came in with a huge pile of cushions and started scattering them on the sofa and chairs. Lily and her cushions. As long as he'd known her, she'd loved to snuggle down into cushions and pillows, making a little bed for herself wherever she sat – a nest to watch TV from, or just to lay and chat to Darren, read a book. They were, in a very real sense, her haven, and gave her security.

There was something odd about how she was arranging them. He watched as she piled two or three into one corner of the sofa, and then stood back, surveying the effect. She frowned, before plumping them up so they sat higher, and hauling the sofa forward at one end so that it was sheltered from the light afforded by the window.

"Something wrong, love?" he asked.

"No, just getting the couch the way I want it," she answered, not really paying much attention to anything other than the sofa's position. She sat down, plumped up the pillows again, and sank into them. "Plus I can see the TV better from here, see?"

Darren frowned. She had a point about the TV, but small as she was, the height of the pillows and position of the sofa now meant she got no light from the window at all. "Too bright for you?" he asked again.

Lily scowled, but quickly turned it into a smile. "A bit," she said. "Thought I might take a nap." She made a show of snuggling down and closing her eyes, and Darren let her be. He'd be watching her, though, and a visit to the doctor was only a step away. He didn't like the recent changes in his wife.

Not one bit.

Life settled back into its previous routine, pretty much –
Darren went off to work in the mornings, leaving Lily to
continue putting the house to rights; adding what she
called the 'finishing touches', which he knew meant
letting her buy pretty things to dot here and there around
the house. He didn't mind. She was always careful not to
spend too much and there was no doubt she had the
knack of making things comfortable. Lily talked
sometimes of going back to work, and he made the
appropriate noises, but that was something she'd do when
she felt up to it, and he refused to put any pressure on her.
She felt safe at home, and that was worth putting in some
extra hours to bring a bit more money in. Her job was
being held for now, and if it went – well, she'd find
something else, he was sure.

One thing wasn't the same. More often than not,
now, when Darren came home the house would be empty
– and Lily would be standing under the shade of a huge
willow tree that stood halfway down the garden, staring
nervously at the wilderness that marked the bottom end
of it. They'd managed to clear that far, but the garden
seemed to resist any effort on their part to get further.
They'd gain a foot or so across its span, but somehow the
next day the jungle was back up to the tree's level.

Having done her best to ignore its presence up to
now, these days the garden seemed to draw her to it, at
least as far as that tree. And the nightmares, as a result,
were getting worse. Night after night he woke to the
sound of Lily screaming, begging him to find her, rescue
her from the garden. "Don't let it get me," she'd sob,
"please don't let me get lost in it." And there was nothing

215

he could say or do to console her – yet still she couldn't stay away.

They'd been in the house a couple of months when, one morning over breakfast, Darren announced: "I've got a gardener coming."

"What?" Lily froze in the act of bringing a forkful of bacon up to her mouth; she just sat there, staring at him with wide eyes, food forgotten.

"To clear the bottom half. You know, like we talked about?" He kept his eyes firmly on his own breakfast, not wanting her to get too uptight about it.

"Wha… well… when's he coming?"

He'd taken the wind out of her sails, he knew, but they *had* discussed this, and he couldn't let her just ignore the garden forever. The bottom half of the garden was still a swamp despite their best efforts, and they needed to clear it, see what was buried – literally – under the overgrown grass and weeds. It looked like there were rushes in there, too, which suggested water somewhere.

"Saturday. Not too early, we can lie in a bit – thought we could have a quiet weekend while he clears the ground." Now he looked up at Lily, and smiled at her encouragingly.

Her eyes crinkled, and her lips moved in the right direction, but she didn't look happy – not happy at all. "It'll be nice," she said, "to see what we're dealing with."

So why did she look frightened?

Saturday came far too soon. Darren seemed to have spent most of the preceding days trying to convince Lily that a gardener finishing the job they couldn't was a good thing. Now the day was here, he didn't want her to spend too long worrying. He woke long before Lily and crept down to the kitchen so she could rest. As usual, she'd been tossing and turning most of the night.

Lily woke around ten and wandered downstairs, sleepily accepting a cup of tea and some toast, which she took into the living room. She barely spoke, and Darren wasn't in the mood for another argument about the garden, so he left her to rest. The gardener, a sullen forty-something guy called Nigel, turned up on time at ten thirty, ready to get to work.

Darren opened the side gate and led him through to the garden. The top half didn't look too bad now, he and Lily had dead-headed and weeded for all they were worth, and Darren had invested in a lawnmower to bring the grass back under control – at least as far as the bottom half, where it had become overgrown on an epic scale and resisted all efforts made to tame it.

Nigel stood by the back wall of the house, surveying the task before him, and let out a sigh.

"Something wrong?" Darren asked.

"Nah," the man replied. "Nothing I can't handle." He stared out at the undergrowth for a few moments longer before saying, "Might take a while, though."

Darren was amused to hear a hopeful note in the man's voice. "Can I help?" he asked.

The gardener shook his head. "Nah. Let's see how it goes." And with that Nigel was gone, back to his van for supplies.

Leaving the gate open for him, Darren went in search of Lily – and found her in the kitchen, making tea. Or so she said. In reality, she was hovering between the kettle and the window with a troubled frown on her face.

"Why so worried?"

Lily turned to face him, tried to smile. "I'm not, I…" She turned to the window again, and crinkled her nose in disgust. "Can't you smell it?"

"Smell what?"

"Something's off; like drains or a septic tank or something."

He sniffed, waited, then sniffed again. "No, love, I can't. Sorry."

"Really? It stinks."

He stared at her, wondering what was going on here. "We can get the drains checked if it carries on, okay?"

She nodded. "Okay." Then, going back to his first comment, "I'm not worried, though, I promise."

"Yep, you are." He moved forward, took over the task of making the tea. "I promise you, it'll be fine. You'll see."

As he spoke he was ushering her out of the kitchen and into the living room, where he led her to the sofa and made her sit down. "I'll bring you a cuppa in a minute, love. We'll watch a film, eh?"

She smiled up at him, nodded, but her expression was uncertain. Darren left her to it while he wandered back into the kitchen in search of cake.

By the time he brought a tray with tea for both of them and some dubious-looking fruit cake into the living room, Lily was flicking through channels with the satellite remote; although judging by her blank expression he didn't think she was actually seeing anything. He put the tray down and placed a cup of tea on the coffee table in front of her, alongside a side plate with a slice of the fruit cake.

"Here you go," he said, and smiled at her. "Found anything?"

"Thanks love; not really."

She waved the remote control in his general direction and he took it, turned the channel to one that seemed to have her favourite sitcom on repeat. Ten years after it had finished, and it was still permanently available to view, somewhere. He sighed – whoever had come up with that idea would never have to work again, if they didn't want to.

Lily had made herself a nest, as usual, and sat – feet curled beneath her – ensconced amongst her beloved pillows, with a blanket over her legs. Her tea sat beside her cooling off while she nibbled absent-mindedly at her cake.

Darren sat down in an armchair and pretended to watch with her, in the hope he could draw her into conversation somehow.

"Blimey, we've seen this one a few times," he said.

"Mmm."

"Still, it's a good one."

"Mmm."

He gave up. Darren leaned back in his chair and sipped his tea, musing on TV's soporific qualities – at least as far as a programme like this was concerned. It was Lily's equivalent of comfort food, and he didn't mind, really; she'd been living on her nerves for weeks now. It would do her no harm to relax a bit.

He was roused by a shout from the back door, and opened his eyes to see an amused Lily staring at him from the sofa. The TV was still showing her sitcom, and she seemed much happier than she had in the last few weeks. He started, thinking for a moment that he'd surely spilt his tea all over his lap, but then he heard Lily laugh and saw the cup safely placed on the coffee table alongside her own.

"Sorry," he said. "Must have dropped off."

"It's Nigel."

He blinked, tried to process what she was saying, but it didn't seem to make any sense. "What?"

Lily sighed, and tried again. "Nigel. He's calling you."

Darren blinked and sat up, then registered Nigel shouting again. "Mr Smith! Mr Smith! I need to show you something!"

He didn't sound happy. Darren managed a strangled "Coming!", then hauled himself out of the armchair and rubbed his eyes, trying to rout the last traces of sleep.

"Do you want to come?" He was pretty sure Lily would say no, but figured she'd be annoyed if he didn't at least ask her.

Her eyes widened, and she stared nervously at him for a moment before nodding. "Okay."

He tried not to show his surprise, and smiled at her before heading for the back door. Darren was dimly aware of Lily padding down the hall behind him, her footfall so light he could barely hear it.

Nigel was standing at the back door, one hand holding it open, the other on his hip. He was sweating, and extremely red in the face – although whether that was a result of working in the sunshine or anger at his apparent deafness, Darren couldn't be sure.

"I was calling you," the man said, his tone abrupt.

"Sorry," Darren answered. "I must have dozed off for a moment."

"Hmph," the man said, and no more. He might as well have shouted 'it's alright for some', Darren thought, his disgust was so plain to see.

"Anyway," Nigel went on. "I've found something."

With that he was gone, striding up the garden towards his discovery. As Darren followed he could see how hard the man had been working; the overgrown mix of grass, rushes and weeds was gone, piled high to either side of the lawn's edge. In their place was a neat lawn, with what looked like a roughly circular planked area in the middle. The planks were dark and rotten, and there was a smell seeping out from underneath. The air stank of something rotten, or of a blocked drain nearby. It was foul.

"Odd place for a deck," Darren ventured, and was rewarded with a snort from the gardener.

"Ain't a deck," he said, his tone supplying the 'stupid' that was missing from the sentence. "It's covering something up, innit."

"Is it?"

"Course it is." He moved forward, grabbed the nearest plank and heaved.

The smell of putrefaction swelled, a cloud of rank air roiling towards them in seconds. Darren heard Lily gag, and turned to see if she was okay – she had her hand over her mouth and had gone a sickly yellowish-white, but she waved him forward and stood her ground.

Darren cleared his throat, not trusting himself to be able to open his mouth without vomiting, and then – making sure to take very shallow breaths through his mouth so as to avoid the smell – said, "What the hell is that?"

Nigel coughed, turned and hawked up a plug of phlegm, resulting in more gagging from Lily, standing well back from the proceedings. "That, Mr Smith, is a pond."

"A pond?" Darren tried not to feel stupid at this habit he seemed to be developing of just repeating the gardener's words. "Well…what do we do now?"

Nigel let the plank fall back down, and the smell started to recede. "Well," he said, "we need to drain it, obviously."

"And…um…can you do that?"

"I can," Nigel answered, scratching his head with one fat, sweaty hand. "But it'll cost you."

Darren groaned. Of course it would. How could he have thought otherwise? "How much?" he asked.

Nigel tilted his head and considered the planked area as if it contained the world's last treasure. "Well, we'll have to hire the drainage equipment," he said, "although I can work it, so that'll save a bit." His words trailed off as he considered the matter. Then, turning, he grinned happily at Darren. "£300, how's that sound?"

Darren didn't know what to say. Three hundred pounds was a fortune to them, at least at the moment. With all the expenses of moving in, decorating…

"Mr Smith?" Nigel was staring at him, his smile narrowing, his expression becoming markedly less humorous.

"That sounds…fine. Thank you. How soon can you do it?"

Nigel's smile returned, happy now that he'd managed to inveigle a higher fee from them. "Tell you what, I'll do it tomorrow."

And with that he was gone, the garden gate swinging shut behind him.

Darren turned to Lily, unsure of what to say, and stopped short. She was staring at the planks, a frown creasing her forehead. "What's the matter?"

She said nothing, just stared at him, her expression just short of terrified.

"Lily? What is it, what's wrong?"

Now she looked directly at him, really *focussed*, and Darren flinched back from the sight. Her skin, always pale, looked somehow *curdled*, a greenish-yellow underlying her normal pallor.

"I should have known there'd be a pond."

"Eh? How on earth…?"

"I dreamed something splashed," she said, "remember? And that smell… It's the garden I dreamed, Darren, can't you see?"

Darren couldn't see what she meant. He saw the planks, soil-stained and warped, looking almost splintered in places. He saw the darkness of the ground underneath the willow tree further down (*he should have realised there was a pond*, he thought. *Weren't they normally near water?*) and the general mess that was still at the far end, the detritus of Nigel's efforts so far piled high on either side of the garden.

He took Lily's arm, turned her gently towards him. "It's just a dream, love. It's not this garden."

"But…"

He saw she was starting to panic, and stepped in, desperate to head this off. "It's just a pond. You'll see, once everything's cleared away and we've made it nice, you'll see it's not this garden you're dreaming about."

Lily said nothing, just stared at the rotting planks, but her disbelief was plain to see.

Darren woke to screams, and the sound of someone begging for their life. He sat up quickly, fighting free of the covers as they sought to pin him down.

His breathing was ragged as he slammed a hand down on the button that flipped the bedside lamp on, and whirled to face the room as it was flooded with light, intent on facing whatever menaced them head on.

There was nothing. Lily was the source of the screams; she sat there, staring blindly into the room, scream after scream pealing from her throat.

There was nothing there. Darren tried to see what she was staring at, what she was so scared of, but there was nothing there. He eased an arm around her shoulder, stroked her cheek as he whispered, "Lily, it's okay. It's just a dream. Lily!"

Slowly, her screaming tapered off to whimpers, and colour started to rise in her cheeks as she blinked and rubbed her eyes before turning to Darren.

"You didn't see it?"

"See what, love? There was nothing there." He kept a hand on her back, rubbing gently in an attempt to calm her down.

"It was right there!" she said, and started to cry. "It was standing at the bottom of the bed!"

"No, love, it was another dream, that's all. Just a dream."

She buried her face in her hands and sobbed, her ribs shaking with the effort. Darren kept a hand gently on her back and made comforting noises, but couldn't stop thinking about how thin she was – he could see every rib, pretty much; and there were bluish hollows in between each of them where the flesh sank in.

Finally she leaned into him and let him wrap his arms around her, her sobs tailing off as she got herself under control. "It was so real," she said, and burrowed against him, eager for his warmth. "It was just standing there, reaching for me. Staring at me with its icy eyes."

"Icy eyes?"

No answer. Darren shook her gently, but there was no response. Exhausted by the nightmare and her tears, she'd fallen back asleep. Darren eased his arm from around her and laid her down, before lying beside her and pulling the duvet up over both of them. She turned towards him, and he wrapped an arm around her shoulders, pulled her close – as much to free himself from a sudden chill as to keep her warm.

Icy eyes, she'd said. What the hell had icy eyes?

He was woken by sunlight streaming through the bedroom window, and the sound of the back door slamming shut behind him. He fumbled his feet into his slippers and reached for his dressing gown before thumping down the stairs.

"Lily?"

She was nowhere to be seen. Darren glanced quickly into the living room on his way to the kitchen, but both rooms were empty. Crossing the kitchen, he grabbed the handle of the back door and swung it wide.

There she was. Lily was standing very still, head cocked to one side, just this side of the planking at the bottom of the garden. She seemed to be listening to something, but Darren still couldn't hear anything. The sun was already warm on his skin and the garden was calm, secluded – and as it was a Sunday there didn't seem to be much traffic. Darren sighed and stepped forward, slowly making his way across the lawn to his wife's side.

She didn't notice him at first, just kept staring ahead at the willow tree, head cocked to one side.

He spoke gently when he tried to gain her attention, fearful of scaring her. "Lily?"

She shivered, and slowly her eyes started to focus on her surroundings. As she did this, her disquiet grew, until she stared at Darren with eyes like moons – terrified.

"How did I get out here?"

"I'm guessing you walked," he said, and smiled; hoping to defuse her terror.

It didn't work. She took a step closer to him, grabbed his hand. "I don't remember…"

"Maybe you were sleepwalking, love," he said. "Don't worry, eh? Big day yesterday, bound to upset you."

"You think?"

"I do." He started back towards the house, leading her firmly by the hand. "Cuppa?"

"Please." She came with him willingly enough, only looking back once. When she turned to him, he saw Lily wanted to put it behind her; she didn't want to think about sleepwalking, or why she might have done it. She smiled at him, and his heart leapt. "Toast?"

"Dunno," he said, and looped an arm around her shoulder. "I mean, it might be a long day again; Nigel's doing the pond."

"Still?"

"Course," he said. "How do you feel about a fry-up?"

"Silly question."

They reached the door and stepped back into the kitchen; Darren pretended not to notice Lily locking the door firmly behind her.

He made for the fridge and started rummaging. "Have we got any bacon?"

"Yup, bottom shelf. Don't forget the butter."

"As if I would."

While he'd been searching in the fridge, Lily had found the eggs and a crusty loaf. The big frying pan sat ready on the hob, and Lily had already put some oil in it and turned it on to heat before grabbing the kettle and heading for the sink.

Darren slipped some bacon into the pan and broke in a couple of eggs, then cut four slices of the bread and stuck them in the toaster. Behind him, he could hear the kettle starting to boil, the sound of Lily retrieving cups and the milk from the fridge. She'd already started to hum, a sure sign she'd forgotten about wandering into the garden, about whatever fright she'd had. He decided not to mention the locked door; if it made her feel safe, then so be it.

Ten minutes later they were sitting at the kitchen table eating breakfast; Lily's nightmare and subsequent wandering seemed very far away. She looked at the clock, then at the garden, before turning to Darren. "What time is Nigel coming?"

"Same time as yesterday, I expect; he didn't say exactly. Why?" he asked, slathering butter on a slice of toast.

"I just don't want to have to rush," she said, and gestured towards the food.

"We should have plenty of time," Darren said. "And we'll have a better idea of what we're dealing with once it's all drained."

"Dealing with?"

"You know, do we want it cleaned out and re-lined, re-filled; or do we want it filled in and turfed over?"

Lily stared, mulling over what he'd said. "I hadn't thought of that."

"You hadn't?"

She shook her head. "No; I'd only got as far as Nigel draining it and cleaning it all out." Lily stood, taking her plate across to the sink and leaving it on the worktop. As she came back for her tea, she said, "I guess we wait and see what Nigel's dealing with."

Nigel turned out to be dealing with quite a lot. He showed up halfway through the morning, as he had the previous day, and made much of having hired a lorry armed with some kind of pump so that he could drain the pond. Darren and Lily tried to stay out of his way as he tramped from the lorry to the planking, lugging a massive hose over his shoulder, muttering all the way. They watched as he pulled some of the planking up and dropped it at one side of the pond, then fed the hose down into the thick mess that passed for water in its depths.

At that point, Lily flat out refused to go outside until it was all done. "Think of the stink!" she said, and that was it – she wanted nothing more to do with outside until everything smelled as it should again.

Darren watched, bemused, and decided he wasn't entirely sure when that was going to be; and he had to wonder if part of the reason she was hiding indoors was that she was still frightened of whatever they might find. Nigel had gone back to the lorry, and after tinkering inside the cab for a moment or two, had rushed back to the yard with a shouted, "Won't be long now!"

When Darren had gone to the back door to view things better, he'd seen Nigel struggling to keep hold of the hose, which was now pulsing as whatever was left down there was sucked back up into the depths of the lorry. The damn thing looked like it had a heartbeat.

Finally, it was done. The hose was now making the kind of noise that the dentist's drain did when there was no more saliva to suck up; it was causing Darren to feel more than a little sick. Then Nigel went back to the lorry and the pulsing stopped, followed by the gardener's return – he dragged the hose out of the hole, its end now covered in a black, tarry substance that, judging by Nigel's reaction, stank. He lifted it over his shoulder, holding the end up, and slowly made his way back to the lorry one more time.

A few minutes later, there was a knock at the front door. Darren moved through the house to answer it, and found a sickly-looking Nigel standing there, breathing heavily. His sweat-soaked T-shirt was clinging to him, and some suspect black stains dripped down its front. The man smelt as if he'd been dipped in mildew.

"I'm done," he said, keeping his eyes just south of Darren's.

"Great. Shall we have a look?"

Nigel's expression grew even more pained, but he nodded, and grunted in assent. "I'll meet you round the back," he said, turning away.

Darren shut the front door and wandered through the house to the back door, making sure he closed that behind him before slowly making his way towards the reeking mess which had once been a pond. The closer he got the more offensive the stench grew, until by the time he reached an annoyed-looking Nigel, he was once more breathing as shallowly as he could through an open mouth.

"Sorry about the smell," the man said, though he looked anything but.

"No, please, my fault – bit of a dodgy stomach."

The gardener looked unconvinced, but let it lie. He gestured at the hole in the garden left now the planking was up. "I got it clear."

Darren leaned forward, gazed down into the hole. "So I see."

The pit was about ten feet deep, the sides irregular and covered in a black, tar-like substance. The bottom was full of the same oily mess, with no sign of how deep it was. Presumably ancient pondweed or something, Darren thought. There was an old bicycle wheel jutting out of the slime at the bottom, and he could see several shoes off to the sides. He looked carefully, but couldn't see anything bigger, and only realised how stressed he'd been about what still lurked within the pond's depths when he let out a huge, shuddering breath.

"You alright?" Nigel was looking at him as if he'd broken down in tears.

"Yeah, sorry. It's just…" He waved vaguely at the deep hole in the garden, but said nothing more.

Nigel nodded. "Fair enough. Bit of a mess, isn't it?"

"It is, definitely."

For a moment, neither man spoke. The cavernous hole between them lay empty, almost as if it were waiting for something, sending up clouds of foul-smelling air.

In the end, Darren broke first. "So, what do we do now, then?"

Nigel grinned. "That's the million dollar question, alright." He waited for Darren to react, but when no answer was forthcoming the grin slipped, and he went on, "You've got two options, mate. I can fill it in with topsoil, turf it over… That's the easy option."

Darren waited for him to continue, then, sensing he was being set up for a massive fall, sighed and asked:

"Or?"

"Or I can do you a new pond."

"And what does that entail?"

The grin was back. "Now that's a bit more work. First I have to get down there, once it's dried out, and clear out any debris. Then we concrete the hole, or put down a plastic liner – both work, up to you – then we refill, get a pump, stock it with pondweed, fish and the like. See?"

Darren did. He saw the pound signs glowing in Nigel's eyes as he stared hopefully at him. He did a quick calculation of how much was left in the bank, then brought out his next question. "If we did go the second route…"

"A new pond, you mean?"

Darren nodded. "Exactly. How long would it need to dry out?"

Nigel sucked air through his teeth, and did his best to look as if that was a massively complicated question. "Ooh, that's a hard one. Let's see." He made a show of staring down into the chasm, brow furrowing as if engaged in some strenuous calculations, then stood back and stared at Darren, bottom lip stuck out pugnaciously. "Fortnight, if the weather keeps nice?"

Darren tried hard not to smile. In another fortnight he would have been paid again, and so would Lily. He still had one more question, though: "And how much do you reckon it would cost – for the liner, let's say?"

Nigel's face fell, just a little – Darren had correctly surmised the plastic liner would be the cheaper option of the two – then he recovered and said, "I reckon around five hundred, the lot. Take me about a fortnight to do."

Darren smiled. Nigel had confirmed what he'd

thought; the job was going to take a while, which meant he had some time to get the money sorted – and Lily wouldn't have to think about it for at least a fortnight, which was even better. The price seemed too cheap, somehow, but Darren didn't want to quibble over that – or where the materials were coming from. Lily would have a new pond, and a garden with no areas you could hide in. He just hoped that would be enough to allay her fears, and maybe even stop the dreams.

"Let's do that, then," he said. "So I guess we see you in a couple of weeks?"

Nigel nodded, his expression bemused. He was aware on some level that he'd been outsmarted, Darren was sure, but he couldn't for the life of him figure out how that was. "I'll ring you in a fortnight, then," he said. "Let's hope the weather stays dry."

Darren ushered the man out, then made his way back to the living room to bring Lily up to speed. He found her curled up on the sofa amongst her beloved cushions, blanket pulled over her legs and held to her chest.

"You okay, love?" he asked.

She nodded. "Has he gone now?"

"Yeah. He won't be back for a couple of weeks; the ground has to dry out before he does anything else."

"Even if he's filling it in?"

"Well, no," Darren said, and glanced up at her, wanting to see her face when the import of what he said now sank in. "He's coming back in a couple of weeks to put a new liner in, sort you out with a new pond."

"A new one?" She thought about that for a moment, and Darren could see the emotions flitting across her face. On the one hand, the existing pond had overwhelmingly negative connotations for her now. On the other, they could make it so nice, and it would be such a peaceful spot.

"It'll be lovely when it's done," he promised her, "and we can put in a little bench beside it, and some koi. You can train them to eat from your hand, I think."

She smiled. "Sounds nice, I'm sure you're right."

Lily wanted to believe him, he could see that. He just had to hope she'd be convinced once it was all done.

A week later, he was starting to wish he'd got Nigel to just fill the damn thing with topsoil. The smell was finally starting to subside, and the detritus in the depths of the hole were starting to dry out; but Lily had taken to pulling the blinds down in the kitchen to blot out the view, unwilling even to look at it in its current state. She was convinced there was something down there, waiting to be found. And the dreams – far from subsiding – were growing worse. Night after night she woke, crying about being lost and cold. One night she'd even been choking; he'd woken to find her frantically flailing her arms over her head, choking for breath. When he'd managed to calm her, all she'd say was, "I can't swim! I can't swim!"

Darren tried to assure her she was wrong, there was nothing down there, but she wouldn't be swayed. "It could be in the mud," she said, "you don't know, Darren. You don't know *what's* down there."

"I *saw* what was down there!" he said. "Nothing, I promise!" But she wouldn't be convinced, and he couldn't seem to change that.

The nights were worse. Every time she fell asleep Lily tossed and turned, whimpering in her sleep, begging him not to let it find her – whatever 'it' was – hands batting at some unseen foe she thought was coming for her.

Every time, Darren tried to calm her, pulling her close when she was at her worst so that she didn't hurt herself somehow.

The dreams were having a visible impact on her now, and the knock-on effect for Darren was almost as bad. They were both hollow-eyed, clumsy; exhausted by mid-afternoon. And they were starting to get angry with each other, knowing it was because they were tired but too shattered to do anything about it other than let it carry on.

Monday. Eight days since Nigel had sucked the dregs of the pond into that lorry and driven it away; eight days since either of them had had a proper sleep. They got through the day without snapping at each other too much, but both were glad when it was time to go to bed; another day defeated, another day closer to rebuilding the pond and hopefully putting all this to rest.

Fat chance.

Two a.m. and Darren was woken by the sound of sobbing. He sat up in the dark, flesh crawling as his fingers stabbed helplessly at the bedside table in search of the button that switched on the lamp. Finally, he found it and the bedroom was lit by its warm glow.

The room was empty. Lily's side of the bed was cold, the duvet thrown back; the sheets chilled by the wind blowing through the open window. So where was the crying coming from?

"Oh God, *Lily!*" Darren lunged for the window, lifted the sash, and pushed his head through the gap as he searched the ground below.

He saw bare flagstones, the bench under the kitchen window...but no Lily. He gazed further into the garden, but could see very little. He belatedly realised his face was wet, and cold air was buffeting his cheeks; it was raining, heavy droplets of freezing water pummelling his face. Cursing, he withdrew his head and went into the bathroom in search of a towel to rub off. Then he made his way carefully downstairs, searching for his wife.

The living room was empty, as was the hallway and the kitchen – the back door stood open, swinging back and forth in the wind, letting in the rain and the cold.

Darren went and stood in the doorway; he still couldn't see her.

"Lily!"

No answer.

"Lily! Are you okay?"

Someone was definitely crying, the sound was louder out here. Far away, at the end of the garden, someone was sobbing fit to break their heart.

"Lily?" He moved slower now; scared of startling her, and scared too of what he might find. The darkness swelled around him until the house behind felt far away, locked in some different reality, unreachable.

The darkness lessened in front of him, slowly, and he realised he was seeing Lily. She was standing at the edge of the pond, white nightdress flapping around her legs in the storm, shivering. She was crying as if she could never be consoled, and it looked... Darren stopped, then, afraid he might be right, in which case *what was it?*

It looked as if she was holding someone's hand.

A small someone, as she was leaning down towards whoever – or whatever – she was holding. Still she cried, and now Darren could make out words in the keening; or at least he thought he could.

"I'm sorry," she was saying, "I'm so sorry..."

He couldn't see who she was talking to. The air beside her was unrelieved by anything concrete; he could see the grass under her feet and all around her; he could see the willow further back, and the blackness in front of her that was the old pond.

Then he saw it.

As he stood there, shivering, a form started to coalesce. First he saw tiny fingers gripping Lily's, the fingers becoming part of a hand, the hand joined to a thin wrist and bony little arm, then a shoulder… Gradually, the form of a child took shape – a boy, no more than four or five years old. He was shivering, clad only in a thin shirt and short trousers, his feet bare.

"Oh my God, Lily…" Darren reached out to his wife, tried to take her hand, make her *see* him. Then Darren snatched his hand back as the child snarled at him, his face transformed from an expression of loss and innocence to something vicious; with ice-blue eyes and oh, those *teeth*…

Lily turned, then, and Darren realised that she could see him after all. Her eyes were red and puffy from crying, yet her expression was puzzled – and on some level, he thought, she was aware of what was holding her hand, and was screaming.

"I'm sorry, Darren," she said. "He was lost."

"What? Lily, no…" He tried once more to take her hand, and this time she let him; he shuddered at how cold it was, almost blue.

"He needs me," she said.

"He?"

She looked down at the boy, smiling, and squeezed his hand.

The child was staring at Darren, lip curled back to

show his teeth, frigid eyes glaring at him.

"This is..."

"He needs me, Darren." She gestured toward the pond behind them, and Darren saw it was now somehow, inexplicably, full of water again – oily black wavelets lapping at the pond's edge as the water roiled.

"He got lost and didn't see the pond until it was too late. He fell in and drowned here," she said. "He's all alone."

Darren tried to reason with her. "Surely his family..."

"...couldn't find him," she said, her voice far away and somehow vacant. "You've seen what it's like; everything's so high and the water's so dark..." She stared out at the water, her expression blank. "They thought he'd run away," she whispered. "In time, they moved. And he was left here, all alone." Her hand went protectively to her belly, as if cradling something within.

Darren shivered. "Lily, he's not ours. Remember? We lost..."

She whirled around to face him, angry now. "I don't want to remember! I know we..." Lily turned again, to face the boy. "But we could still have... don't you see?"

"Lily..."

"Sshh," she said, and squeezed his hand gently. "He needs a mother." She turned to face the boy once more, and smiled. "And I need him."

The boy was pulling Lily away now, urging her towards the water. The water that was starting to bubble in the middle as if... as if something was rising from its depths.

Darren saw, and everything in him was trying to run away; he could barely force himself to stand still, to keep hold of his wife's hand.

"You're *not* his mother!" he said. "Lily, he's *not* our child!"

And she saw, finally, what he was saying. She saw the expression in his eyes and turned to face the water, realising belatedly that the boy was inching forward towards the pond – a blue light glowed in its depths, drawing him towards it.

Darren tried to pull Lily back, but it was too late.

"Stay with me, Lily," he whispered, and flinched as the creature hissed at him in warning. He held her wrist tighter, determined not to let the thing in the water scare him off. "We can try again, Lily. Please. This isn't our boy."

The boy raced back from nowhere to confront him, hissing and snarling and trying to get Darren to let go of his wife. He wouldn't. He couldn't just let her go, not without trying his best to save her.

"Darren…"

Lily was torn, standing on the edge of the pond with her husband holding her back by one wrist and the creature in the pond beckoning her forward.

Darren didn't know how it could entice Lily this way, but it had a fierce hold on her – the pull was immense, in fact. Lily turned to face him, and he could see the agony on her face as she tried to fight free…

The boy bit him, and he yelled as he drew his wrist back, nursed the throbbing wound against his chest. Aghast, he realised too late what he'd done.

"Lily…"

"I'm sorry," she said, and now she was holding the boy's hand again – the child was grinning, his expression triumphant as he pulled her back towards the water, towards his home…

"For God's sake, Lily!" he cried. "He's not ours! Listen to me! It's not too late for us to try again!"

Lily shook her head, sadly, and yet still took one more step back. The water closed over her ankles, and the boy laughed in triumph as he enticed her ever deeper.

Lily closed her eyes, then, and let the creature pull her back into the water, down into its depths.

Darren cried out and knelt at the water's edge, calling his wife's name, but it was too late. He watched as she sank down and down, far deeper than she had any real way of doing, until the glow disappeared and she was out of sight, leaving him kneeling by the remains of a cleared-out pond, empty save for an inch of rainwater.

The morning dawned clear, and found Darren lying on the ground, unconscious. As the sun rose he opened his eyes, and for the longest time just lay and stared at the sky, before disappearing into the house.

Now, as Darren wandered through the house, picking up items of Lily's clothing – her favourite book, her blanket from the sofa – he realised he knew what to do.

Nigel was true to his word, and turned up the following weekend, having rung to make sure he still wanted the pond put back to its former glory. Over the next few days, the liner was laid and the pond filled, the pump put in… then Nigel came to Darren, to let him know he'd be back later to put in pondweed and anything else he might want.

"Any idea what you might want planted around the edge?" he asked, "any plants you like, or that your wife wants?"

Darren nodded, not willing to let Nigel know it was just him now. "Yes," he said. "I want lilies." He looked out at the pond, beautiful now as it lay neatly edged by a perfect garden; sometime soon he'd get Nigel to build that deck Lily had always wanted, and a rockery for her. Then he'd wait, and sometime – hopefully soon – he had to believe she'd return. And when she did, she'd be coming for him.

He stared at the willow, overhanging the water, dipping down and darkening its surface. Lily hated the dark; always had. He turned to the bemused gardener, waiting for further instructions. "And I want this pond lit," he said.

SAFE

The snow covered her body with a whisper and Nick stood there, shaking, wondering how he would explain it. He supposed he could always fall back on the old favourite: "She ran off with her boss." People liked that one – it fulfilled their sense of symmetry.

There was something about telling someone your wife was a secretary, or PA. They'd nod and smile, and say with a slightly worried look, "What's her boss like?" It was obvious what they meant. So he used to tell them she worked for a gay guy. The relief on their faces was palpable.

The reality, of course, was slightly different. Her boss was fifty if he was a day, had an ever-present sweat problem, must have weighed twenty stone and didn't stand higher than her shoulder, which made him about five feet tall. He had a permanently reddened face, and the worst comb-over Nick had ever seen. His name was Malcolm, of all things. And Hannah was disgusted by him; he was a lech. Worse, an unfulfilled lech.

Still, no one would believe she'd been cheating with a Malcolm.

The wind sobbed at his back, and he huddled further down into the enormous black woollen coat that swathed him in warmth, his breath hitching in his chest as he tried to control his panic. Hannah looked so cold lying there beneath the snow; what little he could see of her skin already turning blue, her lips bled dry of colour. He couldn't, wouldn't, look too close – her features were obscured by a mask of blood, crimson staining the pristine snow beside what was left of her head.

He shifted slightly, took a step back so that he couldn't see the ruin of her face anymore. From where he now stood, so that she was lying with her back turned to him, he could fool himself into thinking she was asleep.

Something cracked behind him, and Nick whirled round – aghast at the sight of Malcolm, breathing hard, a wrench in his grubby little hand. He was standing on a patch of ice that had cracked under his considerable weight – shame he hadn't been on the frozen pond rather than the path. He stood there, chest heaving and a rueful grin on his face, his shirt pulled out and the tattered front of it spattered with Hannah's blood.

"Nick."

He nodded in spite of himself. "Malcolm."

"I expect you're wondering what I'm doing here," Malcolm said, a nervous smile playing around his lips.

"I think that's fairly obvious, don't you?" Nick nodded at the wrench.

"Ah yes," he said. "I can see how that would be misleading."

"That's a bit of an understatement, Malcolm, don't you think?" Nick stared down at Hannah's body and willed her to move, to twitch even, to give some sign that he was wrong. She wasn't dead, this was still… salvageable.

"What, you think *I* killed her?"

Nick studied his opponent, suddenly unsure. Malcolm certainly *looked* shocked. His complexion, usually so ruddy – especially when exerting himself – was now pallid. Sweat stained his shirt and even the neck of his jacket. His expression had turned absurdly mournful, and he looked like he was about to burst into tears.

"I didn't kill her, Nick," he said. "I *loved* her."

The laughter had escaped before Nick could stop it, and now it stained the air with its presence. It seemed profane to laugh with Hannah lying there, her head caved in and half her face gone. He coughed, and tried to steady himself, but the laughter bubbled upward every time he imagined Malcolm and Hannah – *his* Hannah – together.

Nick watched as Malcolm stood straighter, his pudgy features drawing themselves into a frown. Colour had started to return to his cheeks; a sickly, puce hue that made him look dangerous. He took a step forward, ice crunching under his feet, tapping the wrench against the meat of his thigh, and Nick took a corresponding step back.

Malcolm had almost reached Hannah now, and Nick groaned at the thought of that bastard touching his wife – hadn't he done enough? He watched in disgust as Malcolm dropped to his knees – flinging the wrench aside – buried his face in his hands, and started to cry. Great, coughing sobs and snorts. *As disgusting as ever*, Nick thought, then winced. He edged forward, cleared his throat.

"Get away from her."

Malcolm wiped his eyes and looked up; piggy eyes squinted in the sunlight.

"What?"

"You've done enough, for God's sake. Get the fuck away from my wife!"

Sitting back on his haunches, snot hanging from his chin, Malcolm began to chuckle. "You still think I killed her!" He struggled to his feet, coughing and gasping as he fought to get himself under control. "You bloody idiot!"

"*Of course* you killed her!" Nick wailed. "You had a fucking wrench in your hand! Look at it, it's covered in blood!"

Malcolm raised his palms in a placatory gesture, glancing towards the wrench where it lay on the snow, blood blossoming around it. "I can see how it looks, mate," he said.

"I'm not your mate!" Nick yelled. "I never was, you moron! Hannah would come home and tell me about your clumsy efforts at getting her into bed and we'd *laugh*! We'd laugh and laugh, because she wouldn't have looked at you in a million years. She loved *me*!"

"That's what you think, is it?" Malcolm's voice was quiet now, barely audible, and he spoke in a tightly controlled monotone – his words like bullets. "You think she loved you?"

He stared down at Hannah, his features softening, just for a moment. When he glared back at Nick, they were like stone – his eyes boring into Nick's weary face. "She was tired of you," he said, his voice flat and uninflected – and Nick flinched. "I knew she didn't love me," Malcolm said. "That never mattered; we were friends."

Nick sneered, and Malcolm frowned and clenched his stubby little fists, snarling: "She made those stories up, you idiot! She knew what a jealous prick you were, and didn't want an argument!"

"I don't believe you," Nick muttered. "Of course you tried; I mean, look at her!"

"It didn't matter because I'm gay," Malcolm said. "She just didn't want an argument, that's all. She just wanted a quiet life."

Nick stared. "You mean I was right?"

244

"What?" Now it was Malcolm's turn to look blank.

"I told my mates you were gay, to keep them quiet."

Malcolm just gaped, not understanding.

"You know; you're the boss, she's the secretary…"

Malcolm shook his head. "Oh, naturally. So I had to be sleeping with her, or at least trying."

Nick nodded. "That's right. Stands to reason."

This time Malcolm actually howled in amusement. "You absolute cretin." He glanced around, taking in the bleakness of the landscape, the frozen-over pond, trees reaching for the sky with bony fingers… and not a living soul in sight, apart from the two of them. He giggled again, and looked over his shoulder at a holly bush by the pond, overhanging the water. "Can you believe this?" he called.

A familiar voice answered. "I can." Nick's mistress rounded the bush and walked towards them, smiling. "He never was bright."

"Claire?"

"Well done, Nick; you got one right." She reached Malcolm and put an arm round his shoulder, kissed him on the cheek.

The little man smiled, gripping her round the waist. "See, sis? I told you he'd fall for it." He turned to Nick and the smile faded, his hatred plain to see. "You were so worried your beautiful wife was going to cheat, even with a loser like me."

Claire tutted, and shook her head. "No, Malc, you're not."

"I am," he said, and smiled. "Look at me. I know what I am."

He turned to Nick. "But Hannah never treated me like a loser. She was my friend. And week after week I had to listen to her crying about some suspicion or other: she'd looked too long at the barman when you took her for a drink; why was she wearing make-up, when she just wanted to look nice for you. You're a fool, Nick; you never once saw how lucky you were. Most blokes would give anything to have what you had."

"She was mine," Nick snarled. "I know what blokes are like. I was just looking out for her."

"With your fist?" Malcolm screamed at him now. "You hurt the one person who never would have hurt you back, you fucking moron! She loved you. Even when you hit her." He shook his head. "The excuses she used to come out with."

Nick turned to Claire, unwilling to believe. "So how do you fit into this? What was your part?"

"To keep you busy, lover," she answered. "While you were sleeping with me, Hannah and Malcolm could plan a new life for her."

"You didn't even *like* me?"

She stared at him, her eyes hard, contemptuous. "Of course not, you're an idiot." She let her gaze travel down his body. "But you're not a bad-looking idiot, and it was all in a good cause."

"What cause? You fucking killed her! How the hell did that help?"

The first blow glanced off the side of his neck, numbing his shoulder and driving him to the ground. Nick knelt beside the body of his wife, stunned, a trickle of blood working its way inside his shirt.

This close, he saw that something was wrong. Hannah's skin looked shiny under all that blood, waxy. Her eyes stared blindly upward, but had no depth.

The second blow hit him squarely in the back – high up – and he pitched forward, fighting for breath. Something had cracked, and now each breath was a struggle. He hoped it was just a rib or two, not his spine. He rolled over, and groaned as he saw Hannah standing over him with the wrench. Tears stained her cheeks, cutting a line through her foundation; mascara had run halfway down her face, blackening her eyes – she looked like a living skull.

"You bastard," she spat, and raised the wrench above her head. "Why couldn't you just believe I was dead?"

"Hannah…" he reached for the body, and felt at last what they'd done, how easily they'd deceived him. It was a dummy, nothing more, the face smashed in and covered with blood so he wouldn't look too closely. Add a wig that mimicked Hannah's own hair, and her clothes, and cover her body with enough snow that he didn't think anything of her being so pale, or rigid… He *was* stupid. They'd been right, and now it was too late.

The wrench came down again; this time it hit his jaw, breaking it and smashing out several teeth. There was a dull *thump* inside his head as something burst, and the power went out of Nick's body. Blood sprayed into the air, the last colour Nick saw. Things were going dark, and Hannah stood in front of him, her bloody weapon held tightly in both fists. She was sobbing.

She raised it once more. He tried without success to raise a hand to stop her, succeeding only in making his fingers twitch. Hannah paused, just for a moment, and whispered: "All you had to do was believe, Nick. I'd have been gone, and safe. And so would you."

He shook his head, trying to show it wasn't too late, she could go, he'd let her… but the wrench came down, obliterating his face and ending it.

Ending everything.

Hannah dropped the wrench, and watched as Malcolm and Claire soaked her husband's body in petrol.

Malcolm hesitated, lighter in hand, and looked at her. "We don't have to do it," he said. "We can leave him like this; they'll think it's a robbery or something."

"No," Hannah said, and shook her head. Claire picked up the wrench and wiped it down with her scarf, then stamped a hole into the ice and dropped it in to the pond. "I need some time to get away, start again."

Malcolm nodded, clicking the lighter. Flame bloomed, and he dropped it onto the body. Nick erupted into a beacon of light, and was consumed.

Finally, she was safe.

IN MY MIND, MINE UNDERSTANDING

It was the brittle sound of her fingers snapping that brought him back to his senses. He looked down to see his fingers digging deep into the flesh of her hand, blood welling out of the wounds. He felt sick. Her screams echoing through the tunnels brought him back with a jolt; and he realised with a growing sense of despair that it had happened again. He could feel the rage deep within his brain – like a pulsating, icy cold nugget of hate, desperately grasping for control. While exhaustion had lulled him, cocooning his senses, his hands had once more succumbed to its grip – had taken on a life of their own; and this time they weren't giving up without a fight. Try as he might, his grip would not let up. He could see splinters of bone grating against each other deep within the raw, sundered meat of her fingers, and felt sick. Sobbing, he tried to explain, but was prevented from even doing that. All that came out were a series of moans and guttural ramblings; sounds that were easily drowned out by the cacophony of the girl's manic screams. Thank God there was no one around at this late hour to hear her.

The blood streaming down her fingers and his finally greased her hand enough for her to be able to wrench away from his grasp, and she was gone. Running down the platform to the exit, cradling her crushed hand against her body, still screaming. He was left standing there, tears streaming down his face at the hurt he (no, not he, this *other*, usurping the use of his hands) had inflicted. His hands lay inert by his sides, now his once more, but he knew no relief. Control had simply been relinquished, for the moment. Custody was only temporary, and he knew it.

He could feel it still. Deep within his mind, a throbbing globule of hatred, slowly seeping its pus; infecting the surrounding cells, spreading its influence by the second. He could think of no way to stop it. It was there, seething, like the humming of a generator, just below the level of consciousness. His hands fluttered once, twice, waiting for the right signal to goad them into action once more.

A train pulled slowly into the station, trundling its way to a weary halt. The doors sighed open in front of him, and he stepped gratefully into the harsh glare of the interior; ready and waiting to be swallowed by the tunnels, away from prying eyes – and hopefully, at this time of night, from further victims. Thankfully, the carriage was empty. He sprawled across one of the double seats and closed his eyes, willing the night's events to disappear. Maybe it was all a bad dream, and he'd wake up in bed next to his wife. Memory prodded him mercilessly, and new tears rolled down the still sticky tracks left on his face. He wouldn't be waking up next to Sandra any more, not now. That was where all this had started, and there could be no going back. He wondered if the police had found her yet, stiff and cold in their frigid parody of a marital bed, with her face all black and swollen, the imprints of his fingers embedded deep in her throat. Exhaustion whispered softly once more, and he hurtled gratefully into oblivion. But he couldn't forget, not even in the darkest recesses of his mind. Then again, maybe there, at least, he didn't really want to.

He was Robert Leary, and everyone always said he was the nicest man you could ever wish to meet. A deeply Christian man, he was always the first to offer aid where it was needed; and he tried his best to live by the Lord's Commandments. He was honest, God fearing, and kind – and he would not countenance any failure in himself to meet these ideals. Any evidence of his sinful, if human, condition was remorselessly pushed down, and he endeavoured to find the right thing to do in any such circumstance. When he married Sandra, he thought life was just about perfect. Alright, so she had her faults; but no one was flawless. Therefore, on the occasions (more and more frequent) when he considered she had been unkind or untruthful, or just un-Christian, he endeavoured not to judge, and made a real effort to forgive and understand; and things went along just fine, at least as far as Sandra was concerned.

True, he finally realised what a prize bitch (God forgive him) he had married, but by then it was too late. Divorce was not an option, so he saw his marriage as penance for some long overlooked sin, and devoted his life to trying to convert her – and to bear his lot with fortitude. Fat chance. She was a bitch, and she liked being a bitch, so that was that. An uneasy truce had been reached; she had her domain – the house, where she ruled triumphant with a rod of iron; and he had his, the garden – where he sat in solitary peace whenever possible. Life, of a sort, had gone on.

And then he had woken this morning to find Sandra still warm beside him, but most definitely dead. His hands were wrapped around her throat, digging deeply into the flesh. When he had tried in revulsion to pull his hands away, they had not wanted to let go at first; and he couldn't really blame them. It took real effort on his part to make them release her, to subdue the voice that had won control, at least temporarily. They had then hung like dead things at his sides for the best part of an hour, completely unresponsive to any attempts to move them. Then his hands were his once more, if a little clumsier than usual, slower to do his bidding. He put that one down to shock. If he'd but known then what he knew now, he'd have ended it then and there, once and for all.

The sound of the doors opening stirred him from the haven of sleep, and he looked up just in time to watch the doors close - and the woman that had got on move to the furthest end of the carriage before sitting down. He couldn't blame her; he probably looked like a drunk - assuming she hadn't seen the blood drying to a rusty stain on his hand. He tried to conceal it, and a spasm of ice-cold fury shot through his brain as his hands jerked back to life. He suppressed a groan. Not now! Not again! He fought to regain control, and the woman at the far end of the carriage grew visibly more apprehensive. She was no longer sure whether he was just extremely drunk, or whether he was having a fit of some kind. She was just glad that the next station, Camden Town, was coming up any second now. She'd be able to summon help for him, if necessary. More to the point, she'd be safe.

Robert knew he'd lost the battle when his legs decided to join the fray, and he was brought lurching to his feet. Struggling, he was forced relentlessly down the carriage towards her, his wayward hands already grabbing, eager with anticipation. He could see the fear in her eyes, and wanted to warn her – tell her to run, but he was struck mute. Where was the fun in telling the prey to run? The murmuring that was by now incessant in his mind swelled to a shout – a hateful hallelujah bidding his errant limbs to further violence.

Like some still-living zombie, albeit barely, he was dragged inexorably forward. His hands reached towards her throat, and then ...

With a clatter, the train pulled jerkily into Camden Town. His limbs were immediately his own again, the voices quieted. A façade of normality he knew from bitter experience wouldn't last. The doors opened and he fled. Out onto the platform and up the escalators, into the haven of the myriad streets above, where he could hide, fade from sight. The woman left behind in the carriage had pulled the emergency cord and sat slumped in her seat, sobbing hysterically. A few good souls came quickly, though many more passed by, embarrassed, not wanting to get involved. The police and an ambulance were called – but when they arrived, all she could tell them was of the hands, reaching, and the eyes behind them, pleading even as the mouth uttered foul suggestions and obscenities. And about the dark blood all over one of his hands, soaking his sleeve as far as the wrist.

Robert wandered aimlessly through the back streets of Camden, thankfully as dark as his blackest imaginings. The streetlights seemed to match his mood. The light they provided was insipid, fitful even. There were large inky pools of solace between each light, where he could hide his tears and confusion. His legs were numb once more; they belonged to this other now, moving as they were of their own volition. Where they were taking him remained a mystery – he wasn't sure he even wanted to know. He could warn no-one, either, if the need arose. Even speech had been taken away from him. All he could hope and pray for, locked in his cranial prison as he was, was that the police might catch up to him before he hurt anyone else; and put an end to his misery. His body was now a stranger to him. His mind dwelt in a strange land, and was locked there in solitude, while the beast raged without, spoiling and destroying what he had always held sacred.

It had reversed itself. His brain was now a seething mass of palpable malice – with his consciousness (his self) locked in a protective pocket of calm – unwilling and afraid to even attempt escape. Safer by far to stay where he was, and pray for some external source of deliverance.

Sandra's body had indeed been found. The police, acting on the neighbour's reports of how Robert had been seen running, sobbing, from the house that morning, were actively searching for him. When the reports of the day's occurrences on the underground had begun to filter in – of the woman whose fingers had been mangled by a madman who had sobbed all the time he was doing it; and the tale coaxed from the woman found crying hysterically in a train carriage at Camden Town, of being stalked by someone that sounded like a refugee from a very bad horror film; officers were dispatched to each bearing a photograph for identification. When the I.Ds came back positive, Camden Town was saturated with patrol cars and officers on foot, travelling in pairs. It was only a matter of time, now.

Robert was scared. He had walked all the way from Camden Town up to Tufnell Park, through streets that were, for the most part, deserted. Now he was stalking his way up Dartmouth Park Hill. His senses were attuned to the scent of prey, and oh, it felt fine. In his mind's eye,

Robert cringed from what his body was experiencing, wanting no part in its shame.

He could feel the air, caressing his skin – raising all the minute hairs in a tactile response that was completely unfettered in its unlimited imagination. The body's desires had been chained too long, and were eager to add experience to imagination. His body felt as if it were aflame with possibilities, each one baser and more perverse than the last. The night air on his face felt like a lover's embrace, more shockingly intimate than any he had enjoyed with his wife when she would consent to his amateur fumbling. It felt like hundreds of tiny electric shocks were shooting through his veins – a fix, if you like, of life.

Jolting him into recognition of the world as it really was, not the humane, pristine little box he had always seen before, in his blinkered state.

He saw it now in all its complexity – a maelstrom of malevolent intent. The narrow streets he walked, and the blocks of flats stretching back and back, became warrens of hidey-holes for unseen assailants. The cars that passed seemed to slow as they passed him, then accelerate away with a screech of tyres. In the state of paranoia in which his body now existed – it seemed to Robert's body that they were going for help, intent on alerting the police to his whereabouts. Time to live, really live, was growing short. Not long before they forced it to relinquish control to that prat once more, to live the rest of its life out in penance and guilt; afraid to experience. That, or shoot it dead. Then it would feel nothing, not even the toned down version of things that Robert saw. (Locked deep within, Robert wept and prayed for deliverance – whichever way it came.) It determined to go out fighting, to experience to the last; to the full. It would deny itself nothing.

The few people he had seen had looked like sheep to his altered sight, all possible prey. His body had made no move in their direction, however, because none of them had been alone. They had been groups of young lads, weaving their way home from their local pubs, singing and laughing; unaware of the horror that eyed them so benignly. They had left him alone, he thought, because he looked as drunk as they were. His body moved with a jerky, unnatural motion – as if he had been paralysed and was only now re-learning the skill of walking. His tongue had refused to give voice to his pleas for help, and they remained locked in his throat, unspoken; but no less fervent for that.

Halfway up the hill, he came across a young couple, snogging against a wall outside the New Brunswick pub. He could hear sirens in the distance, and instinct told him they wailed for him. Someone had seen him, recognised him, and the battle was about to commence. His decision made, he fell on them.

The boy was dead before he hit the ground, Robert's keys jammed deep into his brain and left dangling from his ear, like some outlandish earring. The girl drew breath to scream, and then he was on her. He was screaming inside as he watched his body throw her to the floor and kick her in the stomach. The air flew from her lungs with a *whoomph*! There would be no screaming now. He fell on her and began to bite and scratch, savouring the feel of each tender mouthful. The texture of her skin as it ripped, welling scarlet, although in this light it looked more like black ink, tracing its secrets in a weird hieroglyph, unknown even to him. He grabbed her dress and tore it straight down the middle, exposing the swell of her breasts. Forbidden fruit no more.

When the police finally caught up with him, some minutes later, he had bitten out her tongue and was chewing it with barely contained glee. He spat it out and sat grinning up at them, teeth gleaming white against the gore dripping down his chin. All he would say was one word, over and over. "Sweet."

The next day, Detective Sergeant Maloney watched impassively through the two-way mirror as the creature that had once been Robert Leary cursed and slavered; trying with all his might to throw off the straitjacket that was binding him as he flung himself against the padded walls of his cell. Their eyes met briefly, though only one was aware of it. Maloney looked deep into the face of madness and was sure he saw, deep down, Robert – the real Robert – crying for release from his prison; desperate to take up the reins of his life once more. Then his gaze was wrenched away, and the ranting began again.

The psychiatrist in charge of Robert's case looked up in time to see a tear of compassion trickling down his worn, weary face.

"Sergeant?"

Maloney turned to the doctor, silently daring him to make something of it, some flip comment. Wisely, he decided not to.

"What went wrong, doctor? What happened to him?"

"We don't know what triggered him, sergeant. It could have been anything. Something completely trivial."

Maloney sat down in the armchair to one side of the psychiatrist's desk, and covered his face with his hands. The admission, once made, softened the psychiatrist's tone immediately.

"He's my nephew, doctor. My sister's child. She's now under sedation at home. The priest's with her. I'm not here in an official capacity, you understand. I just need to know, for her sake. And for my peace of mind."

He looked up at the psychiatrist, and the bleakness in his face said it all.

"I'm sorry. Robert is, as you can see, uncooperative, to say the least. The records we have been able to compile show no indication of anything like this. He doesn't appear to have been under any particular strain, as far as we have been able to find out. Do you have any ideas? Anything that might have led him to.... this?"

Maloney sighed. "Robert was the gentlest soul I ever knew. He wouldn't hurt a fly." He paused to look at the beast in the adjoining cell, and the tears came once more. Neither man acknowledged them. Rising and making his way over to the mirror once more, Maloney continued:

"Robert lived for his wife. A bitch if ever there was one, though he couldn't see it. He took anything she cared to dish out. Saw it as his lot, I suppose. He had a deep and abiding faith, doctor. Did his damnedest to live a Christian life."

The psychiatrist nodded. "That would tie in with what his friends and neighbours have been able to tell us. He was always making a conscious effort to be a good person. Wouldn't give a bad thought house-room. That may be the only explanation."

"What?"

"All his life, Robert sublimated, denied, his bad feelings. All his bad thoughts."

"So?"

"So now they've taken over. They want out."

He stared at the doctor in disbelief. "Oh, come on!"

"I'm serious," he replied. "All the hate, all the rage…all the bad stuff has boiled up and taken control, and what's making it last is that his conscious mind, his good side if you like, has hidden. It's still there, of course, but it's burrowed down so deep it might never get back out again."

Maloney felt his own anger start to rise. "So much for 'the meek shall inherit the Earth.'"

The psychiatrist rose from his seat, and joined Maloney at the window, watching the thing that had been Robert as it wailed and hurled itself against the walls in a vain attempt to loosen its bonds. "He's still in there, don't forget. There's always hope." As he spoke, Robert stilled, and tilted his head towards them. He turned towards the glass, still calm, and Maloney saw the despair deep in Robert's eyes.

"Look at him, doctor. He knows full well what's happening to him. That's not buried very deep."

"Ah well, we can but hope." The glibness of the doctor's response sickened him, and Maloney felt his hands twitch in response. He took a deep breath and looked again at Robert.

Robert wasn't home now, he saw. The creature that was staring directly at him now was a creature of impulse, of pure evil. And it was smiling; he could feel its joy, could feel it swarming, infecting him. He felt his hands twitch again, and went cold. His voice, when it came, sounded different – it wasn't his own. "You should remember one, thing, doctor, about places like this. And what happens to people when they come here."

The doctor was oblivious to anything but his star patient, Robert, watching gleefully as if he could see exactly what was happening in here. "What's that?"

And now Maloney's hands were rising, intent on reaching the doctor's throat. The thing that was Robert howled in glee, and started dancing about, demented in anticipation.

"Hope dies, doc. Just like everything else."

THE CRADLE IN THE CORNER

Mary stared in horror at the monstrosity standing before her.

"Do you like it?" Alan asked. He stood there, all proud of himself – chest puffed out, huge grin on his face. How was she supposed to destroy that?

She released a breath that shook on its way out into the world, surprised not to see actual smoke. *Calm, woman. He thinks he's done a good thing.* "It's... different, I'll say that for it."

The smile froze, and she rushed to smooth things over, make it better, as usual. He was only trying to do something nice. "I haven't seen one like that before. Where'd you get it?"

The smile returned and Adam knelt by the cot, eager for his wife to share his enthusiasm. "In a little antique store in town; I know how much you love old things."

She laughed. "It's definitely got that going for it."

Alan sat back, his face serious now. "I know this needs work, love, but that's what I want – a project. And once it's been painted, got the right drapes and stuff – you'll see; it'll be beautiful." He leaned across and passed her a leaflet he'd picked up from the carpet. "See? That's what it should look like when it's done."

The cot in the picture was far from today's image of a wooden cot with bars up the sides and a high mattress. This one looked more like a laundry basket on legs; wire frame on crossed iron legs that resembled the bottom of a laundry rack – a precursor to today's Moses basket, sort of. A cradle, rather than a cot, and in lamentable condition. Mary smiled, feeling slightly better – a cradle was only for a little while. "It's beautiful, love. Will it be safe, though?"

He nodded. "Yep; by the time the baby's big enough to sit up, she'll have moved on to a cot. The cradle can be stored away at that point." He looked up, then, eyes sparkling as he asked, "Where do you want it?"

Looking round the bedroom, with its low eaves and quirky corners, Mary was at a loss for a moment. Then she saw the perfect spot. There was a recess by the window on the east side of the room that featured a cushioned window seat that she could sit on while she fed the baby, or sang her to sleep. The window itself was double glazed, secure from draughts, and caught the sunrise every morning. "Over there," she said. "In the corner, by the window."

Alan grinned, and hefted the cradle over to the indicated spot, angling it so that it wasn't too close to the window itself, yet would catch the sun's warmth during the day. "Perfect," he said. "Looks like it's always been there."

Mary shivered as a shadow passed in front of her, obscuring the sun and letting a sudden chill into the room. The cradle looked wrong, now – cold and hard – bare as it was of any drapes or covers. The metal seemed to darken before her eyes, and there was an odour of mildew, and decay. "Put it away for now, love," she said, and moved away. "Let's go downstairs and have a cuppa."

Alan looked up, then, and frowned when he saw his wife. "You okay? You look really pale."

She crossed her hands over her bump, protective of

her child even as it kicked playfully against her palm, and backed towards the door. "I'm fine, just a headache..." then she was gone, her footsteps thudding down the stairs as she headed for the kitchen.

"Feeling better?"

Alan's voice broke Mary's concentration, and she blinked as she registered his presence. She was sitting in the rocking chair by the fireplace, rocking blankly back and forth as she stared into the dormant hearth – her concentration had been absolute, but she couldn't for the life of her remember what she'd been thinking about. She nodded, and took the cup of tea he offered gratefully, cupping it in her hands, eager for warmth.

"I am, thanks," she said. "I can't think what came over me."

"You're bound to get queasy or achy now and again, I suppose," he answered. "You've still got what, six weeks to go?"

"About that," she agreed. "Maybe I just need something to eat."

He grinned as he put a plate of toast beside her. "Thought you might say that."

"You know me too well," she said, "thanks, love." She took a piece of toast and grinned as she sat back. "This baby's going to be the size of a whale, I'm sure. All I do is eat."

"It's nice to see," he answered. "At least you're not being sick all the time now."

"True."

Mary cocked her head as something creaked overhead. "You know, we really ought to get those floorboards checked." The noise came again, louder this time, as something moved across the bedroom floor.

Alan sat quiet, listening. "Either something's wrong with the floorboards or the cat's so heavy she sounds like a person, now."

Mary choked on her toast, laughing. The laughter died when she saw Rags lying on the rug in front of the fire, looking like nothing more than a huge, furry cushion. "Definitely not Rags."

There came the sound of a door closing, and then the house was quiet. Both Mary and Alan sat watching the cat, listening to the usual sounds – the clock on the mantel ticking, the boiler clicking on as the temperature dropped, water rushing in the pipes – but no more creaking overhead. For a moment Mary wondered if it might be sounds from next door, but then she remembered this cottage was detached. It had been their dream home, and they'd only bought it when they started trying for a baby.

"This is an old house," Alan offered. "Bound to make noises; it'll be the floorboards settling, or something like that."

Mary nodded. "Must be." She smiled, and turned to the toast again, her voice a little too bright as she continued, "Must be boards relaxing in the heat or something."

Mary lay in bed that night, twisting and turning as she tried unsuccessfully to sink into a deep and blissful sleep. Alan lay next to her, snoring gently, oblivious to her restlessness. The cherry blossom tree in the garden cast shadows that walked across the walls and ceiling, spindly branches reaching for the door on the far side of the room. The wind moaned as it sought entrance to the house, failing miserably thanks to the new windows they'd put in just before finding out Mary was pregnant. A door banged and Mary flinched, jerked into full consciousness. There was no further sound, and gradually she relaxed, happy to believe Rags was on the prowl, probably after some small creature that had braved the cat flap and gained entrance to the kitchen. She heard a faint yowl, and smiled. There was nothing Rags loved more than to present them with whatever she'd chased during the night as a gift over breakfast. Hopefully this time she'd offer it to Alan, before Mary got downstairs.

Something creaked, closer this time, and Mary froze. The creaking came again, and something moved fitfully in the darkness. Mary gazed around the room, and saw the cradle move. Shocked, she watched as it rocked, ever so slightly, in the shadows. A faint creak came again each time it swung, and Mary got out of bed, making for the window, normally draught-free; perhaps Alan hadn't shut it properly?

She reached the window and rattled the handle; nothing. The lock was securely fastened, and there was no trace of movement in the net curtains that hung there. Looking down, Mary could see the cherry tree's branches whipping back and forth in the wind, but she could feel nothing of the night's fury standing by the glass.

She tested the cradle, then. It creaked once more as she rattled the frame, the noise instantly recognisable. Perhaps a screw was loose somewhere? She resolved to get Alan to check everything carefully whilst he was absorbed in his restoration project – it had to be safe before the baby came.

A wave of dizziness swept over her, making her sway. Her left hand moved automatically to protect the baby; her right finding its way to her back, which was starting to complain at this nocturnal wandering. She crept back into bed, chilled, and curled up against Alan's back, resting her icy feet against the warmth of his legs. True to form, he just pulled the duvet further up, making sure she was covered even in his sleep, and she smiled as his arm came up and rested on her hip, patting it. The baby kicked again, this time connecting with his back, and he huffed half-heartedly before settling back down. Sleep hurtled towards her, and she realised as she fell helplessly into its grip that somewhere a baby was crying.

The next few days were filled with the sound of Alan's off-key humming as he first sanded, then painted the cradle a beautiful shade of very pale pink, and – at her insistence – carefully checked all the screws and fastenings he could see. Humming was a habit of his when happy, and Mary liked to hear it. He insisted the cradle was safe, nothing was loose now (if anything ever had been), but she still heard creaking in the night and pictured the cradle rocking – even though she couldn't actually see it doing so. And sometimes there was a whining noise (it must be the cradle, she reasoned, it couldn't be anything else), making a sound eerily reminiscent of a fussing infant. "It must be the wind," he said, and she could hear the patience leeching out of his voice a little more every time he had to say it. Finally she gave in, and didn't mention the creaking any more – but night after night, there it was, taunting her. She couldn't sleep, and when she did manage to doze, her dreams were filled with the sound of a baby crying, and someone – a woman – wailing in the night.

Tuesday morning, and Mary woke to find Alan already dressed, ready to put a third and final coat of paint on the cradle. Fabric swatches were laid out on the dressing table for her to look at, and the window was open, letting in a chill wind.

"Morning, sleepy," he said, smiling at her. His smile faded as he looked at her, and she spoke more sharply than she'd intended.

"What?"

"Nothing," he said. "At least..."

"What, Alan?" She sat up and rubbed her eyes, shivering as the draught reached her sweat-soaked skin.

"Another bad night?"

She groaned. "Is there any other kind, these days?" Heaving herself upright to rest her back against the pillows, she blinked and focussed on her husband's worried face. "Do I look that bad?"

"You don't look good, love, I have to say. You're feeling okay, aren't you? Apart from the sleep thing, I mean."

Mary nodded. "I'm just tired, that's all. I keep hearing that thing creaking at night –"

"It's not the –"

"I know you say it's not the cradle, but what the hell is it, otherwise?" She'd snapped before she could stop herself, and stopped before she could say something else, something hurtful.

Alan's face fell as he replied. "I don't know. I've checked the cradle, the floorboards... nothing seems to creak. Maybe you're just dreaming it?"

"Maybe I am," she sighed. "I know I'm dreaming a baby crying, but either way the result's the same. I'm shattered!"

"You stay there," Alan answered. "I'll bring you breakfast in bed."

Mary spied the cradle behind her husband, and told herself it wasn't a rocking motion spied from the corner of her eye that had attracted her attention. The cradle was still now, no sign of having moved. But she could have sworn... She smiled brightly at Alan, to show him just how okay she was, and threw the covers back. "No, I'll come down. I'd rather eat at the table, with you."

Bemused, Alan could only watch as she hurried past him and into the bathroom. The door clicked shut and he heard the lock turn. And his wife started to cry. Standing by the bathroom door, he leant against the wood, put his hand to the door and listened as she tried to stifle her sobs. Silently, he willed his wife to let him in, to talk about what was causing all this. Nothing, just the sound of Mary's hitching sobs as she tried to get herself under control. Sighing, he gave up and went down to the kitchen to make them some breakfast. He could at least make sure she ate properly.

When Mary ventured into the kitchen her face glowed pink, scrubbed clean to hide her tears. She couldn't hide her eyes, though; their watery stare showed him just how upset she was, and he tried once more to solve this.

"You've been crying," he said.

Mary shook her head. "Not really. Bit weepy this morning, that's all."

"Why, love?"

"Just tired." She peered at him over her cup, her expression vague. "Probably hormones."

Ordinarily, the mention of hormones would be enough for him to leave the subject well alone. It wasn't unusual for her to get weepy at times, and pregnancy had certainly played its part in that. On the other hand...

"Are you sure that's all it is?"

Now she concentrated on the table cloth, tracing its pattern with a slightly shaky hand. She noticed its weakness and placed her hands on her lap, where the fingers proceeded to work at each other, intertwining and unlocking ceaselessly. "What else could it be?" she asked.

"The cradle, maybe?"

She flinched, and shook her head. "Don't be silly."

"I've seen the way you look at the cradle, love," he said gently. "I know you don't like it. I guess I hoped that would change when I'd finished."

She sighed. "It's not the cradle, as such," she said. "But I hear the thing creaking, night after night, and I know you say it's not the cradle but sometimes –"

"Sometimes what?"

"Sometimes I see it rocking."

Alan stared at her, shocked. "That's impossible."

"I know," she wailed, "but it does!" She was crying hard now, and he didn't know what to do. She hiccupped as she went on, "and... and... and that baby keeps crying! It's driving me nuts, Alan!"

"That's... crazy, love," he whispered.

"I know it is. I know how it sounds." She wiped her eyes and took a deep, shuddering breath. "And yet it's true." She attempted a smile, then, and her next words broke Alan's heart. "Maybe I am crazy."

"No, love," he said, and went to her. He leant down and wrapped his arms around her shoulders, held her tight. "You were right the first time, I think. Hormones. You're just worried about the baby, and it's coming out

269

in dreams."

She snuffled against his chest. "You think so?"

"Of course," he said, willing himself to believe it. "We'll ask the doc tomorrow, when we go for your check up, okay? I'm sure everything's fine."

Mary pulled herself out of his grasp, and smiled up at him. "Hope so." She sniffed, and then grinned. "Can I smell bacon?"

Alan laughed. "You and your stomach. I cooked a full English; hang on." He busied himself with the business of sorting out the meal, and tried to look happy. Mary needed him to be strong. He could do that, if it meant she relaxed. Her face lit up as he brought her meal across, and he sat back and watched her eat, aware that this woman was his world. And he wouldn't, couldn't, let anything happen to her.

Night time once more. Mary tossed and turned, and Alan watched – intent, this time, on making sure she wasn't disturbed. The cradle was silent, unmoving, and he'd pulled the curtains tight shut against any possible draught. The house sat inert – joining him in his vigil.

Midnight. The floor creaked, and Alan turned towards the noise's source – a narrow wedge of light gleamed under the door. Was someone in the hall? Noiselessly, he rose and crept towards the light, freezing as it was cut by two black bands. Someone was standing on the other side; he could hear the rasp of their breath in the dark. The bands shifted to the left, paused, and then moved back. Alan shivered, aware the temperature had plummeted – his stomach fluttering frantically as he fought to regain control of his will. His body locked itself in position just beside the door, and refused to let him try to turn the door handle. The floor creaked once more, and Alan saw the handle turn slightly. He couldn't move. Mary moaned and stirred – and the light went out, leaving everything in shadow. For long seconds he watched, and waited, but whatever had been there had been banished by his wife's movements. They were safe once more. Distantly, he heard a baby whimper, and a woman's voice shushed the child as even that distant noise faded away.

Then silence.

"Alan?"

He cried out at the sound of Mary's voice, and slumped against the door as he tried to catch his breath. "Jesus, you frightened the life out of me!"

"What is it? What's wrong?"

There was panic in her voice, and Alan switched the light on, trying to smile but terrified that his expression must be nearer to a grimace. Mary was staring, owl-eyed, at him; her face so pale. "It's all right, love. I'm sorry." He crossed over to her, sat on the edge of the bed. "I thought I heard something, that's all."

"And did you?"

"No," he lied. "Well, maybe the cat. I guess Rags needs to go on a diet after all."

She didn't smile, and he knew he wasn't fooling her for a moment. He got up and turned his bedside lamp on, then turned out the overhead light and got into bed. "It's okay, love, really. Go to sleep."

She wormed her way under his arm, and soon fell asleep there. Alan lay wide-eyed in the dark, waiting for what might come next. He heard the usual sounds of a house relaxing, but nothing more. Time passed, and the light in the room went through gradations of shadow as the sun rose and tried to peek through the curtains. Still he lay, unmoving, unwilling to disturb his wife as she rested – he couldn't shake the feeling that something was coming. Something wanted to announce itself, and their lives would never be the same.

The next few weeks were quiet, for the most part, and Mary almost began to believe that they'd imagined it all. The birth of their daughter wasn't far away now, and life seemed to consist of hospital visits, shopping trips for last-minute 'essentials' such as armloads of nappies, babygros, creams... you name it, they bought it, eager to be fully prepared. In between those trips and spring-cleaning the house to make sure everything was done ahead of time, there hadn't been much time for anything else to intrude. Now, all was finished, and her thoughts began to turn to what it would be like to greet her child. As they pulled into the hospital car park for a final scan, Mary felt the baby *shift*, not so much kicking as turning around entirely, forcing her to stretch out in the car seat, something that wasn't exactly easy.

"You okay?" Alan asked, alarmed.

"Yeah," she answered, sighing. "She's just having a kick around in there, I think." The baby shifted again, and she winced. "Now I need to pee."

Alan grinned, and pulled into a parking space. "Hang on, then. Won't be a minute."

He was true to his word, and five minutes later she let herself into the Ladies and locked herself in a cubicle. Pain lanced through her abdomen, making her cry out – then the baby *lurched*, and Mary passed out. When she came to, she was leaning against the cubicle wall, and her head throbbed. She put her hand to her forehead and it came away bloody. Had she fainted? Gingerly, she stood and looked into the bowl, fearful of what she might see. There was nothing there, and the pain had abated; perhaps all might yet be okay. She heard a murmur of voices outside, and realised Alan was probably out there, worried. How long had she been out? She tidied herself up, washed her hands, and wadded some tissues against the cut on her head. Then she let herself out into the corridor, where Alan stood, concern etched on his face.

"Mary!" He came to her, and looped an arm around her waist, coaxed her hand away from her forehead. "What happened?"

"I fainted, I think," she whispered. "I feel a bit sick."

"Come on," he said. "Let's sit down for a minute." He led her to a chair, and busied himself cleaning the cut on her forehead, then got her a cup of water from the cooler in the corridor. She drank it, then nodded, a little bit of colour returning.

"Thanks, I'm okay now."

"Are you sure?"

She nodded again. "I'm fine. I just got woozy for a sec, that's all, and the next thing I knew I was waking up."

"Well, at least we're in the right place," he said. "Come on, let's get this scan done, and let them know what happened."

The scan went without incident, and Mary found herself watching the movements of her baby in wonderment, Alan by her side. The child kicked and turned, and Mary saw her daughter was sucking her thumb. It still didn't seem real, yet within a couple of weeks she'd be here, and they'd be a proper family. Things would never be the same.

The baby turned towards the probe again, and Mary froze as she opened her eyes, seeming to look straight at her. "Can she do that?" Mary asked.

"Do what?" the nurse asked, her attention on whatever it was the scan was telling her.

"Can she open her eyes?"

The nurse looked at the scan more closely, then, her brow furrowed. "I don't think so, dear. Perhaps she was just fretting, eh?"

Mary watched as the baby stirred, then went back to the normal foetal position. Dimly, she could hear a baby crying again, and wondered how close they were to the maternity ward here. "Is everything okay with her?" she asked.

The nurse hummed and ha-ed for a few moments as she went over the results, then nodded. "Looks good to me." She looked at Mary then and smiled. "You'll be able to see for yourself soon." She gestured to Mary's clothes and said, "You can get dressed now, you're all done. The doctor will have these in time for your next clinic appointment."

Mary busied herself getting dressed, while Alan looked at the picture the nurse had given them of their baby. He had a beatific smile on his face, and Mary felt a pang at her misgivings. She was letting her imagination run away with her; the baby was fine. And it was all theirs.

Mary's due date was close now; the baby was only days away. She woke, restless, on the Monday; and lay quiet for a while so that Alan could sleep. After a few minutes she couldn't lie still anymore and got up quietly, careful not to disturb her husband. She wandered into the hall and prowled through the upstairs of the house. Nothing stirred. The cat lay comatose on the hall carpet, purring gently as it slept.

The wind sighed in the eaves, and Mary paused. Something rustled, and she looked behind her. Rags had sprung to her feet and was crouched, fur bristling, hissing at some unseen foe. There was nothing there. The hall was empty, and the only sound was the sighing of the wind, and the distant rumble of Alan's snoring.

The wind grew louder, and Mary heard the creaking start in the bedroom. She whimpered, and told herself it was a draught – the double glazing was faulty, that was all. They'd have to call the builder back and get him to fix it. Alan shifted in his sleep, and moaned, and Mary took an involuntary step forward. She couldn't leave him alone in there. *Squeaaaaak... squeeeeak...* the sound was louder now, more insistent. Mary became aware of a shushing sound, and stopped – she didn't want to go into that room. She didn't want to even be in the house, let alone in the bedroom, but Alan was in there, alone, and she couldn't desert him.

The bedroom door was ajar; had she left it like that? She couldn't remember. She pushed it further open, and stepped inside.

The bedroom was in shadow, save for a shaft of dim light that fell on the cradle from the window. Mary moaned as she saw that the window was different now... the modern glazing was gone, replaced by an old-fashioned sash window; paint peeling and rust patches clustered around the lock. The wind howled through a crack in the glass, and the cradle rocked faster.

Mary's feet moved without conscious instruction,

and as she edged closer she saw a dark shadow squirming in the depths of the cradle. The crying was louder now, and Mary saw a darker shadow open in the midst of where the phantom infant's face must surely be. This was the source of the crying; the cradle bore some remnant of a child that had expired in its depths, the sadness palpable around it now, a cloud of misery that reached out to devour everything around it.

A shadow moved past Mary, and she flinched. She watched as it moved towards the cradle, spectral arms reaching out to pick up the dead child and clutch it to its phantom bosom. Mary saw skeletal fingers clutching at non-existent tresses as the baby wailed and wailed, desperate for comfort that would never come.

She screamed as she felt the first pains, and simultaneously saw the baby's head turn towards her, arms reaching for her, her body responding even as madness closed in.

Alan woke, then, and found his wife unconscious on the floor. He leapt from the bed, and struggled to lift her, but finally he got her on the bed. Her breathing was shallow, her expression pallid, and he groaned as he saw the dark stain spreading on the sheets. "Oh Jesus, love," he cried. "You're bleeding. Oh God." He went to pick up the phone, but her hand gripped his wrist, and he saw her eyes flutter open briefly.

"Don't leave me," she pleaded. "Please." Her eyes closed again, and she screamed as another spasm ripped through her.

Alan quickly dialled the emergency services, and called for an ambulance. Details given, he slammed the phone down as she rallied once more, and went to his wife.

"Lean on me, love," he said as he sat beside her on the bed. "Help's coming. Just hold on."

Mary smiled, then; her face so sad as she stroked his face. "She's coming, Alan. Don't let it get her."

Mystified, Alan nodded, and held Mary's hands as she breathed through another contraction. He heard a cry, cut off suddenly, and saw his daughter lying on the sheets even as she breathed her last.

Mary sobbed, and reached out to her baby, then screamed and started batting at the bed. "Get away! Get away from her!"

Alan heard the distant whoop of the ambulance's siren, signifying it had found the lane to their cottage. He ran downstairs and unlocked the front door, leaving it ajar for them – they'd be with him in moments. Then he ran back up the stairs to his wife.

When he opened the door, he stopped in his tracks; unable to process what his eyes insisted he was seeing. Mary was crying, stroking their daughter's lifeless body – and a shadow was reaching out, ushering what looked like a phantom infant towards her still form. He screamed as the shadow-child reached his daughter, and ran forward. The shadow drew back, clutching the long-dead infant to its chest, and vaguely he was aware of Mary shouting "The cradle! Get rid of the cradle!" He rushed over and lifted the cradle, grimacing as it fought in his grip, the spirit of whatever poor soul had lost her baby in the cradle trying to wrest it from him, to be returned to its place by the window. He wrenched it free, and – opening the window as wide as he could – hurled the cradle out into the night. There was a flash as it hit the ground, and he saw, just for a moment, a young woman clad only in a white shift, holding a screaming infant out to him, pleading for her child. "Save her," she sobbed. "Save my baby!"

The ambulance reached them then, the blue light's strobe casting the nightmarish scene in an impossible light. It drove over the cradle – the spirit screamed and was torn to shreds, fingers of mist dissipating in the wind even as the sound was fading, fading. Then the night was still, apart from the normal sounds of the wind, and of the ambulance parking and its crew getting out and coming to the door.

The child on the bed mewed and moved, mouth open in a maw of distress as its little arms and legs waved around. The ambulance crew took one look and, while one went to Mary and started to examine her, the other wrapped the infant in a blanket and gave it the once over. Satisfied it was a healthy birth, he offered the child to its father, who was crying in the hall.

"This one's a fighter," he said, smiling. "She wants her mother." He looked back into the bedroom and then held the child tighter. "You can give her to her in a minute."

Alan smiled. "Mary's okay?"

"She's fine, sir. A bit shocked, hysterical, really; but then she's been through a lot." The man smiled at him, then, his expression kindly. "They'll both feel better when Mum can give baby a cuddle."

Alan nodded, and took his daughter from the medic's arms. He looked down at her face, pink and distressed, and took the waving fist in his own. The baby quieted, and he smiled at her as she watched him, curious now rather than afraid. "Come on, little one," he whispered.

"Let's go and see Mummy."

Afterword

The last evening of the 2010 World Horror Convention is one of those nights that I will always hold very close to my heart. It was the night that I signed with the pen name 'Edgar Allan Poo' on a book written by Tim Lebbon. It's also the night that I think really cemented my friendship with Marie O'Regan and her other half, Paul Kane. I was telling them, and a few others (in a jokey way, you understand), about an idea I had for a story about a dwarf that was bitten by a werewolf and was then turned into a were-dwarf. Now, it might have been a combination of the fatigue everyone was feeling after the end of a very successful convention (the biggest one I have ever been to in my life), it might have been the fact that people may have had a little too much to drink – but something about my silly idea made everyone laugh, and Marie and Paul (from what I can remember,) were laughing the hardest.

And in 2012, my short story 'The Were-Dwarf', was published. It took a long time to write, but I always thought that if the story made anyone titter as much as the idea of it did, I was onto a winner. And I have Marie (and Paul) to thank for it (I've thanked her in public, but here it is in print).

But back to Marie. Us bloody writers, hey? You're asked to do a piece about someone and they always revert it to writing about themselves.

I love Marie's writing. In 2011 I was very honoured to have her write a story for me for a book I was editing called *Bite Size Horror*. The story was 'The Unquiet

Bones' and I can still remember reading it as if it was yesterday. Alex's jittery body twitching around the room, looking at books on shelves although she cannot see. The burning painting. The monk. You'll have read the story now, so you'll know what I'm talking about. Marie's story played out like a demented Hammer Horror, and her tale, along with Reggie Oliver's, are my favourites in that anthology. I was also thrilled to use her story 'Someone to Watch Over You' in the first *Best British Book of Horror*. It was a ghostly tale, tremendously evocative, and as I was reading it; I knew then and there that it would go straight onto the 'must use' list without the need of reading it again.

Marie's writing is crisp, beautiful, but never – not for one second – makes you feel like you're safe. Her writing can be edgy, dangerous even. With 'The Cradle in the Corner' Marie makes you feel real unease, and as a parent, I felt the thrill of nausea course through me. Bravo, bravo indeed!

The highlight of this collection is her novelette 'A Garden For Lily' (previously published as *The Curse of the Ghost)*. Her work on this reminds me of those Mistresses of the genre: Shirley Jackson, Cynthia Asquith and Edith Wharton. Marie's work in *Curse* really is that good.

It would be remiss of me not to mention her other role as editor, and alongside Paul Kane, she has edited some remarkable anthologies. However, for me, *The Mammoth Book of Ghost Stories by Women* is a crowning achievement – it is by far one of the best anthologies Robinson ever published and is the perfect companion piece to Lisa Tuttle's *Skin of the Soul*.

Marie is also very sharp, funny, a brilliant and

sympathetic person to chat to – one of the hardest working people in the genre, and that she's taken on the UK chapter of the HWA just shows how committed she is and how the genre flows through her veins – and how she could never quit it, even if she wanted to!

Marie's first collection was published in 2006, and her second ten years later. I hope it's not a further ten years before we see a third collection. That would be a cruel thing indeed. Marie is an author that demands reading, and in this age where people are going on about moving away from 'proper horror' and turning their noses up at it, I'm glad that Marie is leading the charge, writing 'proper horror' and telling it like it is.

I'm proud to call her a friend, and I'm proud to have asked if we could get a new collection from her. I'm so glad she said yes. I bet you are too.

Johnny Mains 2016

Story Notes

The Real Me.

This story came about because of a chance thought when seeing the ubiquitous pictures of celebrities, both online and in magazines, that had had 'work done', or were suspected of having done so. In most cases, the person concerned is still recognisable; in the best cases, you can barely tell anything's been done. But sometimes, just sometimes, you'll see a picture of someone and realise you didn't even recognise them – not a thing about the face staring out at you with a well-known and remembered name underneath is familiar. I started to wonder how that would affect you; if every time you stared into the mirror a complete stranger was staring back at you, some other 'self' that couldn't even show the discomfort it was feeling at its new appearance. Wouldn't it drive you crazy, seeing a stranger staring blankly at you, day after day, without expression? Trevor Denyer happily accepted the story for publication in *Midnight Street*, #16, and it was reprinted for International Short Story Day on the Horrifically Horrifying Horror Blog in 2012.

In The Howling of the Wind

I wrote this one for a Festive issue of an ezine, *Estronomicon*. It's no secret that I love ghost stories, and this gave me a chance to set one at Christmas – a classic time for such a tale. I had an idea about a boy trapped in a house, the wind howling outside, the boy just waiting for his parents to come home, begging his grandfather for information about when they're going to return. After that, the story almost seemed to write itself, and even now I'm pretty happy with the result. I read this out one Christmas, at an event in Derby. I made half the audience cry.

Cat and Mouse

This one came about because I was asked for a story for the *Femme Fatales of Fright* anthology; something 'fun'. I had an image of a woman pretending to be scared so she could toy with her attacker, the twist being of course that the attacker is really something else. Again, this story came into being very quickly, and hopefully fulfilled its remit. It was reprinted in the *Deadly Dolls* anthology later that year.

Listen

The idea for 'Listen' came out of an image I woke up with one morning; a picture of a young boy listening to a story in a library, rapt with attention, gradually realising that the tale isn't what he thought. From there the idea developed into what you'll have read – a boy who is gifted with a vivid and powerful imagination, and thus can see the reality of what he's hearing. A boy who knows that unless he makes the other children wake up there isn't going to be a happy ending, and enlists the story itself to help him. This story was published in the British Fantasy Society's Spring Journal, 2012, and reprinted in 'Unconventional Fantasy, A Celebration Of 40 Years of the World Fantasy Convention', available to attendees at World Fantasy Convention 2014, Washington USA.

Plus Ça Change

This one came about through a request for a story on the subject of phobias; the anthology *Phobophobia*, edited by Dean Drinkel, consisted of stories that each dealt with a different phobia. After racking my brains for a few days (and watching some phobias I'd have enjoyed writing about get taken by those quicker to nab an idea), I came up with metathesiophobia, or the fear of change. From there I found the neurotic woman who can't abide change in any way, and flipped that to show she had a valid reason for not letting anything get out of control. Bad things ensue when she relaxes her attention.

In Times of Want

This is probably one of the oldest stories in the collection, and it was a tale I dreamed in its entirety. Odd as it is, it's written as it was dreamed, as near as I can remember it. I could never quite figure out where to place it, so it's languished on my computer until now.

The Unquiet Bones

When editor Johnny Mains came to me asking for an 'old-school' horror story, novella length, it took me a while to come up with an idea. As often happens with my stories, they start with a picture – whether that comes when I'm consciously trying to come up with something or whether it's when I'm asleep (this happens a lot). This time it was bones. Lots of bones, little ones, big ones… all trying to escape from their brick prison, all trying to rejoin each other; to reconfigure themselves. Then I started thinking of some of the old-school tropes that I knew Johnny would like, and suddenly I had witchcraft, a castle or monastery… the rest of the story grew easily from there and was published in *Bite-Sized Horror*.

World Without End

This was written around the same time as 'In Times of Want', and it's another story written down as I dreamed it. I had a recurring dream for a long time, that all my teeth fell out one by one, dropping to the bedcovers and leaving my mouth empty. Apparently that's a confidence dream, and I haven't had it for a long time now, whatever that means – but the story reminds me of it, and I still find it quite disconcerting. It was published in *The Thinking Man's Crumpet* in 2009.

Someone To Watch Over You

When editor Paul Finch asked me to write a story for his anthology *Terror Tales of London*, he suggested I might like to write something about Finchley (as I'd lived there for about fifteen years before moving to Derbyshire). I thought about it, and remembered East Finchley station, which is an Art Deco building, still untouched. It's also the first open air station heading north out of the city on the Northern Line (Barnet branch). I love ghost stories, and the more I thought about the station, the more I saw an old-fashioned character saving women who were about to be attacked. I could almost smell the tobacco smoke. Old Holborn, a brand my dad smoked years ago when he tried a pipe. From there the rest flowed quite easily, and this is a story I really enjoyed writing. The story was then chosen by Johnny Mains to be reprinted in *Best British Horror 2014.*

Such is Life

'Such is Life' was written not long after I started to get published, and I could never really find somewhere that seemed a fit for it – so it languished on my hard drive, waiting while I tried to figure out (occasionally) what to do with it. I was intrigued by the idea of life being wasted on the living (paraphrasing that old classic, 'youth is wasted on the young'), and of a bitter ghost seeking revenge.

Play Time

You might have noticed by now that I'm rather fond of ghost stories. I was asked to contribute a story to an anthology called *Darc Karnivale*, with no specific guidelines other than word length and that it should be scary. I started to see a park playground, specifically a roundabout whirling around, alone and neglected. Spinning on its own, in other words. From there I found the character of a little dead girl, Mary. She's fed up of being alone, and blames the world – and adults in particular – for her being in that condition. She likes the playground, and wants to play. She just needs a playmate. And a new mother. The story was reprinted in the *Terror*

Tales anthology.

Inspiration Point

When editor Ian Whates asked me to contribute a story to one of two anthologies he was putting together – *Noir* and *La Femme*, the guidelines were relatively open. He wanted a crime story, a noirish tale with a strong female character – and that was it. As usual, I spent quite a while pondering the guidelines, wondering what would work – and then I thought of Marnie, a damsel in distress with a difference. And I wondered what someone like her would do if they ever found themselves abducted. One thing was certain; it wouldn't be pretty.

A Garden for Lily

With this one, I was contacted by editor Peter Mark May with a request to write a novelette that would fit in with a series he was publishing called 'Curse of...' There'd be a *Curse of the Ghost* (which this story was originally published as), a *Curse of the Wolf, Curse of the Monster* and so on. I was happy to write another ghost story, but struggled with how to start. The 'curse' aspect seemed to be a stumbling block. One day I was looking through my file of unfinished stories and 'A Garden for Lily' leapt out at me. Here was a story of a woman haunted by a garden, and the garden in turn was haunted by a child, cursed to inhabit the pond he drowned in, and desperate not to be alone any more. After that, the story seemed to fly – and I was very pleased with the finished tale. I hope you like it.

Safe

'Safe' was the result of a request for a crime story from editor Johnny Mains for a proposed anthology. The anthology never saw daylight, so the story got filed away and forgotten – when I was looking for tales for this collection I came across it again, re-read it and still liked it; it's a murder with a twist, short and hopefully not sweet.

In My Mind, Mine Understanding

This is another earlyish story – it was commissioned for an anthology called *Dead Ends*, to be brought out by Screaming Dreams Press. Once again, the anthology never came out, and the story got filed away and forgotten. Until now. As with the other early stories, I dreamed this one. What if you tried, *really* tried to be a good person, and buried all the bad thoughts way down deep when they occurred. And what if they got out, then took over?

The Cradle in the Corner

This story was the result of a request for a ghost story from editor Ian Whates, for his anthology *Hauntings*. As happens so often, I started to think about what to do while I was going to sleep; and dreamed of a cradle. A very old cradle, which needed a new baby to go in it – but was still occupied by its previous owner. It was subsequently reprinted in e-book form, again by Ian Whates of NewCon Press, in *Obsidian: A Decade of Horror Stories by Women.*

289

About the Author

Marie O'Regan is a British Fantasy Award-nominated author and editor, based in Derbyshire. Her first collection, *Mirror Mere*, was published in 2006, and her short fiction has appeared in a number of genre magazines and anthologies in the UK, US, Canada, Italy and Germany. She was shortlisted for the British Fantasy Society Award for Best Short Story in 2006, and Best Anthology in 2010 and 2012. Her genre journalism has appeared in magazines like *The Dark Side*, *Rue Morgue* and *Fortean Times*, and her interview book, *Voices in the Dark*, was released in 2011. An essay on 'The Changeling' was published in PS Publishing's *Cinema Macabre*, edited by Mark Morris. She is co-editor of the bestselling *Hellbound Hearts*, *Mammoth Book of Body Horror* and *A Carnivàle of Horror – Dark Tales from the Fairground*, plus editor of bestselling *The Mammoth Book of Ghost Stories by Women* and is Co-Chair of the UK Chapter of the Horror Writers' Association.

Acknowledgements

As always, thanks are due to a lot of people who helped in a variety of ways to bring this collection to fruition. Thanks are due to the lovely Sarah Pinborough for a very kind introduction, to Johnny Mains for the equally kind afterword, and to editor Peter Mark May for taking a chance on me and publishing this book. The various editors who originally commissioned the short stories are also owed thanks: Johnny Mains, Peter Mark May, Ian Whates, Trevor Denyer, Steve Upham, David Byron and Cory R. Scales, Adam Lowe and Chris Kelso, Dean Drinkel, Guy Adams and last but by no means least, Paul Finch. And finally, I'm grateful, always, for the support of my family – including my lovely husband, Paul Kane.

Copyright Information

Hersham Horror Books

Fogbound From 5, Alt-Dead, Alt-Zombie. Siblings, Anatomy of Death, Demons & Devilry and Dead Water. The Curse of the Mummy; Wolf, Ghost, Zombie, Monster & Vampire.

http://silenthater.wix.com/hersham-horror-books#

If you loved the cover art feel free to visit Edward Miller's website below.

les@lesedwards.com

Made in the USA
Charleston, SC
29 July 2016